"Dan Bourne's been having a rough time of it at the ranch."

"What do you mean?"

Dan! Piper had hardly even considered *him* since the news of Diana's death. Dan Bourne... widower.

"Well, I hear there are some dissatisfied customers," her father said.

Piper sat up straighter. "You mean Diana's ranch is in trouble? But that's impossible. It's the best ranch for miles."

"Not anymore," her father said pointedly. "I think he's lost a couple of trainers since Diana's... accident."

Piper pushed her thick hair from her brow. "I don't believe this," she said. "It's as if I *knew* he was bad news the day Diana met him. You know, I feel that if Dan Bourne had never come here, if Diana had never met him, she'd be alive today."

Dear Reader,

Get ready for a double dare from Superromance!

The popularity of our Women Who Dare titles has convinced us that Superromance readers enjoy the thrill of living on the edge. So be prepared for an entire *month of living dangerously!*

Leading off is this month's Women Who Dare title, *Windstorm,* in which author Connie Bennett pits woman against nature as Teddi O'Brien sets her sights on a tornado chaser! But our other three September heroines also battle both the elements and the enemy in a variety of exotic settings. *Wildfire,* by Lynn Erickson, is a real trial by fire, as Piper Hilyard learns to tell the good guys from the bad. In Marisa Carroll's *Hawk's Lair,* Sara Riley tracks subterranean treasure—and a pirate—in the Costa Rican rain forest. And we're delighted to welcome back to Superromance veteran romance author Sara Orwig. Her heroine, Jennifer Ruark, outruns a flood in the San Saba Valley in *The Mad, the Bad & the Dangerous.*

For October's Women Who Dare title, Lynn Leslie has created another trademark emotional drama in *Courage, My Love.* Diane Maxwell is fighting the fight of her life. To Brad Kingsley, she is a tremendously courageous woman of the nineties, and as his love for her grows, so does his commitment to her victory.

Evelyn A. Crowe's legion of fans will be delighted to learn that she has penned our Women Who Dare title for November. In *Reunited,* gutsy investigative reporter Sydney Tanner learns way more than she bargained for about rising young congressman J.D. Fowler. Generational family feuds, a long-ago murder and a touch of blackmail are only a few of the surprises in store for Sydney—and for you—as the significance of the heroine's discoveries begins to shape this riveting tale.

Popular Superromance author Sharon Brondos has contributed our final Woman Who Dare title for 1993. In *Doc Wyoming,* taciturn sheriff Hal Blane wants nothing to do with a citified female doctor, and the feeling is mutual. But Dixie Sheldon becomes involved with Blane's infamous family in spite of herself, and her "sentence" in Wyoming is commuted to a romance of the American West.

Please enjoy A Month of Living Dangerously, as well as our upcoming Women Who Dare titles and all the other fine Superromance novels we've lined up for your fall reading pleasure!

Marsha Zinberg,
Senior Editor

WILDFIRE

Lynn Erickson

Harlequin Books

TORONTO • NEW YORK • LONDON
AMSTERDAM • PARIS • SYDNEY • HAMBURG
STOCKHOLM • ATHENS • TOKYO • MILAN
MADRID • WARSAW • BUDAPEST • AUCKLAND

Published September 1993

ISBN 0-373-70564-6

WILDFIRE

ABOUT THE AUTHOR

Carla Peltonen and Molly Swanton, better known to romance readers as Lynn Erickson, have been writing as a team for more than fourteen years and make their homes in Aspen, Colorado. Their latest Superromance novel, *Wildfire,* is a sizzling adventure set in their home state. "Molly and I drove out to Steamboat Springs to pick a setting for the ranch," says Carla, and the result is an authentic picture of a working ranch and a book that's guaranteed to keep readers on the edge of their seats.

Books by Lynn Erickson

HARLEQUIN SUPERROMANCE

Don't miss any of our special offers. Write to us at the following address for information on our newest releases.

Harlequin Reader Service
P.O. Box 1397, Buffalo, NY 14240
Canadian address: P.O. Box 603,
Fort Erie, Ont. L2A 5X3

PROLOGUE

PIPER HILYARD WAS CRYING. She always cried at weddings. And this was a very special wedding, really special—because her best friend, Diana Kilmer, was getting married.

It was a special wedding, and it was a pink wedding. Everything that warm, sunny September afternoon was pink—the bride's bouquet, the bridesmaids' dresses, the cake, the decorations, the tablecloths, everything.

Diana had wanted pink. Piper had argued with her, trying to tone down the saccharine-sweet, eye-boggling pink, but Diana was as strong willed as anyone on earth. Her folks had died when she was seventeen, over ten years ago, so there was no one but Piper to gainsay Diana. And Piper caved in after one look at Diana's dreamy, love-struck gaze and determined jaw.

"Okay, pink," Piper had said back in June. "I look putrid in pink, but so what? *I'm* not getting married."

"You *could,*" Diana had said excitedly. "We'll make it a double wedding. Oh, Lord, it'll be the best! A double wedding! And you can—"

"Stop, Diana," Piper had said, holding a hand up. "Stop right there, old pal."

"Why not? Marry Dutch. He's crazy about you. He'd do it in a hot second."

"I broke up with Dutch, remember?" Piper had replied.

"That can be easily remedied. A little phone call..."

Piper had shaken her auburn head adamantly. "No way. I don't want to marry Dutch. I don't even like him very much anymore. I'll never go out with him again. You know that, Diana. God, you've been through the whole thing with me."

"Okay," Diana had said, sulking, "but you're wearing pink at my wedding."

Now Piper stood on one foot, eased her other out of the tight pink satin shoe and wiggled her toes. The noise crashed around her: talk, music, dancing, yelling. A good old Western hoedown wedding—a *pink* hoedown wedding. A country and western band played under a striped canopy, and couples two-stepped around the temporary dance floor. The Elk River ran by beyond the band, and the Colorado mountains rose behind that, green and sage dotted.

Piper looked around. God, there were hundreds of people there. Of course, she knew most of them, because they were all Diana's friends, which meant they were her friends, too. Diana and Piper had been raised in Steamboat Springs, Colorado, so their friends were mutual, but—wow—this was really quite a gathering.

"Honey, don't look like your feet hurt," came her mother's voice in her ear. "Wipe your eyes."

"They *do* hurt," Piper said.

"Don't *look* like they do. Smile," Betty Hilyard said firmly. "Don't cry."

"Right, Mom." But she sniffed.

The wedding was being held at Diana's ranch, the Elk River Ranch, the spread she'd bought when she came into her inheritance. She'd bought two hundred and fifty acres along the Elk River ten miles north of the city of Steamboat Springs, built a comfortable log-and-stone house down near the river and proceeded to start an outfit for breeding and training quarter horses.

She'd done it with Piper's help, because the two horse-crazy teenage girls had become fine riders and fine judges of breeding lines, and whereas Diana had the wherewithal to buy a superior stud, Piper had the degree in equine sciences from Colorado State University.

Yes, it had been a terrific partnership and a terrific six years, and horses bred and raised on the Elk River Ranch sold for substantial prices now.

Piper sniffed again, feeling tears well up in her eyes. The music struck up anew, and she could see through the crowd that Diana and her new husband, Dan Bourne, were going to dance this one: John Denver's "Rocky Mountain High."

The newlywed couple stood close, smiling secret smiles, a little nervous, but happy. Dan was thirty-six years old, Piper knew, but today he looked younger. Maybe it was the smile he had for his new wife, or maybe he was just thrilled with his luck, or maybe it was love that showed on his face today. He was a handsome man—very black hair, tanned skin, startlingly blue eyes under black brows. Slightly above medium height but with a strong build, heavily muscled shoulders and powerful arms and wrists. A man who was sexy as the devil and had to have known it.

Piper cocked her head and watched him as he took his wife's hand and they moved together toward the dance floor. His strong bone structure was molded beneath clear skin, a very square jaw and two curved lines bracketing a sensitive mouth, lines that deepened when he smiled at Diana.

Handsome, all right, Piper thought, a veritable Prince Charming in his gray pin-striped cutaway coat and trousers. He took Diana in his strong arms as the music played, and they danced slowly around the floor while the guests all watched, spellbound, jealous, envious, happy for Dan and Diana.

A tear overflowed Piper's eye and her nose ran. What a beautiful couple. What a perfect couple. Dan so dark and masculine, Diana so blond and wholesome and pretty, almost as tall as her husband in her little white satin heels, radiant, glowing with pride and joy.

"Stop crying," Betty Hilyard said again in Piper's ear. "Your mascara is running."

"I can't help it, Mom."

Betty put her hand on her daughter's arm. "Don't be sad, honey. Diana will still be your friend. Marriage doesn't change people so much."

"That's not why I'm crying," Piper said.

"Why, then?"

"Oh, damn, I don't know. Aren't you supposed to cry at weddings?"

"Not me. I didn't even cry when your brother Glen got married. I was happy as a clam. Let Clarissa cook for him!"

"I did. I cried. My big brother, married and gone for good. You're a hard woman, Mom."

Other couples started dancing, thronging the makeshift floor. Men in polyester Western suits and spit-shined cowboy boots, women in silk dresses, teenagers in jeans, little kids in party outfits, old folks dressed in every style imaginable. The who's who of Steamboat Springs, ski resort *extraordinaire* and historical Western town, home of dozens of odoriferous, bubbling hot springs, one of which had given the town its name when early-nineteenth-century fur trappers had thought the chug-chugging noise rising from a hot spring by the edge of the Yampa River had sounded like a steamboat chugging around the bend. Piper had explained the origin of the town's name so many times to visitors she'd lost count.

It *was* a unique town, a hodgepodge of the old and new, part Old West, part new condos and minimalls and old false-front brick buildings nestled between a wide bend of the Yampa River and the green, rolling mountains of north-central Colorado.

The scent of barbecue filled the air. Champagne corks popped. Crystal glasses met beer cans in toasts galore. A baby cried, a man sang along with the band. "Rocky Mountain high, Colorado-o-o!"

Piper sniffed again. She spied Dutch Radowsky's curly blond head above the crowd and quickly turned away. She couldn't deal with Dutch now, she really couldn't.

A hush came over the crowd, then applause. Diana and Dan were going to cut the cake. They were so beautifully matched, more enchanting than the figurines on the top of the elaborate frosting. A fairy-tale couple. Piper bit her lip and smiled. The photographer took pictures, dozens of them. Dan and Diana cutting the first piece, laughing, licking icing off their fingers, Diana trying to feed an embarrassed Dan a piece and Dan patiently putting up with his wife's whim, embarrassed, yes, but obviously adoring anything Diana did.

Diana had wanted a big, bang-up pink wedding, and she had one, Piper thought. She sure as heck had herself one.

More flashes of the camera—the bride and groom kissing. And then Dan tried to wave the photographer off as if saying, "Come on, pal, enough is enough," but Diana tucked her arm in Dan's and insisted on just one more picture taken over the cake, and Dan shook his head, smiling at his wife, and pulling her into his arms. They held their pose too long, and Piper flushed. Sexual vibes flowed between Diana and Dan so strongly that Piper was embarrassed to be around them.

Suddenly Piper was glad of her decision to go to New Zealand for the next year. Yes, it was a wise move. Diana would just have to make do without her, and by the time Piper got back—*if* Piper came back—things would be all settled down around the ranch.

Diana was saying something, scanning the crowd, gesturing. "Bridesmaids, gather all the wedding party for a picture," Piper heard someone say. Oh, well, it was bound to happen, Piper guessed. She pulled at the bodice of her pink silk dress that looked so god-awful with her auburn hair and honey brown eyes and summer tan—really awful—and shook out the bouquet she'd been hanging on to for too long. Then she fluffed up her hair as if that would help mute all the pink.

Pictures. Dozens more of them. Piper smiled and smiled until she thought her face would crack. She stood right next to Diana in every picture and could smell the fragrance of her friend's pink rose bouquet, of her perfume, of the hair spray she'd used on her blond hair. And mixed with it she could sense Dan Bourne's scent—after-shave, man smell, the aroma of dry cleaning fluid from his rented formal wear. Somehow the odors were too personal, too intimate, and Piper wanted to move away, to escape the discomfort she felt faced with her lifelong friend's new allegiance, her new intimacy with a man.

Flashes, images shot through her head unbidden. Diana and Dan alone at night—in bed—undressed. His body would be...

No! she told herself. *Stop! It's none of your business. They're married. Husband and wife.*

When the photographer was finished, Piper stood there, holding a plate, eating a piece of wedding cake. At least the cake didn't *taste* pink. People she'd known all her life spoke to her, to Diana. They were all so thrilled for Diana, so happy. Best wishes and congratulations flew around like a flock of brainless, twittering birds, cute but irritating in large numbers. Piper swallowed cake and responded to people and wished she was having a better time.

Petty of me to be jealous, she thought more than once, but there it was; she did not envy Diana her man—he was not at all what Piper wanted—but her happiness, her passion.

"Always the bridesmaid, never the bride," a man's voice whispered in her ear, and Piper turned, startled. It was Dutch.

"Ready with the clever repartee?" Piper replied lightly.

"Sure, you know me," Dutch said, grinning.

"And you know what my mother always says. 'If you can't say something nice, don't say anything at all,'" Piper told him pointedly.

"Yeah, my mother must have told me that, too, but honest to God, Piper, I've tried all day to talk to you, and you've been avoiding me."

"Yes, I have."

"Why, honey?"

"I'm not your honey, and we broke up, remember?" she said, exasperated.

"*You* broke up. I didn't," Dutch said, sublimely sure of himself, forgetting the scene he'd made, that awful scene, whose images snatched at her mind as she stood there: the crowded singles' disco, the late-May snowstorm outside, Dutch pumped up with anger and disbelief, yelling at her in front of everyone, calling her a bitch, telling her that no one crossed him like that, grabbing her arm painfully, announcing that she was his and no one else would dare ask her out....

Piper stood near the dance floor at the ranch and looked up into his guileless blue eyes and shuddered inwardly. "Listen," she said, "a relationship can't be one-sided, Dutch. Oh, God, we've been through this. Can't you just accept it? I'm leaving soon, anyway, so it doesn't matter."

"Stubborn." Dutch shook his sandy blond head.

"Fine, I'm stubborn. Leave it at that," Piper said.

The band struck up again, Jimmy Buffet's "Margaritaville." Diana had the musicians playing all her favorites, and every song struck a chord in Piper's

heart, twanged memories of her and Diana doing
something while the song was playing on the radio.
Talking about what they'd do when they grew up,
about boys, gossiping, doing homework together,
getting ready for parties. Every word, every note,
caused a pang of reminiscence.

Dutch was asking her something, and she had to
force her attention back to him. "What?" she asked.

"Want to dance?"

"No, thank you. Dutch. Really."

He frowned, shrugged. "Suit yourself," he said,
turning away.

A man was heading toward Piper through the
crowd, a big, red-faced man with thick graying hair.
She placed him mentally—Harry Tegmeier, Dan
Bourne's ex-partner on the Philadelphia police force.
Harry was still on the force, but Dan Bourne, well,
Dan lived in Steamboat now. He'd quit his job.

"Hello, miss. You're Piper Hilyard, aren't you?"
Harry was saying. "Diana's best friend, right?"

Piper couldn't help smiling. Harry was perspiring,
his tie was askew, his jacket rumpled, but he was so
full of exuberance and good cheer she had to respond. "Right, we met last night at the rehearsal dinner, didn't we?"

"Yeah, sure, but I'm sort of on overload here,"
Harry said, mopping his forehead with a wrinkled
handkerchief. "Listen, how about we have a dance?
Best man and maid of honor, you know."

He talked like a gangster in a movie, he sweated and
stepped on her toes, but he made Piper laugh. "Never
been west of Pittsburgh before," he said. "This is
something."

"I'm glad you came."

"Me, too, Piper. Wait till I get home and tell Cindy and the kids. Wish they coulda come, but there was no way. Hell, Lady Di sent me my ticket so Danny-boy would have a best man."

"Lady Di?"

"Diana, sure. Hey, listen, I don't mean no disrespect, but the kid's loaded. Danny hit the big time." Harry whirled Piper around the floor, bumping into people, his collar damp, his forehead glistening, talking a blue streak. Harry was an easy man to like. "Those ponies out there in the fields. Should I know their names so I can bet on 'em when they grow up? Any hot prospects?"

"Those are quarter horses, Harry. They aren't racehorses. We train them for years so they can be shown or worked or whatever, but they don't race. Well, there *are* quarter horse races, but we don't breed for speed."

"I get it. You got intellectual-type ponies, not dumb, fast ones."

Piper laughed. "Close enough."

"What a paradise Danny-boy's got here," he said. "But I'll miss him. You know we worked together ten years? Since he got his detective badge. Ten years. Good years. Heck, before that I was kinda like his father. You know."

They both looked toward the happy couple as if by subconscious agreement. One of Diana's old schoolteachers was kissing her, wishing her happiness. Dan stood by patiently, proud, ruggedly handsome.

Oh, God, was he right for Diana? The whole thing had happened so suddenly. Diana could be incredibly headstrong. If she wanted something she went after it, no holds barred. And Diana had wanted Dan Bourne.

She'd met Dan when he'd come on vacation to Steamboat the previous March. He'd been in the local boot shop looking at cowboy boots when Diana had breezed in to see about ordering another pair for herself. They'd got to talking because Dan, being a dude and an Easterner, knew less than nothing about what to look for.

According to Diana it had been love at first sight. And when Dan had left after his week of skiing, she'd been despondent. Piper knew the whole story. She'd lived through every moment of doubt, every second of elation, every phone call. She knew Diana had wanted Dan Bourne, had flown to Philadelphia to see him once a month all spring, all summer long, until he had resigned from the force and finally moved to Steamboat a few weeks ago.

Piper also knew that Dan had left the force very suddenly, even though Diana had said he was a dedicated policeman. She was aware that there was something odd about his leaving, an internal matter that had left Dan bitter, something Diana either didn't care about, didn't know about or didn't want to discuss. All Piper was sure of was that her friend had been jubilant when Dan had finally resigned, because that had been the one remaining obstacle to their marriage.

Diana had sworn Dan hadn't quit because of her, sworn it up and down. She'd told Piper she could never respect a man who'd do a woman's bidding just like that—or a woman who'd do a man's, for that matter. So things had worked out for Dan and Diana in the end. But then, Diana always got her own way.

Harry was breathing hard, mopping the back of his neck, grinning and bobbing in time to the music. "The altitude's getting to me," he gasped. "What is it, seven thousand feet here?"

"Close enough. You want to take it easy, sit down or something?" Piper asked.

"Hell, no. I gotta live it up. Flying home tomorrow. Back to work, back to the old ball and chain, you know." But Harry's red face looked so cheerful Piper didn't believe his "ball and chain" routine.

"Come on," she said, "you love your job."

"Hey, yeah, you're right. I do." Harry laughed. "And I love Philly, dirty old whore that she is. And I love my wife and kids."

"In that order?" Piper asked.

Harry gave a hoot of laughter. "Got me there, kid."

It occurred to Piper to ask Harry about the mysterious reasons his ex-partner had quit the force, but the notion fled rapidly. This was not the time or place, and besides, Harry probably felt as loyal to his old partner as she did to Diana, and wasn't about to air Dan's dirty laundry—that is, if there really was any.

Well, it was too late now, anyway, because Dan and Diana were man and wife, and Piper would be leaving in a week to work for Sally Cale, who bred horses down under on New Zealand's South Island, where spring was about to blossom. It would be a good break, a good time to get away, to see a new part of the world, to gain experience with a different kind of horse and new people.

"You're a good dancer, Piper," Harry was saying, "and a good sport. I like you."

"Well, I like you, too, Detective Tegmeier," Piper said genuinely.

"I need a drink, some of that cold beer over there. Want something?"

"Oh, no, I'm fine. Go ahead," Piper said.

Her mother and father were standing by the huge, half-demolished cake, talking to the bride. Diana had practically lived at Piper's house after her parents had died; she considered Betty and John her folks, the closest thing to a family she had. There'd been a guardian appointed by the court, a distant relative, but Diana had preferred hanging out at the Hilyards' in the big old comfortable house on Crawford Street.

Piper made her way toward them, holding her pink silk layered skirt up so she could walk normally. *Pink*.

"Hi, honey," Betty said.

"Piper, I haven't seen you for a second," Diana cried. "Are you having fun?"

"Sure, it's a super wedding, Di. Everyone's loving it."

"Oh, I hope so. You know how hard I worked to organize it! Oh, Piper, I'm just floating. I can't believe this is happening! Me, Mrs. Dan Bourne, oh, Lord." Diana grabbed Piper's hand and squeezed, exuberant, high as a kite with pure emotion, two hectic spots of red on her cheeks. She rolled her eyes. "I don't know how Dan is putting up with all this. They're not *his* friends, but he's so nice, so wonderful. Oh, Piper, I saw you dancing with Harry. Isn't he a kick? The way he talks! But he cares about Dan, he's like his father, and Dan wanted him here, I could tell."

"He's funny. I like Harry," Piper said.

"Yes, I agree. We'll go to visit him in Philadelphia for sure." Diana rattled on, her usual high spirits intensified by excitement. She leaned close to Piper. "Is my hair still okay? Do I look like hell? It seems like this . . . this party's been going on for days."

Piper reached up and pushed a strand of fine blond hair behind her friend's ear. "You look absolutely gorgeous."

"No," Diana said breathlessly, "my husband's the one who's gorgeous. Just look at him."

Piper followed her friend's gaze. Dan was talking to Harry, his head bent a little while he nodded. He looked handsome, all right, lost in thought, the two long grooves on either side of his mouth deepening. Piper saw him smile then at something Harry said, but it wasn't a full-blown smile. No, Piper mused, smiling didn't seem to come easily to Dan Bourne at all.

Well, he was Diana's Prince Charming, and he couldn't do a thing wrong as far as Diana was concerned. And then Piper wondered again about the problem he'd had back in Philadelphia when he'd quit the police force. A prince with tarnished armor, she thought a little smugly.

"Isn't he beautiful?" Diana sighed.

"He's very attractive, Di. You know that," Piper said. "He's not my type, though."

"Good thing!" Diana laughed, then whirled to ask one of the waiters if there was enough champagne for everyone. "Oh, good," she said, "there's still lots left. Oh, I've got to go grab Dan before he gets buried by all the locals asking him questions. God, Piper, will you look at that man?" And Diana was off, skimming across the lawn, her white satin dress rustling, her veil floating behind in the golden afternoon light.

Piper stood there feeling ridiculously forlorn, tall and gawky in her formal pink dress. She saw Dan turn toward Diana, saw his face relax, and she felt so alone amid the noise and revelry. No husband, no best friend, not even a boyfriend anymore. How awful of her, to be jealous of Diana's good fortune, to doubt her friend's choice of husbands. It was small and ugly and unworthy of their friendship.

But what made it worse for Piper was the ending of her long relationship with Dutch Radowsky. She'd known him since high school, and he'd been elected the sheriff of Routt County two years ago. She'd gone with Dutch for four years, and she'd thought they were in love, but since becoming sheriff Dutch had shown a new side, one Piper found she simply couldn't handle. He'd become overbearing, possessive and jealous. Piper had always thought having a man be jealous of her would be flattering, but it turned out to be simply repugnant. At first she'd figured Dutch was going through a phase, but the phase never passed.

Oh, Dutch had lots of good qualities. He was tall, good-looking in an easygoing way, kind, a real organizer, a man who knew precisely where he was going and what he wanted to do. He had talent and brains, and in that laid-back Western style he was a consummate politician, a kind of Will Rogers. He was attentive, loving, thoughtful, generous. His one big problem, Piper had come to realize, was that over time his quest for power and control had gotten worse. She'd begun to notice last year that Dutch ran the county the same way he wanted to run her. He was a benevolent despot, lording it over his deputies, keeping his secretary and dispatchers terrified. He treated all the citizens of Routt County as his subjects, under his protection but also under his absolute control.

Well, Piper thought, he was up for reelection in two years. Maybe the good voters would wake up and unseat Dutch Radowsky, although she couldn't imagine him in any role other than sheriff, the ultimate lawman of the county. He was the incarnation of the Western sheriff, Gary Cooper in *High Noon,* John Wayne, all of those staunchly traditional and true-hearted heroes.

Except Dutch was a flawed hero.

Piper imagined that one day he was going to push his power too far, expose himself. Well, she wouldn't be around to see it. Her brainstorm to take a sabbatical in New Zealand had two roots—getting away from Dutch, while at the same time giving Diana some space. Diana was happy for her, and Dutch—well, Piper guessed he'd get over it, maybe even realize that in part he'd driven her away. She wished Dutch well. She also wished he'd mature, mellow with age and his own experience. They'd been friends for many, many years. When she returned from New Zealand she hoped they could again be friends.

Piper shook herself out of her reverie and decided she couldn't just stand there looking so gloomy. A real party pooper. Everyone else was in high spirits—free booze, free food, dancing, old friends. A humdinger of a celebration.

Piper took a glass of champagne off a waitress's tray, pasted a smile on her face and decided to be social. This party was her swan song in a way; after all, she was leaving her hometown in a week. She'd *better* live it up.

She drank champagne and ate hors d'oeuvres, she talked to old high school buddies, the ski area manager, shop owners and bankers, realtors and restaurant owners, all familiar people, good folk who lived in the Yampa Valley and shared in its bounty and closeness.

"Weather's hot for September, think it'll be a late winter?" "Doesn't she look beautiful, and so happy!" "He's a nice-enough sort of fellow, that Dan Bourne, isn't he? Now, where'd she meet him, again?" "So you're off to New Zealand. Boy, that's the other side of the earth. Spring there, isn't it? Say, do the mares breed in opposite seasons there?"

Piper answered questions, talked about the comfortable, familiar subjects, danced with some old friends, talked to her mom and dad a few times.

It was growing dark, and the Japanese lanterns were lit. Dim, flickering lights played on people's faces. It grew cooler, and favorite sweaters were brought out to cover fancy dresses.

Piper knew Diana and Dan were going to leave soon. They were going to Hawaii on their honeymoon, staying in a posh beachfront hotel on Maui. Together, the two of them, drowning in each other in absolute exotic privacy....

"Oh, I've got to change, Piper. Come on and help me. I'll never get away at this rate!" Diana said breathlessly.

They went up to her bedroom, and Piper started feeling sad again. Diana had redone it. It wasn't the frilly, feminine bedroom Piper was used to; it was now done in a tailored Southwest motif, more fitting for the master bedroom of a married couple.

Piper glanced around. No, it was no longer just Di's room. Tossed on a chair in the corner was a pair of man's trousers—Dan's—not blue jeans or anything, but khaki trousers, city clothes. And mingling with Diana's perfume and hair spray was the scent of Dan's after-shave.

"We're only driving to Denver," Diana was saying, pulling off her veil, unbuttoning her sleeves.

"Want me to get the back?" Piper asked, taking her eyes away from the closet, where she could see Dan's clothes through the half-open door.

"Yes, please. You know, I'd rather wear jeans to sit in the car for three hours. Silly to have to put on a dress," Diana was saying. "Oh, God, I'm exhausted." She stepped out of the white satin creation and left it a crumpled heap on the floor. She stood there in her panty hose and bra and white satin shoes, a lock of hair that she loosened as she removed the veil falling over her eye. She stood there and looked at Piper, and her whole being throbbed with life and love.

"I'll always love you, too, you know," Diana said. "Being married can't change that. You're my best friend, always and forever."

"Oh, I know, Di," Piper said, near tears again.

"We've been through everything together. If it wasn't for you and Betty and John, where would I be? You're family."

The two women hugged each other, one quick, tight hug. Piper sniffed, and Diana closed her eyes and swallowed the lump in her throat.

They let go of each other and abruptly broke out in familiar laughter.

"God, I've been crying all afternoon," Piper said, and pulled a tissue out of a box on Diana's dressing table. "I look like hell. *Pink,*" she added, sniffing.

Diana ran a brush through her hair and looked at Piper in the mirror. "You look fabulous, darling," she said, pronouncing it facetiously. "Dahling."

Piper stood alongside her friend and fluffed up the mass of her long, reddish brown hair and pouted her full lips. She opened her dark eyes wide. "Just gorgeous," Piper said in a mocking, sexy voice, and she put an arm around Diana's shoulder, the two of them making faces in the mirror as they had done so many times in high school before a double date when they had pretended to be the ultimate sex goddesses, even stuffing toilet paper into their bras.

The two of them took on the same poses they'd made over ten years ago and then broke out laughing again.

"Pink," Piper said, holding her sides, "I could kill you, Di!"

They finally sobered, and it was Diana who said, "You know, Piper, everything will be the same as before. I mean, it's not like I'm having personality surgery. I just got married, is all."

"I know," Piper said, "It's all going to be fine."

"Now, *you* take care of yourself down under. Don't you dare meet someone and stay."

"Fat chance. After Dutch, the last thing I'm looking for is another man."

Diana narrowed her blue eyes, then abruptly they widened. "Oh, Lord," she said, "here we are up here like it's just another Saturday night! I've got to get ready. I'm a wreck. But I'll be okay. First, the honeymoon. Right. And then you'll be gone by the time I get home. But you'll be back and everything will be normal. Just promise you won't do anything dumb down there and decide to stay. I'd be lost.''

Piper smiled. "Okay, I promise.''

Diana was pulling on a dress, a blue denim camp-shirt-style dress with a leather belt. Instantly she was transformed from the fairy-tale bride into the girl Piper had known since first grade, a casual, breezy, sturdily built girl with slightly tousled hair and pink cheeks and a no-nonsense gaze that boded ill for anyone who crossed her. An independent girl, willful, obstinate to some, pigheaded to others. A girl full of affection and spirit and loyalty.

"Let's go,'' Diana said. "Get it over with. I saw Dutch ordering out a task force to tie tin cans to the car. That man'll never grow up.''

"Probably not,'' Piper agreed.

"Maybe you were right to break up with him,'' Diana mused.

The car was waiting in front of the house on the circular driveway. Tin cans were draped from the rear bumper, tied to strings. Just Married had been scrawled on the trunk. Balloons festooned the antenna. Pink balloons.

Everyone was gathered around the car, waiting. Diana gave Piper's hand one last squeeze and started saying her goodbyes to the clamoring throng. Piper stood back, shivering a little in the cool dusk, feeling a sense of loss so strong it ached in her bones.

She must have been looking grim, she was to think after, when Dan Bourne came up to her. Piper's first thought was that Diana had made him do it, ordered him to placate Piper, and his discomfort, his awkwardness, didn't dispel the notion one iota.

"Thanks for being here today," he started, "for Diana. I know how close you two are."

"My pleasure," Piper said breezily.

"Um." His blue eyes, dark in the evening light, switched away from her. He was dressed now in khaki pants and a pale blue polo shirt. He looked very handsome, very masculine. The gold wedding band on his left ring finger glinted too brightly in the fading light. "Look, I know how you're feeling, but the last thing on earth I want to do is come between Diana and her friends. When you get home next year, everything will be like it was. We both want you to come back to work at the ranch."

"I understand," she said. "Thanks."

He looked at her then, studying her for just a moment too long. A cool, deliberate smile carved itself on the corners of his mouth, and the lines on either side deepened. "I get the feeling," he said, "that I should apologize for something."

"Oh?" Piper said.

"I think you know what I mean."

She'd been looking past his shoulder, calculatingly nonchalant, when she let her eyes travel to his. It was a mistake, that meeting of their eyes, because suddenly, from out of the blue, she felt a dart of electricity shoot through her, and the hairs raised on her body. She tore her gaze from his and felt as if she'd been punched. At the moment she took her reaction to Dan Bourne as the acknowledgment of an adversary, but she hadn't time to really question or analyze or even wonder, because Diana was coming to claim her husband and to give Piper one last hug, and it was so frantic then. Rice was flung in handfuls, the bride and groom were getting into the car, ducking, laughing, protesting. Everyone was yelling, cheering, clapping, crying all at once. Diana was waving from the open window, blowing kisses.

Piper stood there for a long time, staring into the growing darkness at the taillights of the car as it hurried up the long dirt road and under the post and crossbar bearing the name of the Elk River Ranch, cans rattling behind it.

Someone placed a glass of champagne in Piper's hand. She turned, wondering, and saw it was Dutch.

"Nice send-off, wasn't it?" he said.

"Um."

"We could have one just as good. Piper, we—"

But she turned her back on him, not even bothering to reply, and walked away. A knot was forming in her stomach, a hard fist of apprehension, unrelated to Dutch and his fixation. She was worried that Diana, heedless and strong willed, had jumped into this marriage too quickly. There was something about Dan Bourne, something below the surface of those good looks and hard-edged self-confidence. And Piper paused, the glass of champagne halfway to her lips, and wondered just what Diana really knew about the man she'd married.

CHAPTER ONE

PIPER SANK ONTO her old bed in the garage apartment she occupied at her parents' house on Crawford Street and stared into the middle distance. All around her were suitcases and duffel bags, her clothes half hanging out. In one corner of the room sat her well-worn riding boots and hard hat, and the saddle and leather crop Diana had given her as a birthday present years ago.

She sighed, feeling empty and undone by the clutter. So much stuff—how had she accumulated so many things over the past year and a half in New Zealand?

"Damn," Piper said, pushing her hair behind an ear.

She did manage to hang up a few of her clothes, but all the while it was as if the silver-framed photograph that sat on a desk beneath the dormer window kept beckoning her. *Come over here, Piper,* it taunted. And eventually she did pick up the picture, fingering the smooth silver frame, a knot the size of a fist hardening deep in her belly.

Diana and Dan cutting the wedding cake.

Piper stared through blurry eyes at the photo and felt her breath begin to quiver in her throat. Diana had been so beautiful that day. And Piper had been jealous. Now she could kick herself for that pettiness. Piper had all the time in the world, and Diana had... nothing.

Piper's mom had fixed a huge welcome-home dinner, but when Piper crossed from the garage to the big yellow frame house situated near downtown Steamboat Springs, the last thing on her mind was food. Since December, well over a year ago, she'd known it was going to be hard coming home—but this was a nightmare. Everywhere she looked—from the hammock to the white-painted porch furniture, the old tire hanging on a rope from the spreading willow tree— Piper was reminded of Diana. So much of her life had revolved around their friendship. There had been teasing and girlish secrets and so much laughter....

It was all so familiar, the table set the way Betty always did it for company. The smells were the same, the aromas of home.

Her mother beamed, setting down the fork-tender brisket, Piper's favorite. Only her brother Glen's chair was empty, as it had been for some years, because he was married now and living in Santa Fe.

And Diana's chair... It came back in a rush, all those evenings when Diana had sat there and eaten with the Hilyards, one of the family.

"So," John was saying, "how big did you say that ranch was in New Zealand?"

"A couple hundred acres. Not so big. They don't have a lot of room there," Piper answered.

"Well, it sounded like a beautiful place," her mother offered.

"It was. Kind of reminded me of here in a way because of the mountains, but they were farther away.

And it was much more humid there. We had different problems with the horses, more hoof fungus and things.''

''Um,'' her father said, offering her more meat.

They were skirting the subject, Piper knew. A stupid, senseless car accident a year ago last December, and Diana...

There was a knock at the front door. John Hilyard frowned. ''Now who'd be coming around here at dinnertime?'' he said, pushing himself from the table in the cozy dining room.

Piper was lifting a forkful of potatoes to her mouth when she heard the familiar voice, and her hand froze in midair. ''My God,'' she muttered to her mother, ''it's Dutch.''

''Piper,'' Betty admonished.

Piper put her fork down abruptly. *Dutch.* Knocking on the door at dinnertime. It wasn't by accident, either. ''Oh, no,'' she said, horrified, ''you don't think Dad will ask him to...?''

''Well, I'd sure like that,'' Dutch's voice echoed from the other room. ''Haven't had one of Mrs. Hilyard's meals for a real long time. Sure I'm not intruding?''

''No trouble at all, Dutch. Glad to have you,'' came her father's reply. ''Betty always cooks too much.''

She heard his boot heels clump as Dutch followed her father across the living room. *Dutch.* Playing his favorite role, the nice guy. That manipulative...

''Look who's here,'' John said cheerfully.

Piper set her jaw.

Dutch was just as broad shouldered and tall as Piper remembered. And, as always, he was wearing his

Routt County sheriff's uniform, official khaki from head to foot, his aviator-style sunglasses casually dangling from the pocket of his Western-style shirt, his broad-brimmed Stetson held in his hands, his gun belt and holster, highly polished, buckled firmly around his waist. He'd grown into his size, and, instead of seeming awkward, he used his bulk as an emblem of his authority, like his gun or his badge.

Well, she'd have to be polite to Dutch, the last person on earth she wanted to see. She hadn't been home long enough to get over her jet lag, and there he was, as if nothing had happened, as if she hadn't been gone a year and a half.

"Hello, Dutch," she said.

"Piper," he said, breaking into a broad grin. "Boy, am I glad to see you. You're looking great, just great!" And he came right over to her, bent down and kissed her cheek, then sat in her brother's old chair as if he owned the place.

"Well, word sure gets around fast," she said dryly.

"How's that?" Dutch cocked his head innocently.

"I mean, I've only been home a few hours."

"Well, as a matter of fact," he said, taking a plate from Betty Hilyard, "Bob down at the gas station said you'd gotten in."

"Small town," Piper muttered.

Dutch put away the slab of meat like a man starving. "Sure is tasty," he said, nodding at Betty. "I forgot how good a cook you are, ma'am."

"You'll have to come by again," Betty said, then caught Piper's eye for a moment. "Though," she put in quickly, "I really don't do much cooking anymore."

How many letters had Dutch written? A hundred over the past year and a half? It was as if he'd never heard her refusal to marry him, as if she'd come home to Steamboat Springs and everything was going to be the same between them. How could *anything* be the same? Not after Diana—that senseless, horrible death...

"You gonna be working your old job out at Diana's place?" Dutch was asking, his mouth full.

Piper's glance shot up to meet his. It was the first mention of Diana since Piper had gotten home. She could feel the tension, the silence from her parents.

"I—I'm not sure," Piper whispered past the sudden lump that formed in her throat.

"I was just wondering," Dutch said ingenuously, and went back to his meal.

But Piper caught a glint from Dutch's eye just before he turned back to his plate, and she felt a twinge of irritation at the shrewdness behind that innocent, blue-eyed look.

She'd have to remember that Dutch was no country bumpkin. She'd have to keep in mind that there was deliberation behind his apparently easygoing ways, and she'd have to tell him flat out that she was not interested in a relationship.

After dinner Piper walked out with him to the official sheriff's department Blazer. It struck her as they stood there together under the old willow tree that she'd been in the exact spot with Dutch a hundred times before. It was the same, nothing had changed, but it was also utterly different because *everything* had changed.

And Dutch didn't even seem to realize it.

"I'd like to see you, Piper," Dutch was saying, and he reached for her hand. "How about Friday night?"

"Look," she said, clasping her hands behind her, kicking at the gravel in the driveway with the toe of her shoe, "I need some time to myself, Dutch. I just got home."

"Of course," Dutch said, "take all the time you need. But there's this band at..."

He just wasn't hearing her. Piper looked up, shading her eyes from the setting sun. "You haven't changed," she said. "Really, Dutch."

But all he replied was, "Take all the time you need, Piper. I'm just real glad you're home at last." He climbed into the Blazer and smiled at her.

"See you," Piper said and watched grimly as he drove on down Crawford Street.

Piper sat on the porch till well after dark with her parents. Everything else in her life seemed askew, but her folks were good people, caring but not interfering, allowing Piper the space to be happy or sad, always there when she needed them. They'd been the same way toward Diana, too, after Diana's parents had died.

"It *is* nice to have you home," Betty said, breaking the stillness of evening. Somewhere in the lilac bushes a cricket began to chirp.

"I'm glad to be here, Mom. I really am. I wish...sometimes I wish I'd flown home for...for the funeral."

"You don't need to explain," John said. "It was a long way."

"I know," Piper said quietly. "It's just that I guess I still need to... to bury her."

"Of course you do," Betty said. "Losing a friend, and at your age . . . It's hard."

"It stinks," Piper put in, and laughed without humor.

"Visit the grave," Betty said. "It helps, honey. It really does."

"Well," John said after a time, "*have* you thought about work this summer?"

Piper shrugged into the darkness and hugged her knees to her chest. "I don't even know if I want to stay in Steamboat Springs. I can work just about anywhere in the state."

"You're a top-notch horse trainer, that's true," John said from his place in a rocking chair, "but you're needed here."

Piper turned her head.

"We didn't want to alarm you, dear," Betty put in, "but Dan Bourne's been having a rough time of it out at the ranch."

"What do you mean?" Dan, Piper thought, she'd hardly even considered *him* since the news of Diana's death. Dan Bourne . . . widower.

"Well," John was saying, "the man's no horse trainer. I hear he's been having help problems out there. Some dissatisfied customers."

Piper sat up straighter. "You mean Diana's ranch is in trouble? But that's . . . that's impossible. It's the best ranch for miles. Everyone's always waiting for a spot to open up to train their horses there."

"Not anymore," John said pointedly. "Word has it that Dan could use all the help he can get now."

Piper shook her head in disbelief. "That just can't be."

"I think he's lost a couple of trainers over the past year," Betty said. "You know, after... after Diana's accident."

"I know you can find work anywhere," John was saying, "but Dan could probably use your help, honey."

"Dan?" she said, still shocked. "Do you think I give two hoots about that man?"

John leaned forward and put a hand on his daughter's thick, curling hair. "We know you don't care about him, Piper, but you do care about the Elk River Ranch. Diana would want you to help."

Piper kept trying to digest the news. The ranch in trouble. What in the name of God had Dan Bourne done to the place? She got to her feet and pushed her hair from her brow. "I don't believe this," she said. "It's as if I *knew* he was bad news the day Diana met him."

"Now, honey..."

"You know—" Piper walked to the porch railing and stood looking out across the lawn "—you know, I feel that if Dan Bourne had never come here, if Diana had never met him, she'd be alive today."

"That's a terrible thing to say. Why, Dan's suffered, too. For God's sake, he lost his wife, Piper," her mother said sharply.

"And I lost my best friend," Piper said sadly, "my very best friend."

Shortly, Piper crossed the yard to the garage and her upstairs apartment. She'd told her parents there wasn't a chance in a million she'd help that man. And her folks hadn't uttered another word. But they knew, just as Piper knew in her own heart, that in the end she'd give in to the loyalty she felt for Diana and her friend's legacy.

She kicked off her shoes and jeans and put on her nightgown, stepping over the clutter, and that's when she saw the car patrolling the quiet street—the sheriff's car, it headlights swinging across her window as it turned around on the dead-end road. She stood in the darkened room and pulled aside the curtain. It was Dutch, all right. Watching the house? "Great," she whispered.

FINGERS OF PEARL DAWN were reaching over the surrounding peaks of the Rocky Mountains and illuminating the broad Yampa Valley when Piper revved up her vintage Jeep the following morning. Her thoughts were doing battle. Drive on out to the Elk River Ranch and assess the situation, or forget it—without Diana there, Piper wasn't sure she had it in her to face the situation, anyway.

And Dan Bourne. Her parents said the ranch looked fine, in good repair, the fields taken care of, the main house as sturdy as ever, but as for Bourne's handling of the horses and the customers...

Okay, Piper thought as she drove down the Crawford Street hill toward town, so he was a city dude and didn't know a horse from a cow. She couldn't blame the man for that. But the people who boarded their horses at the ranch and expected top-notch trainers could blame him. He should have hired someone knowledgeable to manage that end of the business. For Lord's sake, that's where the money was!

When Piper drove through downtown it was all but empty at that early hour. Only a few pickup trucks and a camper or two sat parked in front of a restaurant. A couple of ranchers and the odd vacationing fisherman, no doubt, having coffee and eggs.

She drove through the blinking yellow lights, feeling the cool air on her face, the freshness of the May morning. The streets had just been washed, and glistened wetly in the pale light. Some of the big old cottonwood trees near the Yampa River that flowed through town were just now blooming—fragile looking still, the leaves so new they were a pale, delicate green.

She saw it then, Dutch's Blazer, parked at a café on the west side of town, and she was glad for the blinking light that meant she wouldn't have to stop. Dutch might see her and come out.... Why couldn't he have at least given her a day or two of peace before coming around?

Then she was free of town, heading west on old U.S. Route 40, the highway that at one time had been one of the only routes across the United States—before interstates. Still, Steamboat Springs filled up with tourists summer and winter. In the winter they came for late deer and elk hunting and, of course, skiing. In the spring and summer they came to fish and camp and hike the many popular sites of northern Colorado. Sometimes the place was a zoo of tourists. At other times, like this morning, it was all Piper's, fresh and cool and springtime green, the rivers rushing, the white-capped peaks standing tall against the pale morning sky.

She turned onto Elk River Road a mile from downtown, and headed up the familiar valley. The road rose, past the airport, on up into ranch country. On the distant mountains thick pine and aspen forests were just being touched by soft gold morning sunlight. On the nearby hills sheep and cattle roamed in the coolness, and horses grazed, some more frisky than others at this hour.

Piper wasn't sure what to expect when she turned onto the dirt road that carved a wide arc out of the fields leading to Diana's ranch house. Everything was achingly familiar and yet alien, too. Perhaps it was because she'd been away a long time. Perhaps it was because she'd never see Diana here again.

The Jeep's engine seemed to groan too loudly as Piper pulled up next to the barn and parked. But even though it was still very early, Dan Bourne and whoever he had working there should be up and about.

She poked her head into the barn. "Hello?" she called. No one. Then out to the corral. A few horses roamed—someone had given them hay that morning. But where was everyone? In the fields? No, not this early. And then it seemed as if she were being held rooted to the spot by an invisible force as she stared out across the rangeland. Yes, over there near that tree, she thought, she and Diana had rounded up Red, the stud, and he'd reared, darn near catching Piper with a hoof.

Piper shook off the memories and strode across the yard toward the house. She had to admit the place *did* look okay. The fences were in good repair, everything that needed paint was painted. Yet it was so quiet. Of course, she thought, with so few horses around . . .

She knocked. Waited. Knocked again. Someone had to be on the premises. And then she wondered just what she was going to say to Dan Bourne when she did find him. It wasn't as if they were friends. In fact, she barely knew the man. And what she did know, Piper wasn't exactly sure she liked. She knocked again, loudly, ready to look elsewhere. Where *was* he?

She shifted, putting her hands on her hips, cocking a knee, biting her lower lip. Patience had never been her long suit.

An image of him popped into her mind. He was dressed in his wedding clothes, the pin-striped trousers, the pleated-front formal shirt, the black tie. She recalled his face: strong features, hard angles, an imperious curve to his nose, straight, fine black hair, a certain toughness.

She knocked one more time and abruptly the door swung open. For some reason she'd expected him to look as he had at the wedding, ridiculous as that was. But the man standing in front of her was clad only in a white towel that was wrapped around his torso. Inadvertently Piper's gaze traveled from his unshaven face to his hair-sprinkled chest, down his lean belly to the long line of crisp black hairs that disappeared beneath the startling white towel.

"Well," she breathed, and caught herself quickly, jerking her eyes up to his.

Dan Bourne's brow creased. "Piper Hilyard," he said. "I'll be damned. I didn't expect..."

"That's real obvious," she observed before thinking.

A slight smile formed on the corners of his mouth and he put an arm up, hooking his hand over the top of the door. "You should have called," he said. "How long have you been back?"

"Yesterday," she answered. "I got home yesterday." She looked past his smooth bare shoulder, unaccountably embarrassed, as if his almost-naked state was an insult directed at her.

"Just yesterday," he said, merely standing there, gazing down at her.

"Yes," Piper replied, and folded her arms stiffly, returning his stare.

Then she remembered it, that mocking way Dan had, the hard look in his eye that spoke of things beyond the ordinary human's experience, a challenge, a derisive curl to his lip that stated unequivocally that no one could ever surprise him again.

With his free hand Dan scrubbed at the heavy dark stubble on his chin. Piper noticed instantly that he no longer wore his wedding band. Of course not, she thought bitterly.

"I just got out of the shower," he was saying. "I'll shave and dress while you make coffee."

"While *I* make coffee," Piper repeated.

But he only shrugged and turned away, showing her the bare, tanned expanse of his back. A drop of water from his wet hair ran down his neck. "Do what you want," he said. "I'll be out in a few minutes." Then, as if it were an afterthought, he said, "Welcome back, Piper."

When he was gone she stepped inside and glanced around the ranch-style living room. Again she was struck with a curious impression of everything looking the same though it somehow wasn't. There was a silence to Diana's place. An emptiness.

She did make a pot of coffee, telling herself she wanted a cup and to hell with what Dan Bourne wanted. While the coffee dripped she wandered around the kitchen, running a finger across the greasy stovetop, even peeking into the refrigerator on the pretense that she was getting cream. If Dan was eating at all, it sure wasn't from the nearly-empty fridge. Finally she poured herself a cup of coffee, laced it with sugar and leaned up against the sink in the painfully familiar kitchen to await the widower.

He came in about five minutes later and went straight to the coffeepot, ignoring Piper. When he turned around, taking a long drink from his mug, she noticed that his shirt wasn't yet buttoned, or even tucked in, and that the top button on his blue jeans was carelessly undone.

Really thinks he's something, she decided, and she wondered if his arrogance, that studied cynicism, was for real or a put-on. Plenty of cowboy types possessed a masculine aura—Piper was used to it—but Dan's brand of maleness was too big-city for her, too jaded. Of course, she recalled, he had been a city cop for a long time. And she wondered then if he was aware of the way he came off around women.

Piper took a drink of her own cooling coffee and met his blue eyes over the rim of her cup.

The silence stretched out between them in Diana's kitchen, a silence that began to pulse in the air. Piper took another sip. Then she noticed the dark circles under his eyes and the fact that he didn't seem nearly as aware of the tension in the room as she was. No. He looked preoccupied. That and somewhat tired. Had he been up all night?

Abruptly Piper put her cup down and turned away, disgusted. She folded her arms and wondered what in

God's name Diana had seen in this man. Without turning back, she said, "I see you haven't got too many horses left around here."

There was a long moment of silence. Then, "No, I've lost a few customers."

"Why?"

"It's not too hard to figure out," he said. "I'm not a horse trainer. The customers know it."

"So, hire one."

"I did."

"And?"

"It didn't work out."

"I see." Finally she came around to face him again. "You can't run a ranch," she said, "and get up in the morning any old time you please."

"Is that a fact."

"Yes," Piper retorted. "Don't you have *any* help around here?"

Dan shook his head slowly, that mirthless smile tilting his lips. "I've got a couple of local Mexican guys. They do the best they can."

"Well, that's just great," Piper put in. "And where are they now? Were they out on the town with you or something?"

The minute the words were out of her mouth she knew they were unfair. But it was typical of Piper, when she was in a difficult situation, not to back down. When she was right, she could be self-righteous; when wrong, she was hostile. So she stood there, stuck her chest out and met Dan's angry gaze boldly, daring him.

"Out on the town," he said, with a sharp edge of irony.

She waited, arms folded, dark eyes smoldering.

"It so happens," he said, "we were up all night with a newborn foal that was in trouble."

"That's life on a ranch," she said curtly. Somewhere in her subconscious a small, timid voice was saying, "Ease up, don't be a jerk," but she studiously ignored it.

Dan Bourne gave his head a little shake, as if not quite believing her. "So to what do I owe the honor of your visit?" he asked finally, keeping his tone carefully even.

Piper let her arms drop and focused her eyes at a spot over Dan's shoulder. "I heard you needed some help," she said.

"That was kind of you," he remarked dryly.

"Well, I thought..." She pivoted on her boot heels and looked out the window at the familiar scene. "What I mean is, you need help and I'm free. I know the ropes and I could..."

"It won't work."

"What won't?"

"I can't pay you." He put his mug in the sink and shrugged, starting to do up the buttons of his shirt. "No money, Piper, and I'm sure you don't come cheap."

"I'll..." She thought a moment. "I'll do it for free. You can pay me later if you want. I can start—"

"No," he said, his tone sharp. "I'm not a goddamn charity case." And then he faced her full on, the power of his statement reverberating in the room.

There it was again, Piper thought, that hard-boiled male arrogance. "You know," she retorted, her chin jutting forward, "from where I stand, buster, that's just what you are."

The look she got in return was glacial, but Piper stood her ground, facing him, trying to pull her five feet eight inches up to his nearly six foot height. Brown eyes met icy blue ones for what seemed an eternity.

It was Dan who finally spoke. "Listen," he said in a steel-hard voice, "you've got some kind of a wild hair going. I don't know if you're always like this, or if it's me that's got your back up, lady. The fact is," he said, "I don't really give a damn. I'm tired, and I've got enough problems. I think you just better go on home, kid."

Piper locked her jaw. She could feel her whole body begin to tremble. Words formed in her mind, smart-alecky retorts, but even Piper knew they would come out as spiteful. She realized she was standing there too long, staring at him, saying nothing, two burning spots of red staining her cheeks.

He watched her, leaning negligently back against the sink, arms folded, waiting. He wasn't going to say another word. He wasn't going to apologize or back down or reopen the subject. There was an absolute finality to his stance.

Piper pressed her lips together tightly so she wouldn't say something stupid. She drew herself up, shot Dan a poisonous look and walked very slowly, very deliberately, toward the back door. She opened it, stepped through and couldn't help letting it close just a little too loudly behind her.

On the drive home a dozen questions pummeled her: How could Diana have failed to see what a self-centered jerk he was? And what was more, why *had*

Dan come west, anyway? He'd quit the police force in Philadelphia, but why? Had he been forced to quit?

Still seething, Piper arrived home to find her parents eating breakfast. When she walked in, her mother raised a brow. "I thought you were going to work today, honey," Betty said.

Piper plumped herself into the kitchen chair opposite her mother's. "Tell me something," she said in a hard voice, "did Dan Bourne inherit Diana's ranch, lock, stock and barrel?"

CHAPTER TWO

PIPER LAY ON THE HAMMOCK under the big willow tree in her parents' yard, one foot on the ground, gently rocking, her hands behind her head. It had been almost a week, she was thinking, seven days since he'd kicked her off the ranch, and she didn't feel any better about it now than she had then.

Yesterday she'd visited the cemetery. It had helped. Just as her mom had suggested, visiting the site was a way to let Diana go once and for all. Piper had found it an odd experience, standing there in the late-May sunshine on the side of the hill above town. There was Diana's headstone, all nicely carved and engraved, sitting directly in front of her parents' graves. She had expected to be utterly undone by going there, but she hadn't been.

Piper pushed herself with her toe and gazed up through the branches of the willow. So now what? she wondered, asking herself for the hundredth time, her litmus test: *What would Diana want me to do about the ranch?*

She knew now that Dan Bourne had indeed inherited the place, every fence post, every stick of wood and slab of stone, the water rights, the acres and acres of pasture, the house, the barn, the horses. All the grieving widower's now.

Was she jealous? In all honesty, maybe deep down inside she was envious and that's why she disliked him so intensely. But that notion didn't feel right—she'd never really craved to own a place of her own, as Diana had wanted. No. She wanted to train horses, and that she could do anywhere.

Except Diana would want her at the Elk River Ranch, working alongside Dan, helping him.

Piper's father drove up the driveway and put the car away in the garage shortly after five. She knew he'd wanted to talk to her all week but had kept his distance, biding his time. When he called across the lawn, asking if she'd have a soda with him, Piper was not surprised. She called back, "Sure," then sighed. She only hoped he wasn't going to lecture her. *Piper, honey, maybe you should give Dan a second chance....*

"Piper, honey," her dad said as he pulled up a lawn chair next to the hammock, "I've been giving this business about the ranch a lot of thought. I think—"

"You think I should give Dan a second chance," she put in, looking heavenward.

"Now, that's not what I was going to say."

"But I'll bet I'm real close, huh?"

"I've seen you in action since you were two years old and could voice an opinion. I've watched you launch into just about everything feet first. Oh," he added, "I know you consider yourself honest, frank and all that, but there's a time and place."

"Should I lie to people?" She shook her head, smiling at him.

"Not lie, Piper. You know what I mean."

"I can't be someone I'm not."

"No one's asking you to be. I'm just saying that you could try waiting and seeing before voicing those opinions."

"I'm right about Dan," she said, growing defensive. "I mean, here he comes traipsing out from the big city, and I hear he had problems with his job, and then next thing you know he's married to a wealthy rancher, and then boom, she's gone and he owns it all."

"He was one very sad man when Diana died, Piper."

"I didn't say he wasn't."

"Then what's the trouble? What really happened to get him to kick you off the ranch last week?"

"You sound like it was *my* fault."

"Was it?"

Piper frowned, and then, as always, she examined her father's questions deeply. Maybe, she thought, it *was* possible that she'd been too hard on Dan.

"I don't know. I really don't know, Dad." She sat up, raked her fingers through her long tangles and sighed. "Maybe," she said, "maybe I did provoke him a little."

"Provoked him."

"Well, okay," she said, "I was pulling one of my brutally honest acts on him. Does that satisfy you?"

Her father only smiled.

The following morning, bolstered with determination to mend her ways, and equally determined to save the failing ranch, Piper drove back out the familiar road, past the airport, beyond the river's sharp curves, out to where the Elk River Valley broadened, turned lush and green and rolling, backed by sharp peaks crowned with white, and dark forests climbing the slopes. Horses and cattle and sheep dotted the land. They thrived in the high, cool, dry climate of the Rockies where insect pests were few and the humidity didn't torture them.

God, it was beautiful country, Piper thought. New Zealand had been beautiful, too, but different, of course. And the scope here was huge—miles and miles, acres and acres, endless land where there was space, room, freedom. This was no finite island; it ran north and south, east and west, for thousands of empty miles.

Halfway up the valley Piper's expansive mood deflated. She passed a sheriff department's white Blazer going in the opposite direction, and she saw instantly that Dutch was driving it. He recognized her Jeep, too, and she noticed in her rearview mirror that he pulled off the side of the road, apparently expecting her to stop.

Well, she wasn't going to stop. She wasn't going to encourage him one tiny bit. No men in her life. No men at all, that was her new motto. She'd give Dutch time to get over his obsession. Maybe she'd even explain her new game plan to him. No men, not him, not anyone else, not right now.

She waved her arm casually out the top of her Jeep and continued on, holding her breath and praying he wouldn't turn around and follow her.

Piper drove under the crossbar of the Elk River Ranch and down the long, dusty driveway. She steered straight for the barn and the mares' paddocks, realizing that she hadn't planned a single word to say to Dan. Oh, she wasn't going to apologize for anything.

Uh-uh. But he could very easily kick her off the place again if she didn't come up with *something*. Okay, she thought, she'd confront the problem in due time, but for now she needed to see just what she was getting into, make an assessment of the place—see firsthand the condition of the horses, how they'd wintered, how many there were. She'd already noticed the absence of foals out in the pasture. Surely by now a few should have been born. It was the right time of year.

It could be that Dan hadn't bred any of the brood mares last year. Diana had been gone by the spring when the mares were bred, and maybe he just hadn't bothered or hadn't known what to do.

Then she remembered Dan saying he'd been up all night with a foal in trouble. So there might be a few babies coming. At least there was one.

God! That would mean a whole year lost! And now, right now, in May, the mares would be ready to breed again and someone needed to...

What about last year's brood, the yearlings? Yes, there they were, still with their mothers. Lord, they should have been weaned by now! Oh, what a mess!

She wondered whether anyone had been working with the yearlings at all or if they'd just been left to go wild. How would Dan Bourne, a police detective, know what to do?

At least it looked as if he'd kept the fields irrigated, because they were green, but in May it wasn't much of a trick to keep them green. And the hay fields—how were they? Had he had to buy hay last winter or had there been enough?

So much to do! There were so many details to running a ranch like this. Diana had kept a big blackboard in the barn with schedules, directions, notes, medications for each horse. Was Dan doing that?

Who kept the shoeing up to date? Diana had had a chart, each horse, the date of its last shoeing. Details, details. The place had to run right, because the horses couldn't remind you, and no one could remember it all.

She pulled up in her old parking place by the big barn, turned off the key and sat in her Jeep for a minute, letting the dust settle, steeling herself. Then she tossed her hair back and straightened. "Okay, let's go to work," she said to herself, and, fortuitously not seeing the master himself around, she headed into the barn.

It was neat, raked clean. The black barn cat came to greet her, and she smiled, bending to pet him. "So, Midnight, you're still here. Good kitty."

There was Tansy in a box stall with the new foal Dan must have been talking about. Piper patted the mare and gave the foal a quick look of appraisal. It seemed fine, a bit small. It looked as if it was going to be a chestnut.

She explored further. There was the big blackboard on the wall in its accustomed place, but it was wiped clean except for one cryptic message: Picnic?

What did *that* mean? Was Picnic sick or missing or did she just need shoeing?

The tack room was neat, but dust lay on everything in a fine haze, and motes danced in the light from the window. The room looked unused. No one was riding, then. All the saddles were there, the bridles and martingales and girths hung neatly. The ribbons won by the Elk River Ranch still hung in rows around the walls, along with tarnished trophy cups and horse blankets. Piper opened a cabinet. Liniment and eye ointment and antibiotic cream and hoof protector were all there. Brushes and curry combs and horse shampoo, leg wraps and poultice and blue ice gel for injuries, all the paraphernalia was still in place. Some had been used recently, she could see.

She left the tack room behind and went out the other end of the barn, out the big open door through which a truck could drive. There were the three horse trailers parked in a row. The rear doors on one were open, though, and someone was cleaning it out.

Piper stopped in her tracks, taking a couple of deep breaths. Okay, she thought, it was time to confront him, time to be a little more diplomatic than she had been last week. She walked up to the trailer. "Hello," she called, figuring it had to be Dan working in there. "Hello..."

A figure appeared in the opening, and Piper let out her breath. It wasn't Dan Bourne.

"Hello?" the man said, surprised. He was thin and wiry, Hispanic by the look of it, holding a rake.

"I'm Piper Hilyard. I, ah, used to work here. Do you work for Dan, then?" she asked.

"Yes, I work here for a year now," he said with a distinct accent. "I am Luis."

"Well, hi, Luis. Um, does anyone else work here now? I was wondering, well, because I spoke to Dan about coming back here, to work, and I'm trying to get a feel for what's going on here," Piper said, lying only a little.

"This is a good ranch, good horses. There is only Mr. Dan and me and Rick here."

Piper thought for a minute, then asked, "Luis, is anyone riding the horses, I mean exercising them, working them? And the yearlings—has anyone been handling them?"

The man cocked his head. "There is very much work here. Mr. Dan doesn't ride. Rick sometimes. Me—" he gestured to himself "—I love the horses and I take very good care, but I no ride them."

Her heart sank. It was just as she thought. No one had been riding at all, no one had been doing a darn thing. "Okay, Luis, tell me, are there any other mares about to foal? I saw Tansy in the barn...."

He shrugged. "I think one or two. Mr. Dan try, but we never sure when mares come in their time, you know?"

"And this year? Are you going to breed any of them?"

Luis shrugged.

Piper nodded toward the horse trailer he'd been cleaning. "Have you been taking horses to shows?"

"No," Luis said, "I take a horse to Wonderview Farm over in Kremmling."

"Dan sold a horse?"

Luis shook his head. "This one belong to Missy Trenham. She want more training, so she move her horse."

"You mean Missy's black gelding, Indigo? Indigo's gone to another place?"

Luis was regarding her strangely, bewildered. Here she was, badgering the poor man. The Elk River Ranch wasn't his responsibility, after all. Piper took a deep breath. "Uh, do you know where Dan is?" she asked.

"I think he still in house. You want me to tell him you here, Miss... Miss..."

"You can call me Piper, okay?" she said. "And I'll just look around myself for a bit, to get a feel for the place. Thanks, Luis."

She turned, knowing Luis was happy to get rid of her and go back to his chores. She hooked her thumbs in her jeans pockets and scuffed at the dirt with a boot, planning on going out to the yearlings' field to take a look at last year's brood, the ones she and Diana had bred before she—

"Nice day," someone said, and Piper jerked her head up.

Dan Bourne stood in the cavernous barn opening, one shoulder against the door frame, one leg bent and crossed over the other. A faint smile crooked the corners of his mouth, deepening those two lines.

"Oh, hi," she said, and swallowed.

"Spying on me?" he asked mildly.

"Spying?"

"I heard what you were asking Luis."

"I was just trying to figure out where this place is at, that's all. You weren't around, so I..."

He straightened finally, and Piper saw a flash of anger ignite in his eyes. "Listen," he said, "I don't have time for your games. Why don't you just toddle on home."

It took every ounce of effort to control the sharp words that formed in her head. She told herself that he was being nasty because she'd been so confrontational last week; she reminded herself sternly to think before she spoke. She let out a breath. "I *wasn't* spying," she said finally. "It's just that this place means a lot to me. Diana was my best friend. We put this ranch together . . . from scratch,'' she added, keeping her temper in check. "I—I want to spend the summer helping,'' she said, and raised her eyes to his.

But he put up a hand to stop her. "I put Elk River on the market last week.''

"What?''

"That means that it's for sale. I'm selling out.''

Piper stood there, hot, then cold, then hot again. Her mind whirled sickeningly. "You can't.''

"Why not?'' he asked softly, challenging her.

She groped for words, shocked. "You just can't. It was Diana's. She *loved* this place. It was one of the best quarter horse ranches in the state.''

"Don't start in on me,'' he said evenly. "I'm not in the mood.''

"I'm . . . I'm *not* trying to start anything,'' she said. "I'm only trying to understand.''

"Well, understand this,'' he said. "I'm not a trainer. Diana's dead. I can't run this damn place by myself.''

"*Hire* a trainer,'' she responded.

"I hired two. Neither of them could handle it, either.''

Piper chewed her lip, thinking furiously, her head down, her chestnut brown hair falling in her face. She scuffed her boot in the dirt absently. "Listen,'' she began.

But again he put up a silencing hand. "Why don't *you* buy the place?'' he asked, mocking, bitter.

"Very funny,'' she retorted. "What're you asking, a couple million?'' She pushed her hair back with a hand and held his gaze.

"Close," he said, and shrugged. "It's valuable property. And since all of Diana's money was tied up in it, and I can't get any income out of it, I have what you might call a cash-flow problem."

Piper shook her head. "You can't do it. You have to take the ranch off the market." She heard herself saying the words, hardly believing she'd said them. "I'm a reputable trainer. I'll put the ranch back on a good financial footing. I know what to do. Give me some time and you'll see."

A faintly derisive smile touched his lips, and Piper found herself watching his face, trying desperately to read his expression. He wasn't like Dutch, all swagger and bluster and openness. Dan Bourne was smooth and cold and all closed up inside, a stranger, an interloper who'd never belonged here. But there he was, anyway, owning it all, *selling* it all....

"Give me this one summer," she said quietly, watching him, searching for a sign. The barn was silent; only the sound of Luis's rake on the trailer floor broke the stillness. She waited, holding his eyes with hers, and then said once more, "Just a few months. You'll see, you won't want to sell."

He only regarded her soberly, however, his face all unyielding lines. After an interminable time she finally saw a flicker of something in his expression, as if he'd made a decision. "All right," he said at last, and he folded his arms across his chest, his knees locked, legs apart. "Okay. You can try it for the summer. If you can keep the boarders here and get a few ready to sell," he continued, "get some cash coming in, you get the summer. Understand something, though. If I get an offer, a solid one, I'll sell. Not that

I expect it to happen soon, but I want you to know that."

She nodded, not speaking, her lips closed tightly.

"And I *will* pay you," he said. "You know Bounce?"

She eyed him warily. "Diana's mare."

"She's been bred. She's ready to drop any day, I think. She's yours, her and her foal."

Stiffly Piper nodded. It was fair. Bounce was a fine horse. "Done," she said.

She stood there and felt a smile play on her lips. Two days ago, a day ago, she wouldn't have dreamed that she would be there in the barn with Dan striking up a bargain. Diana would be so pleased, she was thinking. Diana would have wanted them to get along, to be friends. She looked up and was going to say "thanks," but when her eyes met his there was something there she couldn't read. . . .

The memory hit her with a jolt. She was at the wedding again. Dan had come over at Diana's insistence to make conversation. They'd been talking in monosyllables, and something had happened between them. Piper tossed her head a little, trying to shatter the moment, but the same uncomfortable intensity persisted as it had over a year ago, a cold stirring of her senses that raised the tiny hairs on her skin.

"Well," she breathed, and hooked her thumbs in her pockets again, ill at ease. "Well, I guess I better get to work."

Another moment passed. "Sure," he finally said, "you do that."

She escaped. She walked away from him, hunching her shoulders defensively, her long legs eating up the distance to the yearlings' field. When she was finally out of his sight she straightened her back and collected herself. She detested him then; she despised him because Diana was dead and he was alive, because he had power over her, because he could sell the ranch out from under her without a by-your-leave.

It took all day just to sort out what was really going on at the ranch. There were two dozen horses left, including the stud, Red, five boarders, ten brood mares, the new foal in the barn and seven yearlings. There were no horses at all to be trained, the main source of income, and no young stock in training to sell.

No, Dan Bourne had sold all the young horses for peanuts, Piper found out, because he couldn't train them and he couldn't afford to keep them.

Rick had told her that. She'd found him out in the mares' field, herding them in to be grained and checked out for the day.

"Hello!" Piper had called out, seeing a man behind the slowly moving horses. "Are you Rick?"

"Ricardo Salinas, at your service, miss," he's said, grinning widely, showing a gold tooth.

"Hi, Rick, I'm going to be working here. My name's Piper. Glad to meet you."

The short, thickset man, who was totally Americanized from what she could tell, had shaken her hand. "A new employee? Dan didn't say anything."

"Well, actually, I worked here before. I was Diana, Mrs. Bourne's, partner. I'm a trainer."

"Oh, I got it. Well, we can use you. I do my best, but I can't ride them all, and I'm no trainer."

She'd asked him a lot of questions, getting a feel for what had been done at the ranch for the past year and a half, and that was when she'd discovered that Dan had sold off the young stock.

"Oh, God," she said.

"Well, what could he do? They ate and ate all winter, and we didn't have a trainer at the time. He had no choice, really," Rick said, defending his boss.

They herded the mares on ahead of them into a paddock near the barn, and Piper helped Rick fill the feed buckets.

"This one's about to pop," Rick said, patting the rump of a horse with a belly that stuck out on either side like a ripe apple.

"That's Bounce," Piper said.

"Think we should keep her in at night?" Rick asked.

"Wouldn't be a bad idea."

And so the day went. Decisions to make, lists, supplies to check. Piper even started weaning the yearlings, separating them from their mothers, who'd whinny and mope for a day or two. The yearlings were halterbroke, not afraid of people but wild and absolutely ignorant of basics such as standing still for their feet to be handled.

And throughout the entire day Piper was aware of Dan Bourne around the ranch, working. He mended a fence out in the mares' field, irrigated a distant hay field, standing out there in his worn jeans and faded gray gym T-shirt with a shovel, changing the water flow from one ditch to another to flood a new field. He unloaded bales of hay in the barn, emerging with wisps stuck to him, brushing the chaff off with one strong brown arm.

Next she saw him crawling under a tractor, then wrestling with a huge rear tractor tire. She sat in her Jeep, gulping the sandwich she'd brought, and Dan drove to the feed store, returning with fifty-pound bags of the special food for pregnant mares.

He never ate lunch, not that Piper saw, anyway. All afternoon he helped Luis muck out stalls, shovel the manure into a trailer, then unload the stuff in a hay field. Then he had to drag the field with the tractor to spread it.

He never once spoke to Piper. He never looked in her direction. He laughed with Rick once, conferred with Luis, but never, not once, did he talk to Piper.

She avoided him, too. She could play the game as well as he could. But she was aware of him all day, somewhere on the periphery of her vision, bending, straightening, wiping sweat off his brow with a muscular forearm, lugging, hauling, driving the pickup truck or the tractor, his strong brown wrists wrestling with the steering wheel.

By six Piper had had enough. A lot had been accomplished, but there were a few things she had to talk to Dan about. She didn't much like having to ask his permission, but he *was* the owner. She was going to be calm, though, she told herself.

Dan had disappeared into the house finally, gone in without saying a word, or asking her how things were, or if she had any questions or problems to discuss.

She drew in a deep breath, pushed her hair back and went on in after him.

He was sprawled in a kitchen chair, his legs stretched out in front of him, a beer can in his hand, an open can of beef stew, unheated, on the table beside him. He regarded her dispassionately and put the beer can down on the table. He said nothing.

"I'm going to advertise our training services in a few local papers and magazines," Piper began, eminently reasonable. "I just wanted to let you know. Do you want me to put your number in the ads or mine at home?"

"Either," he said, clearly not interested.

"Okay, fine. I'll put your number in. Do you have a machine?"

"No."

"You might want to get one," she said.

"It rings in the barn."

"Okay...well, good." She leaned her shoulder against the kitchen door frame. "I'm going to need some lists. Immunizations, worming, things like that."

"The vet has that stuff." Dan picked up the can, took a spoon and began eating it, cold.

How rude. "But you didn't...? Okay, I'll get it from him. Dr. Dewell, right?"

He nodded, his mouth full.

She pressed down a growing irritation, telling herself he was just tired. "The place looks good," she said. "The horses are healthy. That little foal you delivered seems to be fine."

"Thanks," he said shortly.

"I didn't mean to be patronizing," Piper said, feeling heat rise into her cheeks. "I meant it."

"So did I."

"Oh," she said. Then, "Look, I'm not here to pass judgment on you. We don't have to be adversaries." She'd just been through an entire day of repressing a strong urge to tell it like it was, and she was now tired herself and beginning to lose it. She stood with her shoulder against the frame of the door and watched him eating stew out of that can, drinking his beer, answering her in clipped phrases that sounded as if he was bored to distraction.

An ex-cop, she mused, glaring at him. He was totally out of his element here, a man without the finesse to have appreciated Diana, a man with nothing more than a measure of animal magnetism. He must have used her to escape his sordid life as a cop. Maybe he'd just wanted her money.

"You done?" he asked. "'Cause I really need to shower...."

She narrowed her eyes and abruptly something snapped inside her. "Tell me," she said, "why *did* you marry Diana?" And before the words were even out she knew she'd blown it.

"Okay," Dan said, slamming the can down, tossing the spoon into the sink as he came to his feet. "Okay. This has been coming. Why don't you get it off your chest, lady?"

"You want the truth?" she replied. "*Do* you?" His expression remained impassive as he nodded, but she sensed a sheathed menace in him. "Okay," she said. "All right. I think you wanted to escape your past. Diana was beautiful, not to mention rich." She saw his body grow taut. "Diana owned a ranch," Piper went on recklessly, "thousands of miles away from your problems. *You* figure it out, Dan Bourne."

He said nothing, not one single word. Piper felt her nerves jangle. Defiantly she tossed her head and looked away, reaching for her car keys in her pocket.

"You know what else I think?" she said. "I think, I believe in my heart, that if you'd never come to Colorado, if you'd never met her, my friend would still be alive today."

He stirred finally, moving his heavy shoulders in an impatient shrug. For a moment Piper stiffened, fearing she'd gone too far, but he made no move in her direction. All he said was, "Go to hell, Piper Hilyard." Then he turned on his heel deliberately, calmly, and left Piper standing alone in the kitchen.

CHAPTER THREE

"YOU TOLD HIM *WHAT?*" Piper's mother asked that night.

Piper wiped dry another plate and put it away in the cupboard. "I told him what I thought," she said, "plain and simple. I *do* think he was using Diana."

"So you got yourself fired, is that the bottom line?" Betty's tone was neutral.

"Now there's a good question. I suppose I'll go back out in the morning and find out."

"Do you owe Dan an apology?"

Piper smiled dryly. "That's another thing I don't know."

"Come again?"

"Well," she said, "I tried all day to be civil, I really did, but he was a total jerk when I went in to ask him some questions after work. Important stuff. I don't know who owes whom an apology."

"But you can't possibly *know* that Dan's coming to Steamboat Springs was in any way related to Diana's death. That's just plain crazy."

Piper shrugged. "Maybe," she said, "but there's something . . ."

"Something?"

"I don't know. It's just an itch in my head, is all."

DAN DID LOOK SURPRISED to see her when she pulled up in her Jeep next to the barn the following morning. He glanced up from where he was replacing fence rails around the corral, nails held between his teeth. Piper climbed out of the Jeep, put her hands on her hips and stood looking at him from across the way, wondering what he was going to do. He straightened very slowly and stared at her for a time, the hammer hanging straight down from his hand. The air between them crackled with a kind of current, and Piper tensed, awaiting his anger, ready to argue, to fight, whatever it took—she'd even apologize if she had to. The ranch was just too important to let go so easily.

But to her surprise he merely shifted his grip on the hammer, took another nail from between his teeth, leaned over and began pounding it into a rail. She could only surmise she still had a job—for that day, anyway.

PIPER KEPT HER JOB for a lot of days. The alfalfa sprang up in the fields, thick and green. Summer came into full swing. She told herself that as long as she and Dan avoided each other, it was going to work.

And then Dutch began to drop by the ranch.

At first he made excuses that seemed relatively plausible. "I was up in Clark, checking out some camper's story about his missing sleeping bag. Thought as long as I was passing by, I'd stop and see how you're doing."

Then another visit that same mid-June week. "Kid on a motorcycle up the road a piece said some guy in a pickup, sounded like old Henry Tucker, ran him off the road last night. I had to check out the scene."

He was back the very next day. Although, apparently, it was Dan whom Dutch had driven out to see this trip. Piper was in the barn, but not out of earshot. And what she heard made goose bumps crawl up her limbs.

"Got a minute, Bourne?" Dutch's voice called out.

Dan, Piper knew, was loading manure into his pickup. She heard the clang as he put the pitchfork against the metal tailgate, and she walked to the barn door to see what was going on.

"Where're those two Mexicans you got working here, Bourne?" Dutch had his Stetson pulled low on his brow, his hands on his hips.

"I sent them out to the yearlings' field to mend some fences. Why?"

"'Cause that Luis has me troubled, Bourne," Dutch said in a nonchalant voice.

Dan leaned against his truck, wiped at his sweating brow and neck with a bandanna, then eyed Dutch. "Why's that, Radowsky?" His stance was relaxed, but even from where Piper stood she could see the muscles tighten across his heavy shoulders.

"Can't prove it yet, Bourne," Dutch said, "but I know in my gut the man's an illegal alien. I'd sure like to get a look at his green card."

"Is that so," Dan said. "Well, Luis isn't here, is he? So why don't you catch him out at his trailer some night."

"Oh, I've tried, but his wife's a pretty good liar. She pretends not to understand English. Now, I'm not that dumb, Bourne."

"Sounds like you've got a problem," Dan said. "What I can't figure is if the problem is Luis or me."

"You?"

"Seems like you might be trying to hassle me through Luis."

"And why would I do that?"

Dan lifted his broad shoulders eloquently then let them drop. "Beats the hell out of me, Radowsky."

For a minute Dutch eyed him carefully. Finally he said, "You know who makes the rules around here, Bourne?"

"No. But I'll bet you're going to tell me."

"*I* do. I'm the law in Routt County, and I suggest you tell that illegal you got working here to come on by my office. Tonight would do just fine."

And then Dan laughed humorlessly. "You know," he said, "when I got up this morning I'd have sworn I was still in America, Radowsky. But listening to you, I'm beginning to wonder."

They were baiting each other, the tough ex-cop standing up to the town bully. Piper bit her lip and watched in growing distress—Dutch had started it, but now they were both behaving like two little boys in a dusty schoolyard, ready to start scuffling any second.

"This is private property, Radowsky," Dan was saying. "I'm sure you can read a No Trespassing sign when you see one."

"Don't push me, Bourne, I'm warning you. You might find yourself down in the jail along with your Mexican buddies."

"You going to be the one to put me there?" Dan's arms were still folded across his chest, but he'd straightened, his legs apart, his jaw locked. He was a couple of inches shorter than Dutch, but Piper was sure that wouldn't make an ounce of difference if it came to a fight. No, Dan looked as if he could take the sheriff apart; there was a menacing stillness to him, in the pitch of his head, the tension of his muscles, in the flare of his nostrils.

"I want that Luis in my office *tonight,*" Dutch said. "You hear me?"

"Oh, I hear you, all right," Dan shot back, and suddenly Piper had seen enough. This wasn't about Luis or even Dan—this was about her.

Without another moment's hesitation she strode out of the barn and called, "Dutch! I didn't know you were here."

"Piper." Dutch took off his hat and turned toward her.

"Listen," she said, walking straight up to him and taking his arm, "can we have a talk, Dutch? Over here?" She tugged at him until they were a few paces away from Dan and the truck. She saw Dan eye them for a long moment, and finally he shrugged, picked up the pitchfork and went back to work.

"What are you *doing?*" she snapped, her cheeks flushed in anger.

"I wasn't—"

"The heck you weren't! You're hassling Dan because—"

"Now, why would I hassle him? I'm only upholding the law, Piper."

"*Your* law, Dutch. You've got no reason to be questioning Dan or even Luis. What have either of them done to deserve this?"

"Now, Piper, if I suspect something isn't on the up-and-up, I—"

"It's *me* you're after, Dutch," she said, exasperated. She looked straight up into his pale blue eyes. "I won't have you doing this to them! It's not right. You're being a bully."

"Piper, I—"

"No, you listen to me and listen real good, Dutch. I'm not your woman. I haven't been for two years."

Dutch took a deep breath. "And just whose woman are you, then?" Unconsciously Dutch glanced in Dan's direction.

"I'm no one's woman," Piper said. "I'm off men, Dutch. I don't care if I ever even see one again. So quit harassing me!"

Dutch's face went stiff, but he refused to acknowledge her words. He adjusted his gun belt in an unconscious gesture and said patronizingly, infuriatingly, "I'll phone you when you've calmed down, honey." And then, in an officious voice, he called to Dan, "You tell that Mexican he isn't long for Routt County!" And he strode to his Blazer and drove away.

For a long time Piper stood in the middle of the dust cloud left from Dutch's departure and stared after him. Dutch was going over the edge, was all she could think. Pestering her was one thing, but extending his power trip to include Dan was really out of line. Why, he was becoming a dictator, a crazy, power-mad king.

Piper turned and gazed at Dan. He was ignoring her, studiously loading the truck, sweat separating the ends of his dark hair, the back of his blue-and-white shirt damp with perspiration.

She watched him for another moment and thought about saying something to him, explaining about Dutch. But what could she say? And besides, he didn't much look like a man who wanted to talk. If nothing else, Piper was learning that the lord and master of the Elk River spread was a loner. The strong, silent type, she thought in derision as he continued to throw the heavy forkfuls onto the back of the truck, the broad muscles of his back straining against the fabric of his shirt.

She wondered then exactly how much of her conversation with Dutch he'd overheard. Heck, she'd practically been yelling she'd been so mad. How embarrassing....

Piper let out a breath and went back into the barn. The day was young, and there was a lot to be done, as always. Dutch and Luis and Dan—the problems were going to have to wait.

Late that afternoon Dan walked out into Red's field to fetch the stallion. Lulubelle, a client's ten-year-old mare, had come into heat, and the client, for a handsome fee to the Elk River Ranch, was going to breed Lulubelle this season.

The stallion, as always, was circling the perimeter of his paddock endlessly, his head high, his nostrils flaring. Restless.

Dan caught Red with no trouble, slipping a lead over his thickly muscled neck while Piper moved Lulubelle into a small corral behind the barn.

Dan released Red into the paddock with Lulubelle, then closed the gate and joined Piper, who was leaning against the fence, her muddy boot resting on the bottom rail.

"Do we need to stay?" he asked, and pulled out his bandanna, running the damp cloth across the back of his neck.

Piper shook her head. "You don't have to, but someone needs to see if Lulubelle accepts him." She gave him a sidelong glance, but he was watching the two horses.

"And if she doesn't accept him?" Dan asked, still looking straight ahead.

She shrugged. "She will."

"I see," he replied. He turned his head toward her, but she stared fixedly into the paddock. She felt a slow flush crawl up her neck as he continued to watch her. Ridiculous, she thought, refusing to look at him, the whole thing was perfectly natural; there was nothing to be uncomfortable about.

Piper held her chin up and stared across the paddock to where Red was starting to go through his courting dance. His whole demeanor had changed now. He whinnied, loud, bell-like, his sides vibrating. His neck arched, and he danced on suddenly light feet. The sun flashed copper glints off his quivering flanks as he touched noses with Lulubelle, rumbling deep in his chest.

The mare stood motionless, not even flinching when the stallion neighed again, his clarion call, snuffled, snorted, snaked out his long neck to rub it against her, his muscles taut, his touch astonishingly gentle. He moved around her, excited, his head high, his eyes flashing. And Lulubelle stood there, quiet, acquiescent, her body braced, ready to receive him.

Not yet, though. Red advanced, retreated, snuffled, rubbed his head against her again, his mating dance.

It was utterly primitive, this age-old ritual. Piper felt the breath shallow in her chest. She stared straight ahead, her hands gripping the rail, pretending Dan wasn't there.

Red moved lightly, his mane tossing, moved behind the mare, and then he was over her, covering her, the two arched necks snaking together. His muscles slid powerfully under his shining hide as he fulfilled his task.

Then it was over.

Still, neither Dan nor Piper spoke for a time. Piper was once more aware of Dan next to her. She could hear his breathing, smell the sweat of his labors, feel the breeze that lifted his fine black hair where it grew long on his neck. She cast about for something to say to break the taut silence, but nothing came to mind, so she stayed there, unmoving, her senses too acute, too aware of the sound of flies buzzing in the paddock, the heat of the sun on her back, the scent of sweat-slicked horses and the hay strewn nearby. Her skin prickled, and she wished she could make her throat work.

It was Dan who stirred finally, dropping back from the fence. He cleared his throat. "Was that okay?" he asked quietly, directing his words to the back of her head.

"Yes," she replied too quickly.

"Good." He cleared his throat again. "Good."

She had to move, had to turn to face him. His straight black brows were drawn, his hands in his pockets.

"I'll put Red back in his paddock," Piper said inanely.

"Okay, sure...."

She took a step, but Dan didn't move, his body blocking her. She looked up at him, and they stood there like that, a moment too long.

"Don't you have something to do?" Piper breathed, but he didn't say anything. He only stayed there, his face inscrutable, until she shouldered past him and went to open the gate. Still, even as she caught Red, Dan remained by the fence and kept staring at her.

It was nearly six-thirty before Piper was finished with the chores that day. She cleaned up the tack room, washed her hands and face and combed her dusty hair out from its ponytail, shaking it to hang freely down her back. Dan was sitting on the front steps of the main house when she began to head toward her Jeep. He was talking to Luis, Piper saw, and both of them were drinking cans of beer. It was only then that she remembered Dutch and the ugly scene of that morning. Was Dan warning Luis?

She headed over to the porch as Luis was crumpling his beer can, thanking Dan and saying goodnight. He nodded to Piper, as well, and took off toward his battered pickup.

"Did you tell Luis about Dutch?" Piper asked, shading her eyes from the glare of the late-day sun.

Dan nodded and took a long drink of his beer, looking up at her from where he was sitting on the bottom step. "I owe it to him," he said. "The man's been good to me."

"*Is* he an illegal alien?" Piper asked.

But Dan only shrugged.

"Don't you think you should know?"

"Look," he said, putting the can down on the step, "Luis showed me papers when I hired him."

"They *could* be forged, Dan."

"You're beginning to sound like your friend Dutch." He cocked his head to one side and looked her in the eye.

"I'll ignore that remark," Piper replied.

"Okay," he said, shrugging, acting the hard-bitten, cynical cop. "You know," he went on, "it isn't an employer's job to check the authenticity of a worker's papers. Like I told Dutch, this is still America. Want a beer?"

Piper shook her head. "No, thanks. I only stopped to ask you something."

"I figured it wasn't a social call," he said.

It seemed they were always baiting each other. Still, Piper chose not to play—at least, not tonight. "I was thinking," she said, "that maybe if I talked to Dutch on Luis's behalf, if I found Dutch in a better mood, maybe he would—"

"Don't bother," Dan said, and he came to his feet, a sun-browned hand raking through his hair.

"Why not?"

"Because," he said, "I've seen men like Dutch before. Policemen who take advantage."

"But Dutch isn't really as tough as he comes off."

Dan waved off her explanation as if bored. "Don't bother standing up for him," he said, and his voice was hard. "It's not your fault. It's no one's fault with men like Radowsky. Never is."

She turned his statement over in her mind, feeling that she should understand it better, but then she frowned and decided to let it go.

"That was a little drastic, wasn't it?" Dan said just as she turned away.

"What was?" she asked, pivoting on her heel.

"Telling Radowsky you're off men."

"You were listening?" she asked.

"I couldn't help hearing. You were rather...loud." A quirk of a lip. "Sounded like you meant it, too."

"I did," Piper muttered, clenching her teeth. "Men are all gigantic pains."

He took another drink of beer and leaned his back against the post. "It's your life," he said diffidently.

Piper felt herself grow hot then cold all over. She tossed her head defiantly. "You're right," she said, "it *is* my life," and she turned away again. She took three long strides, heading to her Jeep, then suddenly stopped and spun around. "Do me a favor," she said.

"Oh, and what would that be?" he replied, still leaning against the post.

"Mind your own business," she said, and headed on her way.

AFTER THAT PIPER AVOIDED Dan like the plague, but that didn't stop her from noticing him when he was otherwise occupied. She couldn't help observing the darnedest things about the man—what he was wearing, or the way his strongly curved calves and thighs filled out his worn blue jeans, or that his hair had begun to curl, touching his shirt collar, and needed to be trimmed.

Often Dan had a five-o'clock shadow by noon. It ran from the crisp curly hair above the V in his shirt up his neck and covered his square chin and cheeks, his upper lip and those double lines bracketing his mouth.

Sometimes, unconsciously, he'd rub a hand over his chin, his jaw tightening, and she'd wonder what he was thinking. She'd wonder again who he really was— bereaved widower trying to make a go of a business in which he was out of his element, or a cold, calculating man who was now the sole owner of a very valuable piece of land.

Piper thought about that a lot. As the summer progressed—a hot, bone-dry summer that people were starting to call a drought—she began to dwell on the subject. She'd once accused Dan of somehow being responsible for Diana's death, and at the time the words had seemed just to slip out unbidden. But the question truly was nagging at her.

Piper watched him and studied him and despised his sardonic handsomeness. She knew in her heart it was Dan's offhand, contemptuous maleness, his utter self-confidence, that had first caught Diana's eye.

A year ago Piper had not really thought to question the way in which Diana had met her death. But now she was looking for some answers. Why had Diana been on that icy section of road alone at night? And why had she been driving Dan's pickup truck?

Dust motes danced in the golden evening light that spilled through the barn doors when Piper strode in to find Dan after work one night. He was stacking bags of feed, his shirt off, and she could see the light playing across the rippling muscles of his back. The sweet, dusty scent of hay mingled with his male odor, and Piper found herself pausing, collecting her nerve, waiting until he noticed her approach. She had some questions, all right, and she wanted Dan Bourne off guard. She neared him, her eyes fixed on his broad back, and waited. It was a full minute before he stopped his work, abruptly spinning around, his whole bearing rigid.

Piper stood straighter, taller. "Got a minute?" she asked in a neutral voice.

Dan looked at her expressionlessly, but she could see the familiar tight set of his jaw, and a slight tic above the jawbone. "Sure," he said, "what's on your mind?"

She took a breath. "I want to know exactly how Diana died. The details."

He'd been standing still, but it seemed as if his whole body froze at her question. His stillness was shocking in its intensity, even dangerous.

The moment passed. Dan made an impatient movement, then he finally asked, "Why? Why now, Piper?"

"I just want to know," she replied. Then she added, "Of course, if you don't want to tell me, I can always read the police report."

"Now why does that sound like a threat?" he said.

"It's not a threat," she replied with bravado. "I only meant that if you're reluctant to talk about it..." She let her voice trail off, and for an excruciatingly long moment their eyes locked in challenge, and it seemed as if the air crackled around them.

He studied her for another moment, and then it was as if she could see him relax ever so slightly, though she had a sudden, unfounded impression he was forcing himself to do so.

He did finally tell her the story, in all the detail Piper had requested, though too-vivid images began to form in her mind, and she almost wished she'd let it alone.

"Her car was in Bob's shop in town, so she borrowed my pickup."

"And you said she had this meeting in town that night," Piper said, shifting her weight.

"That's right. I told you, it was a group of ranchers. They were meeting in the town hall to discuss some sort of a legislative bill they were leery of that was coming before the Colorado senate that spring."

"But *you* stayed home."

Dan fell silent a moment, obviously not liking the accusation in Piper's tone. "That's right," he finally said, "I stayed at the ranch."

"Why?" she dared to ask.

"I hate meetings. I sat in on too many briefings in my life."

"When you were a cop," she said.

"Yes, when I was a *homicide detective.*"

"I see," Piper said. Then she asked, "Was it snowing?"

"No," Dan replied. "But it was damn cold out. The road was icy." He turned away then and took his shirt off a nail where it had been hanging. He began to shrug it on. "Why the third degree?" he asked. "It was a stupid, meaningless accident." He began to tuck in the tails of his shirt, sucking his lean belly in. "Diana was driving too fast. She must have been running late. Maybe she wasn't used to the truck. All I know is that the state police told me she was speeding around that curve. What do you locals call it? Six Mile Curve?"

Suddenly Piper felt every nerve fiber in her being quiver. "Six Mile Curve?" she repeated.

"That's right. She hit a patch of ice and lost control. The truck went into the river, and she..."

But Piper was barely listening anymore. Instead, she was shaking her head. "You've got something all wrong," she said after a moment. "Diana couldn't have been speeding around that curve, no way."

"Well, I'm sorry to disagree," Dan said, "but the police report stated that she had to have been doing at least sixty miles per hour to have wound up in the river like she did. Piper," he said in a quiet voice, "the truck was totaled. She had to have been flying."

"No." Piper shook her head. "No. It's just not possible." She looked up into his eyes, imploring him to listen. "You don't understand," she said. "When we were kids, seniors in high school, our friend Nancy was killed on Six Mile Curve. It was New Year's Eve. The road was icy and... Look," Piper said, "trust me on this one. After the night Nancy died we both drove that curve like old ladies. We were terrified of it."

She left him standing there then, looking as puzzled as she was, and walked slowly toward her Jeep, her mind reeling. She turned on the ignition, put the vehicle in Reverse and backed out into the yard.

The next thing she knew, she was pulling into a parking space behind the county courthouse and climbing out of the Jeep, then heading toward the basement office of the Routt County Sheriff's Department, striding, unannounced, into Dutch's office.

"Well, I'll be danged," Dutch said, offering her a chair. "This sure is a nice surprise, Piper."

She looked at him and tried to gather her thoughts, saying, "Not now, Dutch, please, this is business."

"Well," he began, his smile fading, "you do look as if you've seen a ghost, Piper. You're all right, aren't you? No one's been bothering you or..."

"Dutch," Piper said, waving away his words, still trying to make sense of things, "tell me it *wasn't* Six Mile Curve Diana was killed on. Dan Bourne has that wrong. Tell me Diana wasn't speeding around that curve."

Dutch looked at her curiously, as if she'd lost her mind or something. He ran a hand through his curly blond hair and just looked at Piper for a minute. Finally he said, "I thought you knew. Everyone knew. We found the truck in the river just below Six Mile Curve. I really, truly, thought you knew."

CHAPTER FOUR

THE OLD TOWN PUB WAS beginning to fill up with regulars when Dutch escorted Piper in and led her to a booth. She was in a state of shock still, an odd kind of suspended animation in which her body went through the motions but her brain struggled with a whole new version of the truth.

Dutch set a mug of beer down in front of her, slid into the opposite seat and took a long swallow of his own brew. She looked up, a little startled, blinking. "Oh," she said, "we're eating here?"

"Sure, for old times' sake. Why not? I ordered you the special burger, well-done, the usual, right?" Dutch asked.

"Sure, uh, fine."

Dutch leaned forward, his face split in a wide grin. He said, "I knew you'd come around. All this garbage about being through with men, I knew you never meant me."

Piper straightened, her mind suddenly sharp again. "Now, take it easy, Dutch. I only agreed to come here because I wanted to find out about Di's accident, not to start something again. This isn't a date."

"Okay, sure. I believe you." But his smile never wavered.

"Look," she said firmly, "you threw me for a loop back there. Diana speeding on that curve. You *know* she wouldn't do that, Dutch. You know perfectly well Diana never went around Six Mile Curve at sixty miles an hour. No way, not unless..."

"Not unless what?"

Piper tossed her hair back and stared into her beer. "I don't know. Unless something weird was going on." She looked up and fixed Dutch with her eyes. "Didn't it seem strange to you at the time?"

Dutch shrugged broad shoulders. "So, she was in a hurry."

Piper leaned forward and brought a hand up in an angry gesture. "In a hurry! For God's sake, Dutch, didn't you question *why? Why* was she in a hurry?"

"Piper," he said, "my job is not to read people's minds."

"But what if... what if something *made* her hurry, scared her, chased her? Didn't it occur to you...?"

"Something, huh? What something?" he asked.

"How do I know? Isn't it *your* job to find out?"

"I'm not magic." He looked at her shrewdly. "You got a bee in your bonnet, don't you? Come on, Piper, tell me. You suspect something. What is it?"

She slumped back. "I don't suspect a thing."

"It's Bourne, isn't it? You know something," Dutch said.

"I do not," Piper said. "Don't make things up."

Their burgers came. "Hi, Dutch," the waitress said. "Hi, Piper. Gosh, just like old times."

Dutch flashed a broad smile, but Piper only slouched farther down in her seat and mumbled something.

"Look," she said when the girl was gone, "don't make a beer and burger into something it isn't."

"Who, me? 'Course not."

"Darn it, Dutch, I came to you because you're the sheriff and I need answers, not because I want to kick-start our relationship. It's strictly business. I have no one else to turn to. Don't make me feel guilty."

"I wouldn't do that."

"The heck you wouldn't," Piper said, but Dutch was barely listening and his smile had disappeared.

"Dan Bourne," he said. "Interesting. Never occurred to me at the time, but it *was* odd, Diana speeding like that. Odd..." He smiled thinly. "Bourne... I bet I know just what you're thinking, Piper," he said. "Yep. You're thinking Bourne and Diana had some sort of a fight. You're thinking maybe he got abusive, chased her right out of the house in a big hurry. Is that what you're thinking, Piper, that Bourne had some hand in her accident?"

"Dutch—"

"You know," he said, "I like it better and better, now that I think of it. Maybe I ought to haul Bourne in and ask him a few questions."

Piper hung her head and placed her hands in her lap. Now that he'd said it, spoken those words, she realized that precisely the same notions had been forming in her own brain. Unconsciously she'd laid the blame at Dan's feet, and now so had Dutch.

But it was one thing to think it privately; it was another to be the head law enforcement officer of the county and to say it out loud, to threaten to act on it without any real cause. She raised her head and studied Dutch. He returned her solemn gaze with an easy, lazy smile. His luxuriating in his own power was frightening, and Piper felt a fist of apprehension clench her heart.

"Come on," Dutch was saying in a soft, coaxing tone, "you know something. You've been out there every day at that ranch. You heard something, didn't you, Piper?"

She shook her head, swallowing convulsively. "No, Dutch, you're wrong. That's not why I came to you. I want to find out what happened, that's all."

"Well, I figure we pretty much have a handle on that now, don't we?" Dutch said softly. "Although, I *could* be wrong. Maybe Bourne had a more active role in Diana's death. Maybe he followed her, chased her in another car, scared her so badly..."

"Stop it, Dutch!" Piper hissed.

"But it'd be hard to prove. We'd need motive."

"Please, I can't listen to another word," Piper said, but Dutch, like a bulldog, couldn't let go of his idea.

He smiled and dug his teeth in deeper. "Motive," Dutch went on blithely. "He inherits all her money...."

"Dutch!"

"Accessibility—he was with her that evening. And he was, far as we know, the last person to see her alive."

Piper's stomach lurched. "Stop it! One more word and I'm leaving! You're disgusting, Dutch. You don't like Dan Bourne and you're just looking to pin something on him. You're jealous, Dutch, and it's sick."

He shrugged casually, untouched by her vehemence. Oh, God, she should have laughed at his theory, ridiculed it. Instead she'd lashed out, furious.

And all the while she was accusing Dutch she heard in a dark, obscure corner of her brain a little voice crying, "Yes, he's right, exactly right."

Piper took a deep breath and pressed her lips together. She needed time to let everything sink in, to consider the possibilities, to be objective. She still needed Dutch's help, too. Resentfully she raised her eyes to his.

"Okay, I'm sorry, I'll lay off," he said, but his tone belied his words. "Now, eat your burger."

She bit, she chewed. It could have been wood. She sipped her beer. Dutch didn't say another thing about Dan Bourne, but his words lay between them, an opened Pandora's box of dangerous ideas that could never be stuffed back into oblivion.

"Another beer, Piper?" the waitress was asking her.

She shook her head.

"I'll have one," Dutch said, and the girl smiled and told him sure, and it was on the house.

Dan Bourne, Piper was thinking. She pictured him in her mind's eye, tried to read the image she created, tried to remember how he was in person. But all that came to her was Dan's face when she'd first seen him at the ranch: hard, closed, weary.

Could he have abused his wife, chased her out of the house on a cold winter night, caused her death?

It was Dutch's idea to stop back at the office and pull Diana's file. At first Piper told him it was unnecessary, but a little devil was still sitting on her shoulder, too, whispering, "There could be something in the accident report everyone overlooked. You better not leave this stone unturned."

So Piper went with him. She had, after all, started this tonight, and maybe Dutch was truly only trying to help, although knowing him, she suspected it was more like an attempt to get at Dan Bourne in any way he could.

They walked together across the street toward the county courthouse. In the basement offices of the sheriff's department, the girl behind the counter jumped as if stung when she saw Dutch. "Oh, Sheriff Radowsky, I didn't know you'd be back tonight," she breathed.

"Rest easy, Charlotte, just a minor matter. Anything interesting going on?"

"An accident over on Route 40. Car ran off the road. Marv went on that one."

"Okay, fine. Excuse us, okay?"

"Sheriff Radowsky," Piper said when they were in his office. "What the heck, Dutch?"

"Hey, I gotta have some respect around here," he said with heavy geniality. "Think I'm running a Boy Scout camp?"

He searched file drawers, came up with a thick manila folder and dropped it on his desk in front of Piper. Then he sat on the edge of the desk, one long leg resting on the floor. "Be my guest," he said, nodding at the file.

She sat and took the folder. Kilmer, Diana Gay was typed neatly on the tab. Piper blinked, swallowed and opened the file. Papers, charts and typed pages lay in a kind of order. A crude drawing of the road, the river, the truck's trajectory. Photographs, obviously taken the next day, of the truck in the river. Reports, lists, notes in Dutch's handwriting. A statement given by

Dan Bourne, merely a factual listing of his whereabouts, when Diana had left home. A pathology report. All tests for drugs and alcohol negative. A report from the company that had insured the truck.

Piper turned the pages and felt herself choke back a sob. It was all too impersonal. This wasn't Diana; it could have been a file on a Jane Doe.

She was aware then that Dutch had moved and was standing over her, his hand on her shoulder. Gently he leaned over, closed the file and took it away from her. She put her face in her hands.

"Take it easy," he said, his voice low and seductive. "Piper, you okay?" His hand massaged her shoulder, her neck, slid up under her hair and stroked her skin. "Take it easy, babe."

She was suddenly cognizant of Dutch's caressing tone, of his fingers on her skin, of his closeness. She took her hands away from her face and sat up straight in the chair. She felt hot all over, a terrible kind of claustrophobia.

"I'm okay," she said through clenched teeth.

"I shouldn't have let you see that stuff," Dutch was saying, and she knew in that moment that he had planned this when he'd invited her back to the office. Well, she had asked for it.

Carefully, shakily, she got to her feet. "I think I'll go on home," she said. "Thanks for helping out, Dutch."

"I wasn't much help."

"Well," she said, "I don't know what I really expected to find."

"I still think I ought to talk to Bourne."

But Piper shook her head, suddenly weary. "It wouldn't be right."

He shrugged as if she was being naive. "I'll see you to your car."

"Sure, fine," Piper said, and he followed her out into the cool dusk to where she'd parked. "Thank you for dinner," she said. "I was afraid you'd take it wrong, I mean, think I was just using you or something."

"I know you'd never do that," Dutch told her. Then he added, "How about we do it again, say Saturday? There's this new place, wasn't here when you left town. They have the greatest food. I'd like to—"

"No, Dutch, thanks anyway," she cut in, "but really, I'm not going out with anybody. No one. I told you that, and I mean it."

"God, Piper, you're hard," he said, shaking his head.

"I need to be right now. You understand, Dutch? For myself."

"Sure, sure, babe" was all he'd say.

Bone tired, Piper fell into bed that night without even showering. She tried to close her eyes, willing sleep to drive away the many questions plaguing her, but her brain was working overtime. Scenario after scenario of the events that might have occurred the night of Diana's death spun through her mind, and she began to wonder if there were any real answers. Perhaps, she thought, Dan Bourne was the only one with those answers, and he was certainly never going to tell the truth.

And as she lay there, trying to escape her thoughts, trying to flee into sleep, she saw, periodically, the lights of a car crawl across her room, stop, turn, creeping slowly but inexorably across her wall, over chair and bureau and closet door, sliding along the wallpaper and mirror until they were gone. Dutch—playing lawman, guardian, playing God.

WHEN PIPER AWAKENED the next morning everything was as clear as a bell to her. She hadn't gotten much sleep, because she'd sat bolt upright in bed at 3:15 a.m. and known exactly what she had to do.

It involved Dutch. But that was okay, because after his performance last night—driving by her house three times in a row—good old Sheriff Radowsky needed to be set straight, anyway. Just because she'd asked him to help with Diana's accident—essentially to do his job—it sure didn't mean she'd given him a license to hound her.

At 8:00 a.m. sharp she again strode into Dutch's office unannounced. He looked up, surprised, then pushed himself back in his chair, away from his desk.

Piper put her hands on her hips and gave it to him straight. "Dutch Radowsky, don't you *ever* drive by our house like that again. You hear me? Stop it! I order you."

"Aw, come on, Piper, relax," he began.

"I will not. You have no right. And while I'm at it, you can quit stopping by the ranch, too," she said. "I mean it, Dutch."

"Just doing my duty, seeing to it that folks rest secure, that the law is upheld," he said glibly.

"Bull! *Your* law, Dutch, no one else's! You've got to stop it. I need some space, some breathing room."

He smiled, crinkling up his pale blue eyes. "Gosh, you're pretty when you get mad, Piper. Anyone tell you that before?"

"Dutch, I mean it." She stood there breathing hard, mad as the devil, glaring at him.

He put a hand up. "Okay, okay, relax. Good thing one of us has a nice, even temperament. Guess that's why we get along so well."

She ignored him. "You going to stop coming by?" she asked, eyeing him.

"Maybe," he said, enjoying himself thoroughly.

"Damn it, Dutch..." She turned away and fought for control, then spun back to face him. "Can we possibly be businesslike now?" she asked. "I'm serious, Dutch. I don't have anyone else I can turn to. I'm asking you to be fair, to help me. Can you do that?"

"After you've been so sweet and amenable?"

"Will you give me a straight answer?" she demanded. "Please, Dutch, this means a lot to me."

"Um," he said, studying her, "I suppose if you ask all nice like that..."

Even while she stood there longing to turn and walk out on him, Piper knew Dutch was pulling his mastery act on her, thinking he had her just where he wanted. And she would have walked out on him—she would have, but, darn it, she couldn't.

"*Are* you going to help?" she asked.

Dutch looked pleased, pleased with the situation and pleased with himself. "Sure I'll help," he said. "What brainstorm are we talking now?"

"I have an idea," she said. "I want you to contact Dan Bourne's superior officer on the Philadelphia police force."

He regarded her with a raised eyebrow.

"I want to find out what caused Dan to resign from the force. Something happened, some trouble, and he quit."

"Yeah, so?"

Piper strode back and forth in front of Dutch's desk, two long-legged strides one way, two long-legged strides the other. "I gave it a lot of thought last night. I want to know what happened back East, because I think it might shed some light on this whole thing."

Dutch smiled wickedly. "You should have been a cop yourself."

She never stopped her pacing. "Look, Dutch, I don't want you to go off half-cocked, and I don't really believe that Dan...did what you said, but I think it's worth finding out more about him. It's a place to start."

"Well, now, you're big buddies with him. Why don't you ask him yourself?"

She paused in her restless pacing and shot him a derisive look. "Dan Bourne is a real quiet sort of guy. We barely talk. I just have this feeling he has secrets. And Diana knew him for such a short time. I think we should dig a little into his background."

"Hey, you don't have to convince *me*. I don't like the guy. I'd love to nail him to the wall, him and that wetback of his," Dutch said.

Piper leaned her hands on Dutch's desk and stared him right in the eye. "A citizen of this country, and that includes Routt County, is innocent until proven guilty. Don't be too hasty, Dutch, or one day you're going to get into big trouble."

"From Bourne?" he asked.

"From somebody."

"You brought this up, Piper," he reminded her.

"Yes, I did. I want information. You can get it. I want the facts, and I want to be objective."

"A big order, Piper, but then your eyes always were bigger than your stomach. And what if Bourne finds out? He won't like it."

"I'll cross that bridge when I come to it, Dutch. Can you do what I'm asking? Can you call his old captain?"

"What was his precinct?" Dutch asked.

"I don't know, exactly. He was a homicide detective in downtown Philadelphia, that's all I know."

Dutch leaned back in his chair and put his hands behind his head, elbows splayed. "I can try."

"Okay," she said.

"And what'll you do for me?" he asked insolently, still leaning back.

"Cut it out, Dutch, *please.*"

He laughed and picked up the phone. "Denise? Find me the phone number of the Philadelphia police force. If there's not a central number, get them all. Yes, I'll wait. Get back to me soon as you've got them and then hold all my calls." And all the while he talked he kept eye contact with Piper, a smug expression on his face, as if to say, "Look at me, I'm the boss. I have power."

"You want to come back later?" he asked. "Find out what I got?"

"Can I wait?" she asked.

"Might take a while."

"That's okay. I just sort of have this on my mind, you know, and I want to find out . . . well . . . whatever I can."

"And then what?"

"I don't know. Depends."

Dutch shifted his weight in his chair. "It takes a lot to reopen a closed case, Piper. It takes hard evidence."

She turned away, pained by the reality of his words. "I know. But I have to find out. It's as if Diana left this burden on me—maybe because I wasn't here when it happened."

The phone rang, and Dutch held it cradled between his shoulder and ear, writing down numbers. Then he said, "Thanks, Denise," and hung up.

"Okay," he said to Piper, "here we go."

He dialed, and then spoke in that unmistakable, authoritative cop's way he had, sometimes sharp, other times the down-home country sheriff "needin' a bit of info from you all." He had it right on—the professional lawman, the tone, the terminology, the right questions. Piper stood with her back to him, looking out the old-fashioned, tall, oak-trimmed window, worrying her lip with her teeth, twirling a lock of hair around her finger.

God, she hated to do this. It was mean, sneaky. And to make it worse, she had to rely on Dutch, of all people. Where was the man she'd once dated, had gone to high school with? That Dutch had been fun loving, full of bluster and brag, but kind of a big, lovable teddy bear.

Piper heard Dutch's voice change then, and she listened carefully, still not turning around, as if she couldn't quite face what Dutch was doing, what she'd asked him to do.

"Captain MacMurray," Dutch said in his official voice, "this is Sheriff Radowsky, Routt County, Colorado. Yes, sir, good to talk to you. Well, I have a few questions about someone living in my jurisdiction, used to work for you. Yes, sir. You see, I'm looking into this because this fellow, Dan Bourne, has applied for a position with me. That's it, Captain, just checking references."

Piper turned slowly. Shrewd of Dutch to provide such an innocuous reason for asking about Dan, but then, for all his easygoing appearance, he was no innocent.

"Um," Dutch was saying, "I see. And exactly why did he resign? Uh-huh. Rumors, you say, uh-huh, but it was all just talk ... I see. Oh, yeah, I know how it is when the public gets down on the cops.... Yep, someone's going to catch the flak.... Sure, I'd like that if it's no trouble. Our address here is ..."

He finally replaced the receiver and looked at Piper with a smug smile. "Happy?"

She twisted her mouth and turned her head away. "Well, tell me, what did he say?"

Dutch rolled his chair back, put his booted feet on his desk and clasped his hands over his stomach. "Dan Bourne resigned two years ago. Very suddenly. He was a good detective, one of the best, but a maverick, MacMurray said. Had his own way of doing things."

"*Why* did he leave?"

"MacMurray wouldn't say. Some incident that left Bourne bitter, he told me, something about 'one of those things' when the public is down on the cops and rumors get out of hand. Sounded like Bourne was railroaded, but MacMurray was his boss, and, you know, he'd protect the guy even now. I couldn't really push the man, either, or I wouldn't have gotten as much as I did."

"What does it all mean?"

"Only that Bourne didn't do anything illegal, or—" Dutch grinned slyly "—he didn't get caught red-handed doing it."

Piper frowned. "So he *could* have been forced to resign."

"Sure, it's possible. Happens all the time. You know—resign or we'll make trouble for you."

"But MacMurray didn't insinuate that."

"Nope, he said it straight. Dan Bourne resigned, period. But I'll tell you, Piper, something nasty happened that caused Bourne to leave the force."

"It could have been anything, Dutch. It could have been purely personal."

"Could have been," Dutch said coolly.

"Are you disappointed, Dutch? That you don't have anything to pin on Dan Bourne?" she asked pointedly.

"Are you?" he asked.

She looked away. "I'd like to know more, that's all." God, but she felt like a jerk, prying into the man's past, asking Dutch to do it for her because he was the only game in town. And then her emotions flip-flopped. No, she didn't feel bad at all—this was for Di.

Dutch drew his feet off the desk and thumped them down on the floor. He leaned forward, elbows on his desk, and frowned. "You know what I think, Piper?"

"No," she said, "but I bet I'm going to find out."

"I think you're too damn interested in Dan Bourne for your own good. I think you like that guy more than you're admitting."

"Oh, for heaven's sake, Dutch, grow up!"

"And I don't like you working out at the ranch with him and his wetbacks. I don't like the sound of his past. There's something there, something not quite right. Career detectives don't resign before their pensions come up, I'll tell you that, babe."

Anger flared in Piper. "I don't give two hoots what you think. I'm not giving up my job because of your opinion, Dutch."

"That guy's dangerous, Piper, and I want you to quit," Dutch said, emphasizing every word.

"Oh, for the love of God, Dutch! I'm not afraid of Dan Bourne."

"I don't want you around him!" Dutch pounded a fist on his desk. "God, Piper, you are so damn stubborn! You haven't changed a bit. Stubborn and cocksure and pigheaded! Why don't you listen?"

"I'm leaving now, Dutch," she said. "I'm late for work. Thanks for making that call."

"You're going to get into trouble out there," Dutch growled. "Mark my words."

"It's not your problem, Dutch," she said stiffly, holding her temper with effort.

He flung himself back in his chair and threw a hand up in the air. "Go on, then, get the hell out of here. I've got work to do."

She went. Trembling with frustration, her lips pressed together, she walked out of his office, up the

stairs, across the street to her Jeep. She got in, turned
it on and drove away, making an illegal U-turn on
Lincoln Street to head out of town. The tires squealed
satisfyingly.

CHAPTER FIVE

PIPER GOT TO WORK LATE that morning. It shouldn't have mattered; she wasn't on a time clock. But this particular morning it seemed it *had* mattered.

She pulled up to see Dan leading Picnic toward the barn. *That's right,* she remembered, the vet was coming to check out the mare's inexplicable lameness. When he saw her Dan stopped, still holding Picnic's lead rope, and scowled at Piper as she got out of the Jeep.

"Oh, you got Picnic," she said. "Thanks."

"Yeah, and it took me almost an hour. This nag's a pain," he answered.

"Well," Piper said, "I guess she was afraid you'd cuff her and book her."

He narrowed his eyes and shot her a look, then he asked, "By the way, just where were you this morning? *You* were supposed to get this horse."

She stared at him, trying to forget that she'd been in Dutch's office, spying on Dan. It seemed so deceitful now, so terribly out of place.

"Well?" Dan demanded.

Guilt made her react with false bravado. She tossed her hair back, stuck her thumbs in her pockets and put her chest out. Hostility oozed from every pore, and the words came out too quickly—and too loud. "I had errands to do."

"Errands."

"Yes, female things," she said without thinking.

"Female things," he repeated, his eyes pinioning her, "at the courthouse?"

Piper felt shock freeze her blood. She had never, ever, lied before. And now she'd been caught red-handed. "How, how did you . . . ?" she began, totally deflated.

"I had an errand in town, too," he said in a cold voice. "I saw your Jeep."

"Oh," Piper whispered.

For a long time he stared at her, so long a time that she felt like squirming. *I'll tell him the truth,* she decided, but suddenly caught herself. Not yet, she thought, not just yet.

Dan finally shook his head slowly and gave her one more hard, contemptuous look before he said, "I've got work to do," and turned his back on her, yanking at Picnic's lead rope.

Piper and Dan had a ten-o'clock appointment that morning to see a woman who was bringing her daughter's horse to be trained—a new customer. The horse had been expensive, but it was not turning out to be the push-button blue-ribbon winner that Mrs. Rafferty and Jackie had been promised. She'd said on the phone she'd try Piper Hilyard for a couple of months, to see if the horse, Reno, could be improved.

Mrs. Rafferty drove up, pulling a horse trailer, promptly at ten. Her leggy, fourteen-year-old daughter got the horse out and held him while Piper sent

Rick off to find Dan. Then she went to meet the new clients.

"Nice to meet you, Miss Hilyard," the woman said. "I've heard about you, but you were gone for a while there, weren't you?"

"Yes, I was in New Zealand, riding Thoroughbreds for a breeder. What's the problem with Reno?" Piper asked.

"He's been refusing jumps, behaving badly at shows. He won't obey Jackie very well. He was supposed to be well trained when we bought him, but so far..." Mrs. Rafferty grimaced.

"Tell you what," Piper said. "Why doesn't Jackie tack him up and ride him in the ring so I can take a look at them. Then I'll have a better idea what's needed."

"Okay," Jackie said, "but no matter what, I told my mom, I'm not getting rid of Reno."

Piper laughed, recognizing the fierce love teenage girls had for their first horse. "You won't have to get rid of him. You'll just have to work real hard to ride him. Are you willing to do that, Jackie?"

"Oh, yes," the girl breathed, her braces showing, her hand clutching Reno's lead rope.

It was then that Dan came up, dusty, his forehead beaded with sweat, interrupted by Rick in the middle of a job.

"Dan, this is Mrs. Rafferty and Jackie," Piper said. "And Reno. We're going to be working with him this summer. And this is Dan Bourne," she continued, "the owner of the Elk River Ranch." Oh, how it hurt to say that still, even though she'd been saying it all summer.

Mrs. Rafferty gave Dan a thorough once-over, Piper noticed, and raised an eyebrow.

"Welcome to the ranch," Dan said.

"Well, thank you, Mr. Bourne." Mrs. Rafferty paused. "Aren't you...that is...wasn't your wife...?"

Dan smiled tightly, and Piper looked away. "Diana Kilmer was my wife, yes. She owned the ranch originally."

"We were all very sorry to hear about the, uh, accident," the woman offered.

Dan nodded, controlled, polite. "Thank you." Then he said, "Well, if you'll excuse me, Mrs. Rafferty..."

"So," Piper said, "let's get Jackie up on Reno and—"

"Poor man," Mrs. Rafferty said, still looking after Dan.

Piper cleared her throat. "Uh, yes..."

"Widowed. At that age. Left with all this."

"Yes," Piper repeated.

"Well, someone will snatch him up pretty soon, I'd say," Mrs. Rafferty continued. Then she pivoted and leveled her gaze on Piper, unabashedly staring, obviously wondering.

"Yes, it's very sad," Piper said firmly, meeting the woman's eyes, "because Diana was my best friend. I'm just trying to help Dan out here."

"Excuse me, Miss Hilyard," Jackie was calling, "is my girth tight enough?"

And then Piper could turn her back on Mrs. Rafferty's embarrassingly curious appraisal and go to work. "It's okay, Jackie," she said. "Go on into the ring."

And then Piper was able to forget Mrs. Rafferty and Dan Bourne and Dutch and everything else and concentrate on Reno and Jackie and try to figure out what she needed to do for them.

For the rest of the morning Dan irrigated the south fields while Piper finished with the Raffertys and worked with the yearlings in the ring, leading them one by one into the now-familiar enclosure, patiently, skillfully, doggedly guiding them through their training routines. But if her mind was on her work, her heart was elsewhere. There was that persistent ache in her chest, that tightening in her stomach, whenever she thought about Diana and Dan and the night her friend had died.

It was after lunch that Dan found her in the tack room. She hadn't heard his entrance, but, rather, she sensed a presence behind her. Piper spun around. He was standing in the doorway, seeming to fill it, his face obscured by shadows. She held back a cry of surprise.

He was quiet for a moment, then said, "If you've got time, I could use some help with the books."

"The books?"

"Yeah. If this drought keeps up, I can't figure if I'd be better off irrigating or buying more hay for the winter."

"Irrigate," Piper said. "It's got to be cheaper."

"Maybe when you were here two summers ago it was, but last year the ditch-usage prices soared."

"Oh," she said, "I didn't realize."

"Well, you do now."

It was always that way between them, Piper thought as she dusted herself off and entered the house behind him. Dan could push her buttons faster than anyone she'd ever known. Even faster than Dutch—and that was saying a lot. And she had to ask herself if Dan had pushed Diana's buttons after a time, too. Had they begun to fight?

He led her into the office that was located off the living room. There was a leather couch, bookshelves, the cluttered desk. Behind the desk there was also a sunny window with a deep sill, and on the sill were many framed photographs—pictures of Dan and of Diana, and pictures of them together.

Automatically Piper moved around the desk and stood looking down at the windowsill. She hadn't noticed before, but there was also a picture of her and Diana, each with an arm hooked over Bounce's neck, giving Diana's prize mare a big kiss. She reached down and quietly touched the glass with a slim finger.

"Sometimes," she heard Dan say angrily from behind her, "I hate coming into this room."

And it was as if he'd forgotten she was there, as if he'd spoken only to the walls. She stood very still and looked at the pictures one by one and wondered at Dan's statement. She could almost swear he was still grieving over his dead wife....

"Well," he said, "let's take a look at these figures."

Accounting was not Piper's strong point. In school she'd gotten a C. Or had it been a D plus? Oh, well, she thought, it couldn't be *that* difficult. You paid so much per hour of water usage; you paid so much per bale of hay. A field yielded only so many bales. Fairly simple.

But this was a drought year. Maybe in the end of July and during August they'd get a couple of good downpours—and maybe they wouldn't. The trouble was Dan was almost ready to stop irrigating and let the crop go. It was a gamble. Of course, it *could* start raining any day.

Piper sat at the desk with Dan at her shoulder and kept running a hand unconsciously through her hair, sometimes twirling a few strands in her fingers. She was frowning. "I don't know, Dan," she said. "It looks as if you could go on watering for at least another week and then call it quits if it doesn't look like the weather's going to break. I don't really know."

She was aware of his nearness, the male scent of him. He was so close above her shoulder she could hear the rasp as he scrubbed at the stubble on his jaw, and she felt her spine stiffen.

He moved away then and walked to the leather couch, dropping onto it, an arm behind his dark head, his legs stretched out, crossing at the ankles. "Hell," he said, letting out a breath, "this ranching business stinks."

"Doesn't it, though," she agreed.

Then he turned his head toward her. "I'm serious. It's bad enough trying to deal with the horses. But feeding them, too..."

"It would be great to have a bumper crop," Piper said, thinking aloud.

"Fat chance this summer."

"Well, maybe the rains will come in August."

"Have you listened to the weather reports lately?" She shook her head.

"Don't count on a break, then," he said.

"Um," Piper replied, leaning on an elbow, her fist supporting her chin.

"I'd like to get an offer for this place," he said. "I'm ready for a fire sale, in fact."

"Don't say that."

Dan quirked a brow, his head still turned toward her. "You can see how great I am at ranching. Why can't you get it through your head that I'm wrong for this?"

"Anyone can have trouble getting a horse in from a field," Piper said.

"Oh, really? Then why the smart remark this morning?" He gazed up at the ceiling, his mouth set in a hard line.

Piper watched him carefully. "Just trying to keep things light."

He gave a short laugh. "You like that. A real cowgirl, aren't you, Piper? Tough as nails. Funny, you looked different in that fancy pink dress at the wedding."

She felt a jolt of surprise. What a strange thing to say. She could almost believe he'd noticed her then.... She couldn't think of a fitting retort, so she just sat there in Diana's chair, behind Diana's desk, and watched him. She studied his chiseled profile, the strong, muscled length of him as he rested there. And then it came to her with a kind of wonder—Dan had actually let down for a minute, actually allowed her to see what he really felt. She was astonished at the discovery. Yes, he'd said, well, a few things. About how he hated to come into this room, and his reaction had seemed genuine, too seamless, too spontaneous to have been fake. And how he felt about the drought—

he was worried. And that he'd resented her making fun of him today, that he wasn't much of a rancher. And that he'd noticed her at the wedding, her and the pink dress.

"I hated that pink dress," she finally said.

"But Diana loved pink, so you wore it," he replied quietly.

A strange, contradictory man, Piper thought, a formidable opponent. Yet somehow, Piper was beginning to suspect, he'd be just as formidable a friend. "Well," she said briskly, rising, "I've got a few more chores to do. Someone has to get to work around here."

But as she left the house, she thought she must have been crazy to even consider that Dan had feelings, much less that he was letting *her* in on his secrets. It was all an act. It had to be.

IT WAS SIX-THIRTY on a Friday night when Dan strode up to her Jeep as she was leaving. He put a hand on the back of her seat and looked her in the eye. "What?" she said, surprised. They'd barely spoken since that day in the office.

"I need to talk to you," he said. "It's important."

"So, talk." God, there she went again.

"Up at the house, Piper."

"Well, I . . ."

"Look," he said, "I'm not going to rape you, kid, I just want to ask you something."

"Okay, sure," she said, wondering, climbing out.

She followed him across the yard, watching him carefully, asking herself what was so important it couldn't wait till morning. He walked, she decided, like a man comfortable with his body. He had sexy legs and perfect, well-muscled buttocks. Yes, he did have a certain grace and ease of movement. Diana had waxed eloquent about it, trying to describe Dan in dozens of ways to Piper, but Piper had always quipped, "You mean macho, that's the word." But Diana had denied it, saying, "No, he's not aware of his masculinity. Macho men are. God, you're so dumb sometimes."

Diana had even questioned Piper once as to why she didn't seem to like Dan. "I mean," Diana had said, "you've only met him once. What is there *not* to like about him?"

And Piper had tried to put it into words. "I can't quite get a finger on it," she'd said, "but he's...so sarcastic, you know, cynical about things, as if he's seen everything, done everything."

"Oh, that's just his facade," Diana had said. "He's not really like that. He's a little disillusioned from being a cop, I guess, but inside he's a pussycat."

"If you say so," Piper had replied wryly.

Now, as Piper followed Dan into the kitchen, where he popped open two cans of beer and handed her one, she recalled clearly that conversation with Diana. A pussycat. How could her friend have been so blind? But Diana had no doubt learned about Dan—the hard way. God, she wished that police captain in Philadelphia had been more helpful.

"Sit down," Dan was saying, nodding toward the kitchen table.

Piper shrugged and pulled out a chair, sitting in it tomboy-style, her knees splayed. She pushed her heavy hair back over one shoulder, took a drink of her beer and eyed him.

Dan sat down, too, across from her. He was all business. "Okay," he said, "I want to hear more about Diana's fear of that section of road, the Six Mile Curve."

Piper looked at him curiously, and suddenly she felt as if she were in an interrogation room in a police department. "Don't you have a bright light to shine in my eyes?" she blurted out. What sort of a game was he playing now?

"Cut the bull," Dan stated, and she saw the blue of his eyes turn flinty. "I want you to tell me everything about it, from the time your friend in high school was killed there to when you left for New Zealand."

"Why?" Piper asked flatly.

"Do you always have to—" he began angrily, then seemed to catch himself. "It could be nothing. Just, please," he said with difficulty, "humor me."

Now she was really curious. What did he mean—it could be nothing?

"Piper."

"Okay, okay," she said, focusing on his face. She straightened her back. "Like I said before," she began, "it all started on New Year's Eve in our senior year...."

She told him the whole story and recalled in vivid detail an incident when she'd been driving into town in the Jeep, Diana in the passenger seat, and they'd hit a patch of black ice on Six Mile Curve and the Jeep had fishtailed. Piper had pulled over, shaken, and Diana had actually gotten out of the car, refusing to go on another inch.

He asked her more questions, trying to get her to remember other incidents, pressing her with a professional thoroughness that would have been impressive if she'd been watching him do it to someone else. Occasionally he was very silent and very still, sipping on his beer, lost in some unfathomable train of thought. And during those moments Piper kept getting mental flashes of the world Dan Bourne had come from. She kept seeing such ugliness, the fallen, abandoned buildings of the city, the slums and filth and squalor and the death. The shootings and stabbings and drug overdoses, faceless bodies being zipped into plastic bags. And Dan. Oh, she could fit him so easily into those terrible pictures. He wore a suit, dark and wrinkled across the back, and a rumpled shirt, a tie loosened, askew, at his throat. There were circles under his eyes, smudges of gray on pale city pallor. He needed a shave, badly....

Oh, yes, she could see Dan, all right. He'd be questioning suspects, pushing them against grimy brick walls, handcuffing them, shoving them into squad cars. An ugly, miserable existence. Yes, Dan belonged in a big city, a place where it was sometimes hard to tell the criminals from the corrupt cops, when a man's morals were challenged every minute of every day. Dan had obviously thought he'd escaped that life when he'd met Diana. But then, Piper thought, staring hard at him, perhaps his dark side had emerged again.

Dan just looked at her, apparently lost in thought. About what? she wondered. Why in the name of God was he dredging up all this stuff after a year and a half?

It occurred to Piper then that she'd just told Dan, stated unequivocally, that Diana's death couldn't have been an accident. And if her death hadn't been an accident, then it had been ...

"So that's it," Dan was saying. "That's all you remember?"

"Yes," Piper was quick to reply, "that's it."

Dan was staring into space, a frown creasing his forehead. Then he turned his gaze back to her, and his face smoothed out, unreadable now and very still.

Piper's blood stopped in her veins, and her heart gave a heavy thump, then another. He knew what she was thinking. He could read her mind—a cop, an experienced cop like Dan, could see through her as if she were transparent. He was good, oh, boy, was he good! With that small-boy, vulnerable act. Poor bereaved Dan. The good cop-bad cop routine, only he hadn't even needed the bad cop. She'd sat there in his kitchen and blurted out that his wife's death had been ...

"Is that it?" Piper asked, and she realized her voice was shaky.

"No," Dan said after a moment, "that's not quite it." And he regarded her with silent intensity.

Piper felt as if all the air had been suddenly sucked from the room. He wouldn't dare ...

"I'm leaving," he said, still staring at her, "for a few days."

"You're ... what?" she asked, trying to collect her thoughts.

"I *said* I'm leaving for a few days. I need you to handle things while I'm gone."

"You're leaving, just like that?"

"That's right. *Will* you handle the place?"

"I . . ." Piper cocked her head, utterly confused. "Where are you going?"

"Never mind that. It doesn't concern you."

"But—" she began.

"Will you be okay for a couple of days? Come on, Piper," he said, crumpling his empty can of beer, "I need to know. If not, I can—"

"I'll be all right," she said. "I can run this place with my eyes closed."

"I never thought otherwise," he remarked. He tossed the can toward the trash basket by the back door. It hit the wall and bounced into the plastic can. "Okay," he said, rising, "I've got a lot to do tonight. Mind if I kick you out?"

"I was going, anyway," Piper retorted.

He walked outside with her, but it was only because he'd been heading to the barn. Piper ignored him, climbing up into the seat of the Jeep, fishing out her car keys. He made her so darn nervous sometimes she just didn't know how to deal with him, and now there was all this business about Diana's accident and his announcement that he was leaving. What was going on? Why all the mystery?

She put the key in the ignition and her foot on the clutch, then glanced up at Dan as he started into the barn. A devil kindled angry flames inside her; resentment glowed red-hot. The words just seemed to pop out by themselves. "Hey, Dan, have a nice trip," she said with heavy irony.

His stride slowed, stopped, and she could make out that familiar twist of his mouth as he turned and eyed her. She put the car into gear, noisily, irritated. "I suppose it'd be too much trouble to leave a telephone number where you'll be staying," she said coolly, "just in case."

He came over to the Jeep and rapped his knuckles lightly on the hood, thinking. "I'll be in touch," he finally said, looking at her through the windshield. Then he rapped his knuckles on the hood one last time and turned toward the barn. He said over his shoulder, carelessly, a last-minute thought, "You have a nice time, too, Piper. But I'm sure you and Dutch will find something to keep yourselves occupied...."

Piper stared at him, bewildered, for another long moment, then let the clutch out and drove away. All she could do was wonder if she'd heard Dan right.

CHAPTER SIX

PHILADELPHIA WAS AS HOT and muggy as Dan remembered. He walked along Market Street and felt the oily grime of the city center settle on his face and hands and darken the neck of his white shirt. Sweat beaded on his forehead and began to collect on the ends of his hair.

He could have ended up like any of the punks he saw strutting around these streets. He could have been worse off, coming from where he had—except for Harry Tegmeier. He recalled with utter clarity the first time he'd seen Harry, almost twenty years ago. Harry had been a strapping young cop, streetwise, able to gain the respect of the punk Dan had been. And Harry had seen something in that young punk, taken him under his wing, shown him a better way. Yes, Harry had saved him. And that was what made it so much worse that...

Dan wiped a rivulet of sweat off his temple as he walked along Independence Mall and past the Liberty Bell. He crossed Market on Fifteenth Street, dodging cars, horns blaring at him. Yeah. Tempers sure boiled when the mercury rose. He wondered if the weather had changed in Colorado. Not likely. It would be dry—really dry this year—maybe a high of eighty, eight-five degrees. Clear skies, rugged, unspoiled mountains that pierced that perfect blue bowl...

And Piper Hilyard would be there on the ranch. He could envision her clearly as she did her chores, gentled the young horses, rode the older ones, felt a cut knee or a swollen leg, saddled and unsaddled and rode out under the hot sun. Patience, absolute patience, and skill and total control. Oh, he'd watched her, all right.

It was her hands that fascinated him most—strong, brown hands with short nails, hands that could feel the painful heat in a horse's joint with unerring precision, hands that could doctor and heal, that could jab an immunization needle into a horse's neck matter-of-factly, or drive a truck, or whip out a pocket knife to cut the string on a bale of hay, or make a stubborn horse respond.

He'd watched her for weeks now. Toward the animals she was gentle and patient; toward him she was hostile. She'd never liked him, not from the first moment they'd met. Diana had been upset about it, he remembered.

He saw in Piper something unique. She was willing to kill herself working for Diana's dream. Her loyalty never faltered, her instincts were sound. She'd known when no one else had that Diana's death had been no accident. She'd simply known.

Sometimes he wished she'd just pack up and go back to New Zealand. The woman was driving him nuts. She could get inside a man's head like a fever with those long legs encased in tight, worn jeans, her small, fine-featured face and her wild, thick, reddish brown hair that she stuffed under her hard hat when she rode. Dark eyes, thick black lashes. Her mouth too wide, her lips too full, her smile too big, her teeth perfect and white. Although she didn't smile often around him, that was for sure. But he had watched her with Rick and Luis, so he knew how she looked when she smiled.

Piper Hilyard. His wife's best friend. He strode along and smiled mockingly at himself.

HE MET HARRY AT THE SAME old breakfast joint, and it was almost as if the past two years hadn't existed.

"Lookin' great, Danny-boy," Harry said, slapping him on the back, beaming.

"Thanks, Harry, how's the family?"

"Good, they're all good."

They ate breakfast, and Harry filled Dan in on his current cases. Cop talk.

"I gotta see this dude down in Society Hill about his mother," Harry was saying. "Come on, Dan, let's do the rounds together for old times' sake. What d'ya say?"

"Sure, why not?" Dan said, shrugging.

They made a couple of stops that morning before the interview with the newly wealthy, grieving son whose mother had had the accident down in Society Hill. The first stop was for Harry to check up on his latest protégé—Harry was still a Big Brother—a sixteen-year-old kid who had a tendency to shoplift. But as Harry said, the kid wasn't into drugs or alcohol and had potential on his high school basketball team.

Harry introduced Dan to Herb at the boy's front door. "Herb, this is Dan. I was sort of his Big Brother about a hundred years ago. Dan and I even worked together as cops."

"Nice to meet you," Herb said, and gave Dan a firm, confident handshake.

When they were back in Harry's car, Dan couldn't help but think what a big heart Harry had, and that his friend just couldn't have been involved in Diana's death. Oh, sure, Dan thought, Harry had made a terrible mistake two years ago when he'd stood by and watched Joey Washington take that beating. But Dan and Harry's friendship had withstood the incident. They had been, after all, partners on the police force, a bond that was closer than friendship. A cop's partner was his blood brother—they were responsible for each other's lives. Despite what had happened to Joey Washington, despite Dan quitting the force, Dan still trusted Harry.

But Sweet Pea and Frank . . . they'd beaten Joey. They'd lost control in that abandoned warehouse and launched into the man with gleeful vengeance. Either one of them—or maybe both of them—was capable of murder.

Harry and Dan had doughnuts and more coffee at a place Harry frequented on Pine Street, then headed the few blocks over to Society Hill, which was located near the old restored waterfront.

Harry, of course, did all the talking to the young man who offered them coffee in his early-American living room. It was a typical question-and-answer session: Harry as cool as a cucumber, the twenty-six-year-old sweating up a real storm when Harry said, "Don't leave town. We're waiting on the final report from the medical examiner."

"What do you think?" Harry asked Dan when they were back on the street.

"I think the guy better hire himself a helluva lawyer."

They had lunch at a small hoagie shop Dan had always liked out near the University of Pennsylvania campus on Walnut Street. It was an old neighborhood—big, graceful oak, locust and walnut trees standing in yards, the streets quieter, safer than those downtown.

"Heard you stopped by the shop and saw Captain MacMurray yesterday," Harry said, his mouth full of the huge sandwich, a piece of lettuce stuck to his chin with mayo.

"That's right," Dan said. "A few things I wanted to clear up."

"Such as?" Harry ventured.

Dan's eyes met his friend's. "Some questions I had about Joey Washington."

"Joey," Harry said. "Dan, that's ancient history."

"Is it?" Dan said. "I'm not so sure. I honestly thought Sweet Pea and Frank would have had to face some sort of charges after Joey never made it out of the coma."

Harry shrugged eloquently. "It's better you let it lie, Danny-boy. Like I said, it's history. No wrongdoing was found. Don't try to stir things up now."

Dan pushed his plate away. "And you, Harry," he said. "Would my asking questions stir you up?"

Harry regarded him for a moment, then said, "You know better than that, Dan."

AFTER WORK IT WAS off to Pop's Bar. Harry headed to the phone to call his wife, Cindy, with his excuses, and while he was gone, Mike "Sweet Pea" Turner came in. At first Sweet Pea didn't seem to notice Dan. He strode to the bar, seated his bulk on a stool and loudly ordered a boilermaker. Dan watched Sweet Pea in the mirror as the man threw down the shot of whiskey and then took a long draw of his beer. He wiped his mouth with the back of his hand, and then he pulled out a grimy handkerchief and began to mop his brow and neck. That was when he saw Dan in the mirror.

"Well," he said, his hand pausing on the back of his neck. "Well, I'll be damned, it's Bourne."

Dan gave him a thin smile, still looking in the mirror, then turned toward him. "Hello, Sweet Pea, how's it going?"

"Well, I'll be," Sweet Pea said, and he rose, moving down the bar to sit next to Dan, who was still standing. "What in hell are you doing in Philly, kid?" he asked. "Thought you were a happily married cowboy or something."

Dan took a drink of his beer. "I'm just back for a visit," he said, "and a little business. Unfinished business, you know."

"Well, I'll be. It's sure good to see you, kid. It's been too long."

"Yeah," Dan said, "too long," and Sweet Pea patted him hard on the back.

"So how's life in the West?" he asked after a moment.

"It's all right," Dan replied, "though maybe you heard that my wife died a year ago last winter."

Sweet Pea's head snapped up. "No way! I mean, that's a goddamned shame, Dan. I don't know why Harry never told me. I'm real sorry, kid. I mean, what a crime."

Dan said all the right things, as did Sweet Pea, but he hadn't failed to notice that his old co-worker in the central division never once asked how Diana had died. And that was odd. But not so odd if Sweet Pea already knew—not so odd at all. It was just a little slip, but one that Dan tucked away for future reference.

Frank came in then. Frank, the quietest of the three, a tall, lean man in his late forties, was not as effusive as the others, but offered a few words like "It's been too long" for Dan's benefit.

The truth was, Dan knew, they were all lying through their teeth. Oh, yes, after Dan's talk with Piper about Six Mile Curve, the pieces had fallen very neatly into place.

The evening wore on, and Pop's Bar filled to capacity. The air-conditioning was working on overload, and faces became flushed and shiny. Smoke filled the room, turning the air to a hazy blue.

By midnight only Dan was not weaving. He wanted to be sharp when he dropped the bombshell in their laps. As it turned out, Dan didn't have to steer the conversation in the right direction. It was Sweet Pea. Drunk as a lord, swaying and pouring sweat, he stuck his pockmarked face right into Dan's and launched in. "Say, pal, why're you really in Philly? It ain't for a visit, I'll bet."

"Sure it is," Dan said, pivoting on his bar stool to face him. "I just love the heat, and the humidity does wonders for my skin."

Frank was sitting on Dan's other side. He nudged Dan. "Say," he slurred, his head practically resting on his chest, "you hear Joey Washington croaked?"

Dan sat up straighter. "Yeah," he said, "I heard. It was a year ago last December, wasn't it?"

It was as if all three of them, Sweet Pea, Frank and Harry, were suddenly as sober as judges. Harry, who was standing behind Dan, put a hand on his shoulder. "We can't bring Joey back, Dan," he said. "I hope you realize that nothing you can say or do now will change that."

Dan let a minute pass. The smoke from dozens of cigarettes wafted in the warm air around him, and the smell of stale beer thickened the atmosphere. Finally he stood and looked each of them in the eye, one by one, before he spoke. "Well, boys," he said, "I'm afraid the cat's already out of the bag."

There was a moment of tense silence. "Dan," Harry said then, "what have you started . . . not Internal Affairs . . . you didn't . . ."

"Of course he did," Sweet Pea grunted.

"What will you tell them?" Frank asked, his eyes red-rimmed, imploring. "What will you say when they ask you, Dan?"

Dan began to peel money off a wad he carried in his pocket. He tossed a few bills onto the bar. "I'll do what I should have done two years ago," he stated flatly. "I'll tell the goddamned truth." He stared them all once more in the eye, then turned on his heel and strode out, never looking back.

For hours he walked the familiar streets of downtown Philadelphia. A light rain had begun to fall out of the heavy sky, and the city took on a red glow below him. Horns honked, sirens wailed in the distance, though it seemed strangely removed to him, muffled by the rain.

He needed to walk. To think. A lot had come together for Dan since he'd arrived in the city, things he hadn't even considered when he'd told Piper he was leaving. He now knew for certain that *he'd* been the target the night Diana had died. She'd been in his truck; it had been cold, dark, and one of his former co-workers had made a mistake.

But then, Dan thought as he walked on toward the river, Diana's killer had gotten scared off. Another accident so close to Diana's would have aroused too much suspicion. Radowsky might be a small-town cop, but he wasn't *that* stupid.

So the murderer—or murderers—had backed off and bided his time. Sure. Probably waiting to see if Dan would catch on. But Dan hadn't. And he also hadn't done a thing about Joey Washington's death, had he. No, Dan had made it easy for them because, ironically, sickeningly, Diana's death had taken Dan's mind off Philadelphia entirely.

Until beautiful, angry Piper Hilyard.

He walked, his hands thrust into his trouser pockets as the drizzle settled on his head and dampened his shirt. Well, his former co-workers' plans had gone fine for a time. Until tonight. But they had the message loud and clear now. And one of them—or more—was going to have to make a move.

Okay, he thought, it was time the truth came out about Joey Washington's death, and about Diana's—

oh, yes, her death most especially. The trouble was, somehow Dan had to live to tell it.

He walked on into the night, shoulders hunched against the rain, hands in his pockets, into the shadows of the city.

CHAPTER SEVEN

THE PHONE IN THE TACK room was ringing. As quickly as she could Piper buckled the halter on the horse she'd been riding, then tied him to the iron ring with an experienced flick of her wrist. "Okay, I'm coming!" she called out.

She burst through the tack room door and grabbed the phone. "Hello?" she panted, out of breath.

"It's Dan," came his voice.

She took a breath, shifting the phone to the other ear, collecting herself. "Oh, Dan," she said, "are you back? At the airport?"

"No, I'm in Philadelphia."

"Oh."

"I'll be here awhile longer," he said flatly.

"I see."

"Any problems?"

"No, nothing we can't handle. But we could sure use your help. Rick and Luis are maxed, and I'm pretty busy riding. We got two new ones to train and I—"

"Piper," he interrupted.

"Yes?"

"Just listen," came his voice, hard and menacing. "I saw MacMurray. You remember Captain Mac-Murray, Piper, my old boss on the police force?"

Piper's heart stopped, fluttered, then thumped too loudly in her chest. She said nothing.

"I know the stunt you and Radowsky pulled. So I'm trying to get a job, am I? Pretty clever, you two," Dan said harshly.

"Dan—"

But he cut her off, and she could picture his black brows drawn into an angry line, the spark in his blue eyes, the twist of his mouth. "I don't want your lame excuses. You listen to me, Piper. You and your boy-friend stay out of my affairs. Do you hear me?"

"Yes," she whispered.

"What?"

"Yes," she said louder, "I hear you, Dan Bourne."

"It's none of your business," he growled. "You understand?"

"Sure," she said, feeling anger begin to kindle in her.

"Good," he said coldly.

"Is that all you phoned for?" she asked.

"Yes."

"Well, fine, I'll let you go then. Have a nice day, Dan," she said, and then she hung up.

But for all her bravado, Piper was left with a dry mouth and a quaking heart. She'd never heard the dangerous tone Dan had just used with her, the threat, the absolute hardness.

Piper walked out into the barn and thoughtfully stroked the neck of the horse she'd left tethered there. What would Dan do if she continued to delve into his past, and he found out? She shivered and automatically began to untack the horse, while her mind worked furiously.

She knew now, she was positive, that there was something very wrong with Diana's death. She knew that Dan Bourne had left behind something shady in Philadelphia, resigned for no good reason and married Diana very suddenly. Now, conveniently, he was the sole owner of a very valuable piece of real estate, and he'd just warned Piper to leave his past alone.

What was he doing back there in Philadelphia? It was pretty coincidental that he'd up and left for the city the minute Piper had intimated that Diana's death had been no accident. What was the connection?

She lugged the saddle into the tack room and set it on the saddle tree, thinking, thinking. Why *had* he left Philadelphia? That was the key. She had to know exactly why he'd left two years back, what had happened. MacMurray wouldn't tell—if he knew. How could she find out?

She thought about it while she sat in the shade and ate her sandwich. She thought while she handled the new filly they'd temporarily named Star, for the white spot on her forehead. She thought while she doctored a yearling who'd cut himself pretty badly, but not badly enough to call the vet, because she was always trying to keep the bills down.

She racked her brain until her hands fell to her sides and her eyes got a faraway look, and Rick asked her, "Hey, man, you ozoned out, Piper?"

She turned her gaze on him and frowned. "I've got to go into town, Rick, okay? Can you and Luis hold down the fort?"

"Sure, but—"

"It's important or I wouldn't leave you like this. Any messages, write them on the board for me, all right?"

"Sure, Piper." But he stood, hands on hips, and watched as she strode to her Jeep, swung inside and roared away, leaving a rooster tail of dust. And all the time he was shaking his head and muttering to himself in Spanish.

Inwardly Piper cringed with the need to go to Dutch again. She'd gone over every possibility in her mind, examined the problem from every angle, and come up with Dutch. If she had the time and money she could hire a private investigator or go to Philadelphia herself to check things out. But she had neither, and the circumstances surrounding Diana's death had gone unanswered, unquestioned, long enough.

Dutch would call her stubborn, intractable, a bull in a china shop, but she didn't care. It had to be done, and it had to be done now.

Surprisingly, Dutch was in one of his expansive, jovial moods, his "I never met a man I didn't like" state of mind. He'd conveniently forgotten their last angry meeting. *Good*, thought Piper.

Her idea intrigued him. He nodded, one booted foot crossed over the other knee, jiggling. "It might work, sure, why not?" he said thoughtfully.

"Will you try it, Dutch? Please."

"Now?"

"Yes, now."

The dispatcher, Denise, got him the numbers. Once again, Piper stood at the tall window, arms folded tightly across her turquoise tank top, and listened to Dutch ask the questions she couldn't.

"Daily News?" she heard Dutch say. "Good. Well now, I'm calling from Steamboat Springs, Colorado, trying to get some information on a former policeman there." He paused. "That's right, I'm the sheriff here...." But Dutch got nowhere with the newspaper. Nor could he get any information from the next one—both reporters who'd covered the police beat two years ago had gone on to other jobs.

"Try the *Philadelphia Inquirer,*" Piper said, frowning. "They're the big paper."

"Now, how do you know that?"

Piper shrugged. "I don't know, I just do. Like you know the *Los Angeles Times* and the *Miami Herald.*"

"Very impressive," Dutch said and dialed the phone.

Just as Piper had hoped, he hit pay dirt when he reached the *Philadelphia Inquirer.* He covered the receiver with his hand and hissed excitedly to Piper, "Come here. The editor is putting me on to the reporter who covers the police force and organized crime."

Piper went and leaned on her hands over his desk as he spoke. "Mr. Hobey, right? This is Sheriff Radowsky, Steamboat Springs, Colorado. I'm doing a little research on a resident of the county, Daniel Bourne. He was a homicide detective, left the force about two years back. Yes, he lives here now. You do recall, sir?" Dutch winked at Piper as if to say, "We'll get Bourne yet, don't you worry, babe."

Piper held her breath and closed her eyes in a mute prayer.

"So you did a story on Detective Bourne?" Dutch was saying. "Oh, not on Bourne exactly, on a case he was on. Police brutality, huh?"

Piper's eyes snapped open, her heart gave a leap and she leaned closer to Dutch.

"Tell you what, Mr. Hobey, let me just hand you over to my deputy here, and she'll get the information," Dutch said, grinning broadly. He held the phone out to Piper and nodded, but Piper only stared, wide-eyed, at the receiver. "Take it," he whispered. "Go on."

Slowly Piper reached out her hand and took the warm black plastic and raised it to her ear.

"Hello?" She had to clear her throat and try again. "Hello, Mr. Hobey. This is—" she switched her eyes to Dutch, who nodded encouragingly "—Deputy Hilyard."

A man's voice answered. "Okay, Deputy, shoot. I don't have all day."

"What do you remember about Dan Bourne?" she asked.

"Geez, I remember all sorts of things. Can you be specific?" Hobey's voice was shrill, high-pitched. And he was smoking; she could hear the suck and whistle of his breath over the phone.

"All right. Why exactly did Dan Bourne resign from the police force?"

"Lady—excuse me, *Deputy*—the cops aren't saying. It was rumored that something happened, but exactly what is strictly off-limits. Hey, you know that."

"Was he engaged in criminal activity?"

"Look, that Joey Washington case was probably police brutality. I mean, any fool coulda figured it."

"Joey Washington case?" she said cautiously.

"Well, that's what we're talking about, isn't it? Washington was a guy with a record long as your arm. A bad dude. Supposedly, he was found in an abandoned warehouse in a coma. See, the cops found him that way, or so they say. But rumor around Philly has it that they beat him up. Well, common sense'd tell you that, wouldn't it?"

"Sure, right. So, was Dan Bourne involved in this case?" Piper asked, her heart in her mouth.

"He was there, on the scene. Along with three other cops. But they all filed the same reports, and there were no witnesses, so, you know how it is."

"Yeah, I sure do."

"Anyway, I seem to remember a couple of other guys over at the precinct who told me some off-the-record stuff, but it's been a while."

"You can't recall anything else?"

"Not really. I've written one or two stories since then, lady."

"But that's when Dan Bourne quit the force?" Piper asked.

"Right around then, a while after, maybe. Quit and left town, and now I hear he's living in Colorado."

"Yes, he sure is."

"He getting into any trouble up there, Deputy?" Hobey asked nonchalantly, and Piper could hear him sucking smoke into his lungs.

"Oh, no, nothing like that. There's no story up here, Mr. Hobey, just, uh, doing some background checking."

"What is it up there in Routt County, a police state?" Hobey asked humorously.

"Yeah, that's it, ha, ha," Piper said. "Well, thanks a lot, Mr. Hobey, we really appreciate your cooperation."

A stream of smoke hissed in Piper's ear. "Welcome."

"Oh, by the way, uh, Mr. Hobey," Piper asked, "whatever happened to the man in the coma, that Washington guy?"

"Oh, Joey Washington," Hobey said carelessly. "He croaked."

Piper hung up. She stood there, her head hanging, her eyes closed, her hair falling down around her face. She could see the scene in her mind's eye, policemen beating a man on the ground. He was writhing, crying out, but they kept beating him, and one of the policemen was Dan Bourne, his strong body bent over the prostrate figure in the dirty, abandoned warehouse. No, her mind told her, that simply cannot be true. Not true, not—

"Hey, Piper," Dutch said softly, coming around his desk. "What'd he say?"

She shook her head, speechless.

He put his hand on her bowed neck, heavily, caressingly. "Hey, babe."

She moved away from that hand, so sure of itself. Even in her shock she could not abide that heavy hand on her. She shook her head again.

Dutch stepped back and folded his hands across his chest. "Well, do I arrest Bourne or not?" he asked in a hard voice.

"No," she breathed.

"What did the reporter say, Piper?" he asked again.

She swung her gaze up to his. "There was a man, a criminal, supposedly found in a coma, but...but what people think really happened was that some policemen, the ones who found him, beat him up. And then he died."

Dutch's mouth curved into a grin. "And Bourne was there. Well, well, Mr. Goody-two-shoes isn't so perfect, after all. I knew it. I knew—"

"Stop it, Dutch. There was no proof of any wrongdoing. MacMurray told you that himself," she said.

"Then why did Bourne resign? Tell me that."

She took a deep breath. "I don't know."

"Police brutality," Dutch said smugly. "Very interesting."

"There's no proof," she repeated.

"In this day and age there doesn't need to be. No wonder Bourne quit. They were probably going to start a full investigation. Yep, Internal Affairs. Now, there's some tough dudes. And Bourne, well, he'd have done hard time, Piper. Holy cow, nice guy you're working for."

"Please, Dutch," she said dully.

But he didn't let up. He had her where he wanted her, and he kept chipping away, the Will Rogers persona entirely gone now. "Your friend married him, for God's sake, Piper. He preys on women, can't you see that? He's dangerous. He was in trouble and he needed a place to retreat to. Well, he found it, and you're helping him keep it. I want you to quit that job, Piper. I don't want you out there with Bourne."

"Leave me alone, Dutch. You're using this to get at Dan. You're letting your emotions get in the way of your judgment." Piper thrust her hands into her hair. "I wish I'd never asked you to make that call."

"Do you really wish that?" Dutch asked. "You'd rather not know what kind of man you're dealing with? Come on!"

"I have to think. I have to figure this out."

"Okay, I'm willing to be objective. Let's talk about it," Dutch said. "Let's put all our facts together. How about we do it over a beer across the street?"

Piper looked at Dutch, then shook her head. He'd use any excuse on earth to get her alone, wouldn't he? "No, Dutch," she said quietly, "I'm not going out with you. I'm not going out with anybody. I don't want a date. I need to think. Thanks, Dutch, but I'm just going home."

"Hit you hard, didn't it?" Dutch said nastily. "Your golden boy all dirtied up, dragged down into the mud."

"He's not my golden boy," she said patiently, then she turned to walk out of his office.

"When's he getting back?" Dutch asked.

"I don't know. I don't keep track of Dan Bourne."

"Well *I'm* sure as hell going to," Dutch growled.

She drove home, drained, sick inside. The house was empty, as her folks had gone on their summer visit to Santa Fe to see her older brother. Glen had three kids, a business, a nice house down there. Glen was tall and auburn-haired like Piper, and lovable, and he never got into situations like this one. She wished her folks were here. She wished her brother was here. She wished, oh, God, she wished she wasn't so alone.

DUTCH CAME UP WITH the idea around five in the morning. He lay in his bed and a smile curved his lips. Piper was so all-fired against him taking a direct approach with Bourne. Well, okay, he thought, grinning now, he'd just get at Bourne through a back door.

He shaved and showered and thought about it while he dressed, snapping the buttons closed on his khaki shirt, zipping up his pants, buckling on his holster, checking his gun, settling his hat on his head with just the right tilt.

Piper was going to have to understand that Dutch needed to do his job whether she approved or not. And when he confirmed that Luis Santana was an illegal alien and that Dan Bourne was harboring him with full knowledge... Well, he'd have Charlotte look up the law on that, maybe even call the Immigration and Naturalization Service in Denver. Yeah, he'd have Bourne on some sort of abetting charge. It was going to feel real good.

Dutch recalled the expression on Piper's face yesterday when she'd found out her boss was involved in some nasty business back East. Her reaction had hurt Dutch. She'd looked so upset, so full of pain—and for who? That jerk Bourne.

Well, she'd get an eye-opening now, when she found out Bourne was breaking the law on this Luis thing. And, Dutch reminded himself, he also had a duty to the good folks of Routt County. He'd sworn to uphold the law, and that's exactly what he was going to do.

He grabbed a stale white doughnut from a box on top of his fridge and ate it in his Blazer as he drove to the west side of town where the River Run Mobile

Park was located. He knew the way because he'd cruised this area many a time, wondering how many illegals lived there. Yeah, it felt real good to finally be doing something about it.

He pulled up in front of an old aluminum trailer that he was pretty sure Luis rented, and, sure enough, there was the battered pickup truck that Dutch had seen out at Bourne's ranch. Children's toys lay in the unkempt yard and clothes were hanging on a line to dry. Someone had planted flowers by the crooked front steps.

Dutch got out of his Blazer, hitched up his belt and walked briskly up to the front door. As he knocked he was aware of a neighbor peering out at him through curtains that were quickly pulled closed when she saw him take notice.

The door finally opened—outward, like a car door—and he had to step back to avoid it. The wife stood there in a housedress, a baby on her hip, her face surprised, then scared.

"Is Luis here?" Dutch asked louder than usual, as if that would help her understand him.

"Luis?" she asked, her voice shaking.

"Yes, Luis Santana. He lives here, doesn't he?"

"*Sí.*"

"Let me see him, okay, *señora?*"

"*Momento.*" She stepped back and called him. There was a babble of Spanish, somewhere a child cried, and finally Luis came to the door, a skinny man with nervous dark eyes.

"I'm taking you in," was all Dutch said.

The man paled. "You are arresting me? But why?"

"For not having papers. I warned you and your boss."

"I have papers," Luis said. "Here, I get them."

"You can get them," Dutch replied. "But it won't do any good. I doubt they're authentic."

"What?"

"Papers are easy to forge. But I guess you know that," Dutch said. "Now get them and let's go."

Luis disappeared inside for a minute. Dutch heard a drawer being opened, closed, and then another babbling of Spanish. Luis reappeared, his face desperate. His wife stood behind him, the baby crying now, tears in her own eyes. Dutch decided that they should have known better. Sooner or later they all got caught.

He put Luis in the back seat of the Blazer, behind the grille, where the door locks were controlled from the front. Curtains were pulled back in the trailer park, faces just barely showing. They drove into town to the courthouse and Dutch led Luis inside, one big hand on the man's thin arm.

"Do I book him?" Doug, one of the deputies, asked.

"No, not yet. I want to hold him for a while, check his papers, for all the good it'll do him," Dutch added.

"Please," Luis said, "can I call the ranch? I'm supposed to be there."

"Later. I'm busy now," Dutch replied, knowing he was going to find an excuse every time Luis asked to use the phone. He wasn't an American—why should Dutch give him the benefit of the law?

The deputy said nothing.

Dutch got the keys off the hook on the wall and stiff-armed Luis ahead of him and along the corridor to the holding cells. He unlocked the door and pushed Luis in.

"Why you do this to me?" Luis asked, his voice cracking. "I do nothing wrong."

"I swore to uphold the law, Luis, and that's exactly what I'm doing, protecting the citizens of Routt County." Dutch turned the key in the lock, where it made a satisfying click, and turned and strode away, a small grin on his face.

CHAPTER EIGHT

DAN UNLOCKED THE DOOR of the white Ford pickup truck, threw his duffel bag in, slid up onto the seat and put on his sunglasses. It was hot in Steamboat Springs, but at least it was not that stifling summer sultriness of Philly. The flight had been late and he was tired, dragged out from the sitting, the waiting, the airport ennui that deadened the mind and body.

He started the engine, slipped the gearshift into Reverse and remembered his wife. Every time he got into the truck he remembered her. She'd died in a truck just like this. Well, now he knew how and why, but he wasn't sure if knowing made her loss more or less bearable. A senseless accident or a deliberate murder. Either one hurt.

Forget it, he told himself. *No self-pity. First things first.* His number-one priority was to get Piper Hilyard out of the way. She was underfoot, irritating, nosy. My God, she'd even had her lout of a boyfriend call MacMurray!

"So, Bourne, you're getting a job out in Colorado," MacMurray had said the other day in headquarters, squinting up through the smoke from his cigarette.

"A job," Dan had replied carefully.

"Yeah, with the sheriff's department out there. Just got a call from some guy named Radowsky, checking up on you...."

Now, as he drove along, Dan automatically glanced at his gas gauge and swore. The needle was nudging the E—he'd never even make it to the ranch. Damn it. He turned right onto Elk River Road, cursing the time it was going to take him to gas up in town. What he needed to do was confront Piper—there was no telling when his former buddies would make a move. Soon, Dan thought, they'd do it soon, though. And Dan intended to be certain of one thing: Piper wasn't going to be around to catch the flak. It was bad enough having one death weighing on his conscience.

Maybe he'd tell her the whole truth someday when it was all over. He owed her that, but right now he didn't dare. If Piper hadn't told him about Diana being so cautious on Six Mile Curve he'd never have put two and two together. But she had, and it had struck him with the force of a blow. Diana's accident had occurred in December, a year and a half ago. That was precisely the time Joey Washington had died. Washington's death after months in a coma had raised the stakes for the three policemen involved. They'd been responsible for a death, for murder, if the truth ever came out. Frank or Sweet Pea or Harry—he prayed fervently it wasn't Harry—had decided it was time to tie up all the loose ends, to make absolutely sure the truth never came out, to eliminate the sole witness, Dan. Unfortunately, Diana had been driving his truck that night.

He pulled up in front of the gas pumps and went around to the tank to open it. Bob came sauntering out, his grandfatherly gray hair and beard in direct contrast to his alcohol-laden breath. Bob was on the bottle again.

The gasoline chugged into the truck's big tank as Bob approached. "Hi ya, Dan," he said. "Back in town?"

"Yes, I am."

"Where'd you go?"

"Oh, back East. A visit."

"Hmm." Bob regarded him, rocking a little on his feet. "Hear they're busy out at the ranch."

The man knew everything. "That so?"

"They'll be mighty glad you're back."

"Um."

"Saw Dutch heading up the valley not too long ago," he said.

Dan's jaw tightened.

"'Course, he coulda been going to Hahn's Peak or anyplace, for that matter," Bob said.

"Yes, he could have," Dan replied, waiting impatiently for the gas tank to fill.

Dan drove out of the gas station too fast, wrenching the wheel, spurting gravel. Dutch Radowsky. Piper. Harry Tegmeier. Frank and Sweet Pea. Diana. They were all connected in the ugly little drama being acted out, and he was the stage director.

If only Dan had pushed harder for an Internal Affairs investigation back when the Joey Washington incident had happened. If only he'd insisted, threatened to go to the press with it. Then it would have been bad, but it would have been over two years ago. Instead, he'd gone to MacMurray like a good cop, a brother, with his accusations against Harry, Frank and

Sweet Pea, and it had been hushed up, buried, the brotherhood drawing together its powerful protection system. After all, they'd figured, what had happened? A longtime criminal had possibly been beaten up. So what? God knew he deserved it, didn't he? And there was no proof that anyone had done anything wrong. In fact, a phony investigation had been launched, coming up with the even phonier verdict that the three cops were telling the truth, namely that they had found the said offender, one thirty-two-year-old male known as Joey Washington, beaten and unconscious on the floor of the before-mentioned warehouse. And if by chance anyone had dug up evidence that Washington had received his injuries from the three homicide detectives, Dan had no doubt the conclusion would have been similar: that they'd been acting within acceptable parameters of self-defense.

He hadn't had the moral strength to pursue the mess any further, to buck the system that had taken him in, cared for him, rewarded him. The only real family he'd ever known. Harry—he would have wounded Harry mortally.

Harry had stood by him, told him to pay no attention, that in time the guys would forget. And when Dan had asked Harry what he should do, Harry had replied, his beefy red face sober for once, "Do what you have to do, Danny-boy."

And then Diana had come.

Smack-dab in the middle of the whole sick mess. Dan had gone ahead with plans to ski Steamboat Springs with the police force club. And right there in the cowboy boot shop he'd met Diana.

"Quit the force," Diana had said on their third date. "Why would you want to stay with those bums, anyway?"

So simple...

Dan drove up the beautiful Elk River Valley that was turning brown that July under a relentless sun. Yes, it was looking dusty and parched. Guess it hadn't rained, after all. The gamble hadn't paid off, and he'd have to buy hay now.

It had been too easy—his meeting Diana. He remembered so well the day he'd phoned her to tell her he'd resigned. She'd been ecstatic, positive he was doing the right thing. He'd asked her to marry him then—on the phone—and she'd cried. He wondered now as he'd wondered so many times over the past ten days: would he and Diana have taken it more slowly if he hadn't had to deal with the Joey Washington nightmare? And if he'd waited, not quit the force, would Diana be alive today?

Dan rubbed his hand over the dark stubble of his face. No sense asking unanswerable questions. It was too late for that.

Piper Hilyard popped into his mind as he turned under the crossbar that proudly announced the Elk River Ranch. She'd probably be up at the barn, and he could get rid of her on the spot. Send her away. Because something was going to happen soon; he'd seen to that, all right.

It was odd, but the first time Dan had laid eyes on Piper he hadn't paid much attention to her. Oh, he'd heard about her from Diana. Piper this and Piper that. A tall girl with long legs, deep-set, tawny-brown eyes and wild auburn hair. She hadn't impressed him one way or the other. But then, at the wedding, Diana had sent him over to talk to her, because Diana had known her best friend was down and not having a very good time. *Then* something inside him had given way, some warm, primitive melting in his gut. He'd spoken some meaningless drivel, but their eyes had met, and even through Piper's belligerence he'd felt it, that melting deep in his belly. If someone had walked up to Dan that day and asked him to define his sudden, reckless attraction to his new wife's best friend, Dan could not have put words or meaning to it in a thousand years. It had simply, inexplicably, happened.

The incident flashed through Dan's mind as he steered the truck, an uncomfortable memory. He'd turned it over in his head even while he and Diana had been on the plane to their honeymoon. He'd told himself it had been too much champagne—that and seeing Piper all dressed up for the first time in that pink dress. Lousy excuses, but they'd worked for him. And then Piper had been gone, as far away as you could get—to New Zealand. Out of sight, out of mind. He'd devoted himself to his growing love for Diana and his new life. He'd worked hard to forget he'd once been a member of the elite, a homicide detective on a big city police force. He'd tried hard to forget that he'd never in his life wanted to be anything but a cop. He'd listened to his wife read aloud Piper's letters from New Zealand and dutifully remembered her as a very pretty woman, his wife's best friend.

Any man would have found Piper Hilyard attractive. It didn't mean he'd loved Diana less. And he knew he'd made Diana happy. But, damn, they'd rushed into things so quickly, Dan desperate for a new life, Diana impulsive. *I should have had more re-straint,* he told himself. Her death was his fault.

He drove up the long driveway, dodging potholes, the big, empty truck bouncing noisily. Piper was probably there now, at work this time of day. She wasn't expecting him.

He hadn't been expecting her that May morning. She'd shown up like a specter, still hostile, blaming him for Diana's death. He had seen it in her eyes, heard it in her tone of voice. She'd lost her best friend because of him. Piper was hurt, angry, sick at seeing him still alive and kicking while Diana was dead. He hadn't blamed her. And still, even though he'd never expected to see her again, that same crazy melting sensation had shaken him when he'd seen her standing in his doorway—tall, tight jeans, red T-shirt, wild auburn hair. He'd only met her twice in his life, and yet she'd looked as familiar as his own face in the mirror. She belonged there.

At first he'd just seen her beauty and her anger, but working with her these months, being with her every day, he'd learned there was more to Piper than surface beauty. She was a woman who felt things deeply, who cared, whose sense of right and wrong was built into her soul. She was a woman of temper, as transparent as glass, unable to hide her feelings. He'd come to enjoy watching all those emotions ripple across her face, like sunlight chasing shadow across the ocean's surface. Maybe that was why he enjoyed taunting her so much, just to stir up those emotions. But he'd been a damn fool to bait her about Radowsky. What had he said? Something like, "I'm sure you and Dutch will find something to keep yourselves occupied."

Dan suddenly pounded the steering wheel with a flat hand. He could never let Piper glimpse the truth, that he cared too damn much about her. It was far better if she disliked and distrusted him—better in every way. Besides, soon she was going to be out of his hair, anyway, off the ranch, out of harm's way. No innocent woman would ever get hurt again because of him.

He pulled up in front of the ranch house. Piper's Jeep was there, parked in its usual spot by the barn. And next to it was a familiar white Blazer. Just what he needed. He got out of the truck, dragged his bag off the seat and decided to head right inside. *Leave it alone,* he told himself, his jaw tightening. *Just leave it alone.*

He'd almost reached the top step when he heard his name being called. He stopped, took a deep breath and set his bag down.

"Bourne!" Dutch was calling. "Hey, there, I'm talking to you!"

Dan's back tensed at the cop's officious tone. He knew it too well, had used it himself. To have it turned on him by a goon like Radowsky...

"Bourne!" Dutch's voice was nearer.

Dan turned slowly. There was the sheriff, dressed up in his costume, leather gun belt and holster, cowboy boots, Stetson—the works. Radowsky's hands were on his hips, his legs braced apart, his face smug.

"You want something?" Dan asked, keeping his tone neutral.

And Piper was there, over by the barn, hands also on her hips, her long legs in their worn leather chaps, the ones she used for riding. Her hair lifted in the hot wind, and her mouth was set in a grim line. She was beautiful and angry, and Dan could have wrung her neck.

"Yeah, I want something," Dutch was saying.

Deliberately, slowly, Dan removed his sunglasses and stared at the sheriff. "Well?"

"Some questions have been raised, Bourne, about your whereabouts the night of your wife's death," Dutch said flatly.

Dan's eyes snapped over to Piper. What had she done now? Damn her! He put a cold smile on his lips, not giving an inch, and saw her return his look from across the yard. She wouldn't back down, not Piper. She wanted Diana avenged, and she'd stop at nothing to achieve that end. The trouble was, Dan wanted the same thing, yet they were working at cross-purposes.

"Hey, fella, I'm talking to you," Dutch growled.

Dan switched his gaze to Dutch, a slow, insolent look. "Do I need an alibi?" Dan finally asked.

"No one is accusing you of anything, Bourne, at least, not yet," Dutch replied. "Just some questions."

Dan looked from Radowsky to Piper, who had finally walked over, and he couldn't stop the image from flashing in his brain—Piper in that man's heavy arms. Her bare limbs, long legs, strong hands, entwined with that man's meaty ones. He seethed inside, fought to keep his cool.

"Well, where *were* you that night?" Dutch pressed.

"It's all in the reports, sheriff," Dan said. "Why don't you go read them? If you've got a case, you ought to do something about it. If not, get the hell off my land."

Radowsky smiled thinly. "Sure. No problem. Just thought you might want to cooperate." He paused and his grin broadened. "And, by the way, your pal Luis is down at the jail, behind bars until he can prove he's in the country legally."

White light exploded in Dan's head. Even as he started toward Dutch he was aware of Piper's reaction—her shocked expression, the inadvertent move she made. He walked down the steps, striding up to the big blonde man. "Let him go, Radowsky," Dan growled, "or I'll have every state agency on your back."

Dutch shrugged. "We'll see," he said, moving toward his Blazer. He tipped his Stetson to Piper as he got in the car. "See you, babe," Dan heard him say to her, and then he drove off.

Dan's control held only until the Blazer was gone. Then he whirled on Piper, ready to shout at her, to shake her, to pull her into his arms. "I told you," he said, his teeth clenched, his voice shaking with rage, "I told you to stay out of my business."

She should have been afraid of him, but she faced him bravely. "I can't do that, Dan. I've got to find out what happened to Diana," she said, obviously trying to keep her voice calm. But it shook nevertheless.

The little idiot! If only he could tell her. He'd laid a trap, and for all he knew he could have been followed already, stalked by professionals. And here she was, facing him with foolish courage, in the line of fire, for God's sake. What could he say? What could he tell her?

"I'm sorry about Luis," she said then. "I didn't know, really I didn't."

"Never mind Luis for now. I'll take care of it," he said.

She bit her lip. "Well," she said, "it's good you're home. There are some things I need to—"

He gave a short laugh. "You don't get it, do you?" he said, knowing if he put this off he might relent.

"Get what?"

"I want you off this ranch. You're outta here, kid. Gone."

She stiffened. "What?"

Dan stared at her mercilessly, afraid to give an inch. "I'm canning your butt, lady," he said.

She stared at him, disbelieving. "You wouldn't dare," she breathed. "You can't..."

"Oh, yes, I can. I want you off this ranch now. If I ever see you here again I'll personally escort you off. It won't be pleasant."

He made himself stand there and watch her. She was so furious. Her mouth opened and she started to say something, then she clamped it shut. Her brows drew together, her eyes flashed, her hands clenched into fists. "Damn you, Dan Bourne!" she said hoarsely.

"Go ahead, get your stuff and get out of here," he said.

"What're you going to do with the horses, you jerk?" she yelled at him. "Who's going to train them?"

"Not your problem."

"You...you...fool!" she sputtered. "You're crazy! Do you realize what you're doing?"

"Just go, Piper. I'm not in the mood for arguments."

She spun on her heel and headed to the barn, presumably to collect her belongings. Motionless, Dan stood by his truck and stared at the barn door, awaiting her reappearance. If she didn't come out of there in a minute, if she defied him again, he'd have to physically throw her off the place, a task that would make him sick. If she . . .

But Piper did come storming back out, throwing her things helter-skelter into her open Jeep. She shot him a scathing glance then swung up into the driver's seat. Dan still stood at the bottom of the steps unmoving, implacable, merely watching her, as she turned the vehicle in a tight circle, rocking it, spewing gravel from under the tires. He watched, too, as she careened up the driveway in a cloud of dust. He kept watching until she was a speck on the highway and finally the dot had disappeared around the wide curve. And then Dan moved. Standing next to his truck, he spun around abruptly and pounded his fist into its door, once, very hard.

CHAPTER NINE

THERE WERE JUST SOME times when, no matter how hard a girl tried, she couldn't make herself look attractive. That was how Piper felt, and it was Dan's fault.

Fired! He'd fired her.

She stood in front of her bathroom mirror trying to form a French braid in her hair and recalled the incident with a sick lurch in her stomach. Fired.

Alone at her folks' house, Piper had planned to get decked out Western-style and have an evening on the town, maybe run into some old friends, get her head straight.

She'd gone over to the house and soaked in a bubble bath in her mom's big old claw-footed tub. She'd pulled on her tightest, sexiest jeans and found a favorite summer-weight blue denim shirt, Western cut, ladylike, with shoulder pads and an embroidered yoke. Her best wide leather belt and her fancy snakeskin cowboy boots completed the outfit. From the neck down she looked great; from the neck up her face showed every bit of her anger and frustration. And now her hair... Giving up, she brushed it out and let it fall to her shoulders. She picked up her purse and headed out to her open Jeep, put the key in the ignition and took a deep breath, telling herself she was going to have fun tonight despite everything.

But...where to go? Where *did* her old friends hang out?

Piper tried two spots downtown, but both of them were crammed with tourists, and she didn't recognize a soul, not even the bartenders. She walked back to her car and decided there was only one spot—the Timber Parrot Tavern up in Clark, eighteen miles away. *Oh, well,* she thought, the drive would do her good, get her mind off things, and maybe she could even muster a smile or two for some old acquaintances in the tiny mountain village. The only trouble was, she did have to drive up the same valley where Diana's ranch—Dan's ranch, she reminded herself bitterly—lay. She'd just have to drive straight by, not even turn her head.

Piper rounded Six Mile Curve slowly, her eyes inadvertently going to the spot where Diana's car had gone off the embankment. She let out her breath and drove on as she always did, up the valley and past the ranch.

Clark, a town consisting of a few dozen folks, lay around a long curve in the road. It was a gateway to the many national forest trailheads in that neck of the woods, a stopover for fishermen and campers, hikers and even some boat enthusiasts who used Steamboat Lake at the foot of Hahn's Peak. Oh, yes, Clark was a great little place, a jumble of log cabins, a lodge, a bike rental shop and a bar, a few rustic mountain homes. It wasn't much, but Piper suspected she'd run into a local or two in the bar.

What she hadn't expected was Dutch.

Off duty, for once out of uniform, Dutch rose from the table where he was sitting and strode straight up to her. "Piper, come on over, join us. Wow, if this isn't a surprise!"

"Dutch, I..." she began, then relented. He *was* sitting with Judy Kaiser and John Hamon, two old high school friends who'd graduated just a year ahead of them. "Well," Piper said, "maybe for one drink."

"Beer?" Dutch asked, heading past the jukebox to the bar.

"Sure, a light. Whatever," she said, forcing a couple of dollars on him in spite of his protests.

It was pleasant seeing Judy and John again. In fact, Piper realized, Diana's wedding had been the last time she'd seen a group of former friends. For a time they sat at the table in the small, cozy log room beneath a neon beer sign that blinked in the window, and talked about New Zealand and Piper's experiences there. They talked skiing and horseback riding and reminisced about the good old days at high school.

And then Judy and John had to go.

"Now," Dutch said when they were gone, "aren't you glad you came out tonight?"

Piper took a sip from the bottle in front of her. "I am. I guess I've been too involved in work lately." What she didn't tell him was that she'd been fired. And then her eyes came up to meet his. "By the way," she said, "have you let Luis out of jail? I mean, that really was above and beyond the call of duty."

Dutch shook his head and sat back in his wooden chair, hitching his thumbs in his belt loops. "Luis is a free man," he told her. "I had to let him go. That SOB

Bourne got the American Civil Liberties Union all over my back."

"The ACLU?" Piper couldn't help but smile before she caught herself.

"It's not funny," Dutch was saying.

"Well," Piper put in, "it's kind of amusing if you look at it a certain way."

Piper began to study Dutch then, not as an old friend or an old boyfriend, but as a human being, a man. He was very young for his job, and maybe in time he'd mellow out. He wasn't a *bad* man, and someday she was sure he'd make someone a good husband. But not her. Piper knew now that she was too independent to settle for a man who wanted to lock her up and throw away the key. The kind of man she wanted was hard to find—a strong man, secure enough in himself to treat a woman as his equal.

She looked at Dutch, then gazed back down at her folded hands, and the craziest thing struck her. Dan Bourne was that kind of man. Despite his terrible flaws, despite the awful things she suspected about him, he *was* the sort to let a woman go where she needed to go and then be there when she returned.

She felt her knuckles tighten. Why was she bothering with thoughts about that man? She loathed him, she really did. If he had even one redeeming quality, who cared?

"So," Dutch was saying, "you wanna tell me about it?"

"About what?" Piper looked up.

"About this rumor I heard."

"What?"

"Bourne fired you."

"Oh," Piper said, stiffening, "who told you that?"

"I got my sources, babe. Nothing happens in good ol' Routt County that I don't hear about sooner or later. You know that."

"Oh, I *do* know that," Piper said. "Well, I guess Dan and I just don't see eye to..." She suddenly became aware of Dutch staring at something, or someone, over her shoulder. She swiveled in her chair.

"Speaking of the devil," Dutch said, and grinned, and Piper saw him then—Dan.

She turned back around quickly. "Darn," she said, and took a long drink of beer. What on earth was he doing there?

Dutch was still smiling when Piper looked up from her drink. He was grinning as if he had some grisly secret, and she wondered if Dutch wasn't waiting for Dan to notice him—Dutch and her, together. *Oh, God.*

It took some time, but eventually Piper managed to reposition herself so that she could see the bar. Steve Altman was behind the counter, pouring drinks. Kevin and Iris Carridy, two old locals who ran a gas station up near the lake, were sitting, drunk, head to head on the end stools. Next to them was Billy Dinsmore, a young cowboy type who worked at the W/B Ranch out on Route 40. And next to Billy, his foot propped on the brass rail, a drink in hand, looking as carefree and handsome as they came, was Dan, all gussied up in one of his clean, pastel-plaid city shirts.

Piper began to seethe. The wealthy widower, she thought, and she realized that he probably did this every night.

Dan tossed his dark head back and laughed at a joke or something that Billy was telling the group. Piper gritted her teeth. And then Laurel Lee, one of the alternate bartenders at the tavern, sauntered over and put one hand on Billy's shoulder, the other on Dan's.

"Wonder if they know each other," Dutch said.

"How should I know?" Piper snapped.

"He sure is havin' a good ol' time," Dutch couldn't resist putting in.

"Oh, be quiet, Dutch," she said.

"You did tell me you were off men, Piper, but you're sure looking as if—"

"Dutch."

"Okay, okay."

But he'd struck a chord, and Piper knew it. She glared at Dan again and shifted mental gears. It was his happy-go-lucky presence in the bar that was really pushing her buttons. All his talk about the ranch being too much to handle... The way he'd eat his food cold from a can, exhausted, ready to drop into bed... That baloney he'd given her about not being able to walk into the office and see the pictures of Diana.

"Oh, my!" came Laurel Lee's voice, a high-pitched giggle, and Piper saw Dan pull some money from his pocket, toss it on the bar and order a round of drinks. *Diana's money,* Piper thought.

She got to her feet.

"Piper," Dutch began, "what're you..."

But Piper was halfway to the bar by then. She tapped Dan on the shoulder. Laurel Lee took one look at Piper's face and ducked away.

"Piper," Dan said, half turning toward her, looking studiously bored now. "I *thought* that was you over there with your pal."

"Never mind that," she said.

"Can I do something for you?"

"You can tell me just who the heck you think you are, Dan Bourne."

"How's that?"

"You know exactly what I mean. You come striding in here as if you don't have a care in the world when we both know the truth! You think you got away with Diana.... But I'm telling you, mister, if the law can't nail you on something, I sure as hell will!"

"Piper—" his voice had become abruptly low and dangerous "—not here. Not now."

"Oh, yeah? You afraid everyone will know what I know? That *you* forced Diana out of the house the night she was—"

He took her arm. "That's enough," he said. "I mean it, Piper." And something in that tone, so cold and calm and deliberate, gave her pause. "All right," he said quietly, "there's a thing or two I'm going to tell you, for your own damned good. But not in here." Dan glanced around and dropped her arm.

"Look—" Piper started to say.

"Of course," Dan interrupted, his blue eyes locked with hers, "if you're afraid to go with me..."

The words tumbled out, tripping over one another. "I'll go anywhere, Dan Bourne. You don't scare me one bit."

"Then let's do it." Dan finished his drink in a gulp, his throat muscles working. He took her elbow and steered her past Billy, Kevin and Iris, and toward the door.

"My purse," Piper said, coming to her senses, but suddenly Dutch was there, snagging her other arm.

"Wait a minute," Piper began. "Dutch, what're you—"

"Just be quiet, Piper," Dutch said, and his eyes locked with Dan's.

Piper looked at Dutch in surprise. "Listen," she said, "this is crazy. Let go of me, Dutch."

He gripped her arm harder. It was a tug-of-war, Dutch and Dan both holding on to her. Something in her exploded then, and she wrenched herself free, her cheeks flaming. "I'm walking out of here with Dan," she said to Dutch in a cold voice. "It's important. Dutch, you have to..."

But Dutch wasn't hearing her. "She's *my* woman," he said to Dan, "and nobody's going to leave here with her except me."

And Dan. Coolly reasonable. "I'd say that's her choice, Radowsky."

"She's with me," Dutch growled.

But Dan only shrugged. "I think she's made her position clear."

"Will you both please stop this," Piper began, but Dutch took a step toward Dan, thrusting her aside.

"You, *buster*," he said to Dan, "are out of this county." He thrust his chin forward, and Piper could almost feel static sizzle through the heavy air.

"Please," she whispered to Dutch, "don't do this. Dan's right. I'll make my own decisions. Blame me, don't take it out on Dan." With as much dignity as she could muster in the hushed room, Piper went to get her purse. She prayed to God Dutch would just let it go—she was leaving with Dan, she was going to hear those "things" he had to tell her. "Okay," she said to Dan when she got back, "I'm ready." But the two men were still chest to chest. "Let's *go,*" she said.

"You do this," Dutch told her, "and that's it. We're through."

"Dutch," she began, "please . . ."

"I mean it. You go with this guy and you may as well both keep going right the hell out of Routt County."

Piper tore her eyes from Dutch and looked at Dan, but he wasn't reacting to the sheriff's bluster one bit. Instead, he wore a calm, almost amused expression, as if he'd seen men like Dutch too many times before.

Dutch must have recognized it, too, because he backed off, and the tension in the room abated a touch. Piper took a breath after far too long.

"Get out of here," Dutch said harshly, slicing the air with his hand.

"Okay," Dan replied, "have it your way, Radowsky. But mark my words, pal, you're the one that's going to be through in this county. I'm going to see to it personally." And then, taking advantage of Dutch's momentary lapse, he took Piper's arm, pushed through the crowd to the door and thrust it open, and the clean mountain air struck Piper in the face like a welcome blow.

She walked to the rail that ran around the porch and gripped it, leaning forward, her stomach twisted into knots. "He's gone crazy," she whispered. "Stark, raving mad."

Dan came up behind her. "Yeah, well," he said, "power can do that to a man. Listen, let's get out of here, head to the ranch. This is a bad spot, too open. Are you coming?"

"What?" Piper faced him, uncomprehending—but later his words would make complete sense.

In her own Jeep, Piper followed Dan's white pickup along the curving road. It was, perhaps, eight miles back down the narrow country road to where the Elk River Ranch lay. She stayed behind him by several car lengths—a deer could leap out from the night shadows and force Dan to jam on his brakes. But she wasn't thinking about deer. She wasn't even thinking about Dutch's insane threats—she'd have to deal with that later. Instead, she was thinking about these "things" that Dan was going to tell her. It was all very mysterious, almost ridiculous. What was he going to say—that Diana had been a lunatic beneath her very together facade? That Diana had run off to a lover or something the night of her death? How *was* Dan planning to explain away his wife's very curious accident?

She steered around a curve, still following the taillights of the pickup, and asked herself if she wasn't being foolhardy. Dan would have her alone at the ranch. He could do anything he wanted. Another "accident." And maybe, if he was clever enough, the community would buy it. Sure. Everyone had seen Piper leave the tavern upset that night. All Dan had to say was that he'd tried to get her to ride with him but she'd been headstrong, shaken, and, geez, they all knew there was no stopping Piper Hilyard when she had a head of steam.

Dan *could* pull it off. She stood between him and his future happiness, his wealth, because, darn it, she'd told him every which way that she was never going to rest until the truth was out.

He could do it. He could kill her.

But she knew, in her heart she knew, that Dan Bourne would never lay a finger on her. And if he wouldn't hurt her, then how could he have hurt Diana?

If she'd had time to give it consideration, Piper would have known there hadn't been a storm all summer and that she couldn't have been hearing a reverberating clap of thunder just then. And when Dan's pickup suddenly swerved violently ahead of her, she merely reacted, jamming her foot on the brake, watching in stark horror as his truck caught a tire on the shoulder of the road and careened down the embankment.

It had happened so suddenly, shockingly, and yet the events of the next few minutes seemed to stretch out over hours. Her foot was on the brake hard, and the Jeep did some swerving of its own before coming to a stop a few feet from where Dan had gone off the road. And then she was out of her car, running, running, her legs nightmarishly leaden, her heart knocking at her ribs wildly, running to the edge and sliding down, falling onto her rear, righting herself again. Running.

There, over there! her mind screamed. The truck, on its side, its tires still spinning. Everything except the tires, though, was unearthly, motionless. Not a tree stirred, not a night animal chattered. No sounds whatsoever, except the rattle of gravel as it sifted down the bank onto the truck.

"Dan," she gasped through suddenly dry lips. "Dan!"

Stumbling in the dark over a rock, Piper almost fell into the overturned truck. A terrible, dank fear gripped her—he was dead. He had to be dead!

She managed to open the driver's door, though it was smashed and she had to use her foot to push it into a vertical position because the truck was on its side.

Still no sound from within. And she could barely make him out—just barely, his head lying limply on the steering wheel, slouching in his seat belt.

"Dan," she said, a strangled whisper. "Dan, can you hear me?"

Deathly silence.

"Dan." She put a trembling hand on his shoulder—she'd never touched a dead person.... "Dan, oh God, Dan, wake up!"

It seemed as if minutes passed, and how many times she said his name or nudged him, Piper never knew. But finally, mercifully, he emitted a low groan, and his head moved as if he were trying to raise it.

Some wild, unfathomable emotion surged through Piper. "Dan," she said, weeping, "oh, Dan, wake up, please wake up!"

He moaned something, trying to speak.

"Come on," she urged, and she touched his head, easing it carefully away from the steering wheel. Hot, sticky blood covered her fingers. If only she had a flashlight... The glove box, maybe in there...

With great care Piper managed to stretch across him and wrench open the compartment. Everything fell out—even a flashlight. She switched it on and eased back across him, carefully supporting her weight above his. She shone the flashlight on the deep gash on his brow that was liberally pouring blood, covering his eyes and cheeks, the entire front of his shirt. So much blood...but head wounds bled furiously, didn't they? He'd be all right. Maybe some stitches, maybe a few days' rest with a concussion. Or, she thought, shining the light on his limbs, maybe there were broken bones, too. Oh, Lord.

"Dan," she said, "we have to get you to a hospital. Can you move?"

"Fine," he muttered. "I'll be fine."

It took a full ten minutes to get him out of the truck and resting on the ground. Piper pressed a rag she'd found in the truck to the wound on his temple, knowing how dirty the cloth was, but figuring it was better to stop the bleeding than to worry about that. Once, she scrambled back up the rocky embankment to try to wave down a passing car, but the driver roared by, apparently not seeing her. She waited a few more minutes, but no one else came by. It was a seldom-used road, and getting late to boot. She went back down to Dan, afraid to leave him alone.

"We're on our own," she said, kneeling beside him. "Do you think you can stand?"

"Sure, sure." But when he came to his feet he swayed and she caught him, putting his arm around her shoulder, insisting he lean on her.

The worst was getting him up the rock-strewn slope. Though it was only a few feet of vertical climb, the gravel kept slipping out from under their feet, and she was terribly afraid he'd fall, injuring himself more.

"Hold on, Dan," she kept saying. "Put your weight on me."

He was heavy. Though not particularly tall, Dan was solid muscle, and that made him heavier than he looked. Piper sucked in lungfuls of air and bore his weight, wondering what they'd do if she faltered. But she didn't, and somehow she got him to her Jeep.

"Sorry," he kept saying, "I'll be okay in a minute."

She helped him up to the passenger seat and fastened the seat belt for him. "You'll be okay as soon as we get to the hospital," Piper said.

But he waved her off. "Get me home. No hospital."

"Dan..."

"No hospital."

She climbed into the driver's seat and gazed at him. "Listen—" she began.

"I'm all right, just head for the ranch," he told her. "We have to get off this road. Piper," he said, turning to her, his hand, surprisingly strong, gripping her knee, "please. Just do as I say right now."

She looked at him for another moment, then put the car into First and took off down the dark, lonely road.

Dan did seem a little better when she opened the front door of the ranch house and helped him upstairs to the bedroom. Piper barely looked around at the once-familiar room that Diana had remodeled for Dan. She went straight to the bathroom and found peroxide, antiseptic cream, a roll of gauze and tape. She'd patched up plenty of animals, but never a person. And she sure never thought she'd be doctoring Dan Bourne.

"Lie down," she told him, setting the stuff on the nightstand. "Darn, it's still bleeding."

"It'll stop."

He did as he was told. She even helped him, lifting his legs onto the summer quilt, putting a pillow behind his head. "Your shirt's a goner," she said, touching the oozing wound on his brow, pushing his black hair aside carefully. And she felt it then, his gaze on her as she poised above him, her breasts practically touching his shoulder. She moved away quickly, sitting on the side of the bed, opening bottles, readying the gauze and strips of adhesive tape.

"I can clean the cut," Dan said, his eyes still on her. "I've patched myself up before."

"Don't be stupid," she said, and she became aware of the trembling of her fingers as she unscrewed the cap of the peroxide bottle. It was, of course, the aftermath of tension—it had been a long hour since the accident. Then, too, she'd almost had to carry him. Naturally she was shaky. "Now, lie still," she said and turned back to him, a soaked cotton ball in her fingers. "Why you wouldn't just go to the hospital is beyond me."

Dan was completely still and silent as she cleaned the wound and applied pressure to it until the bleeding was almost stopped. He was too still. And it was too quiet in the room. Piper became acutely aware of the funniest things: the way her fingers moved on his forehead, the rise and fall of his chest beneath the soiled plaid shirt, the rise and fall of her own breast. There were the scents in the room: the coppery odor of dried blood, Dan's own scent and hers, a mixture of perfume she'd put on hours ago and perspiration.

He never took his eyes off her, either, as she worked on the gash. The effect of his attention became mesmerizing, and she began to hurry through the process of taping him up.

When she was finished with his head she stood quickly and surveyed her work. "I guess you'll live," she said, wondering at her flippancy. She turned away. "I'll get you a clean shirt and a washcloth or something," Piper added, and walked to his closet, sliding back the doors. She knew she was acting strangely, all thumbs and quivering muscles, and for the first time in her life she felt utterly out of control.

"Here," she said, handing him the clean shirt. "I'll go get a washcloth."

She caught her reflection in the bathroom mirror as she wrung dry the cloth. Her eyes were brilliant, dark and limpid, and there was a flush of excitement on her sun-browned skin. Her hair was a springing mass of loose tendrils and snags.

Dan was sitting on the edge of the bed when Piper walked back into the room. He had taken off the stained shirt and he held it between his splayed knees, his head down. Carefully she took the shirt from his hands and went to put it in the hamper. "I think you really ought to get checked out," she said, returning to his side, gazing down on his dark head, the breadth of his shoulders. "Dan..."

"I'll be fine," he said. "In an hour or so I'll be fine." He looked up and gave her a half smile, a genuine smile. Her heart pounded once, twice, then settled back down.

Somehow she helped him wash the dark dried blood from his face and chest, touching him as she'd never thought possible, as she'd never wanted to. She began to feel dizzy, and wondered if concussion was catching.

She helped him into a clean yellow shirt and stood back, watching as he fumbled with the buttons. Finally she stepped up to him and fastened them herself.

Wild, crazy, forbidden sensations rocked her as she worked with his buttons, his breath soft on her hands, his muscles tensing beneath the fabric. Neither of them said a word. But she knew—she knew that *he* knew she was losing control, adrift in some unfathomable sea of new emotions. Oh, yes, he was aware of her discomfort, aware of it and saying nothing. She felt suddenly ashamed to her core, guilt ridden, standing there in Dan and Diana's bedroom, her pulse racing at his nearness. She was a fool, a stupid, blind fool, and she had to regain her senses because he was the enemy, a man she didn't want, a man she could never have.

Piper dropped her hands and moved away as he stood, turned slightly, undid the top buttons of his blue jeans and tucked in the shirttails, sucking in his belly. He was still unsteady on his feet, and his skin was pallid. But he would live, and she was finished helping him.

"Let's go on downstairs," he was saying.

"Sure," Piper replied, shrugging.

He followed her down the steps and they went to the kitchen, Dan pulling the curtains over the windows before he offered her something to drink. She watched and wondered but dismissed his actions. He wasn't quite with it, after all.

"Water's fine," she said, "but I'll get it." She went to the sink. Over her shoulder she said, "So, what made you swerve like that, anyway?"

"Swerve?" Dan replied.

"Yes." Piper set the two glasses on the table and pulled out a chair. Dan, however, was still standing. "Was it a deer? I didn't see..."

"Piper," he said and stared soberly at her, "you didn't hear it?"

"Hear what?" And then she remembered, the thunderclap. "I did hear something," she said, taking a sip of water.

He watched her for a moment and then seemed to decide something. "Piper," he said, and he sounded grim, "if you could see the windshield of the truck, you'd find a hole in it."

"A hole," she repeated.

"That's right. A bullet hole." He picked up his own glass and took a drink, holding her eyes with his over the rim, and all she could do was stare back in confusion.

CHAPTER TEN

SHE HADN'T HEARD HIM right. She couldn't have. "A bullet hole?" she repeated blankly.

He put the glass down and touched the bandage on his head gingerly, thoughtfully. "Someone shot at me," he said matter-of-factly.

"*Shot* at you? Who?" she breathed. "Why?" *Oh, my God,* she thought abruptly. *It was Dutch.* "Was it ... do you think ...?"

"Dutch?" Dan quirked an amused brow. "He wouldn't have the nerve, much less the know-how."

Relief flooded Piper for a split second, until the reality hit her all over again. "Who, then, Dan? Who would shoot at you?"

Dan sat there at the familiar kitchen table. He was pale, and some dried blood still spotted his cheek and neck. But he wasn't scared, he wasn't panicked. He was absolutely serious, calm, in control. He'd sat there and told Piper someone had shot at him as if it happened every day, and then it occurred to her with a sickening lurch of her guts that it *had* been an everyday occurrence to Dan—when he'd been a police detective. Piper looked at him earnestly. "*Tell* me, Dan," she said, trying to match his cool, "who *did* shoot at you?"

"I think it's better if you don't—" he began.

But she put up a hand. "Oh, no," she said, "you're not shutting me out on this one." She drew her brows together, cocking her head. *Dan takes a sudden trip to Philadelphia,* she mused, *then he's back for less than two days, and someone...* Her head snapped up. "This has to do with the trouble you had as a cop. Tell me I'm wrong."

Dan regarded her with the same studied calm he'd displayed all evening. "I really don't think..." he started to say, and then he pushed back the chair and stood. He looked at her for a moment as if considering something, and walked to the sink, then turned and leaned against it, his arms folded across his chest, one foot cocked over the other.

"Listen," he said, "if I tell you, will you leave it alone then?"

"I..."

"I'm serious," Dan said. "And even though you do have a right to know, because of Diana, I want you to do as I say after I tell you. Will you agree to that?"

Piper was cornered. He was going to divulge his secrets. Okay, fine, but there was a price she had to pay. She let out a breath. "Just tell me," she said. "It's not as if I'm going to make any trouble."

Dan gave her a humorless smile. "Lady," he said, "you've been nothing *but* trouble since the day you walked up to my door."

Piper frowned. "Just tell me," she said.

He watched her for another long moment, pinioning her with that cool blue appraising gaze of his. He was wondering, she knew, if he could trust her with those deep, dark secrets of his.

She held his stare. "*Tell* me," she said.

After another moment he finally gave a faint shrug. "It's not very pretty," he said, as if *that* would change her mind.

Piper tossed her head. "I can take it."

Dan pushed himself away from the sink and began pacing. She noticed he was rubbing his jaw from time to time, thoughtfully stroking the stubble on his chin as if he wanted to put things into just the right words.

He stopped by the back door and gazed at her. "Okay. It all started two years ago, a little over that, in fact." And then his gaze became distant as the months peeled away, and Dan Bourne was transported back to Philadelphia on a raw, rainy day in March. "It was gray out," he was saying, "and the wind was kicking up off the river when Harry and I— you remember Harry Tegmeier—and two other cops, Sweet Pea and Frank, got word from a snitch that this bad dude, a guy named Joey Washington, was holed up in an abandoned warehouse down near the docks. We'd been looking for him for over a month...."

Piper listened as the story unfolded, and she knew in her heart that somehow, in some curious way, Diana's death was intricately interwoven with this criminal and a huge old warehouse in a city she'd never seen.

"Frank and Sweet Pea went in first," Dan was telling her, or rather, he seemed to be reliving the incident himself. "And then it was Harry's idea to go on inside and take a look himself. I didn't like it," Dan recalled, "because we were the backup team, supposed to stay near the car radio, just in case. Anyway, Harry went on in, and I waited next to the car in that damn cold drizzle."

Dan began to pace again, one arm folded across his chest, the other raised, his hand still stroking the line of his beard-darkened jaw. "I waited five, maybe ten minutes," he said, "and then contacted the precinct and told the dispatcher what was coming down. I told her I was going in."

Piper swiveled in her chair, following Dan as he moved around the kitchen, lost in his memories. She didn't utter a word.

The story unfolded slowly, Dan obviously trying to recall the details, his brow below the bandage creased deeply as the scenes came to life in his head. "Joey Washington was there, all right," Dan said, "and so were Frank and Sweet Pea and Harry." He stopped short and swung his gaze onto her. "You really want to hear this?"

"Yes," Piper whispered.

He tipped his head back and let out a long breath. "Okay, then. They were on Washington," he said, "really *on* the guy, punching his lights out, kicking him, the works." Dan shook his head. "I yelled out to them and got there as fast as I could to try to drag them off the man. It was too late, though, too damn late. And then there was Harry," Dan said, shaking his head, "just standing there, watching Sweet Pea and Frank pulverize Washington. Harry did nothing, *nothing,* to stop them."

"And then what happened?" Piper asked quietly.

Dan snorted. "I got them off Washington, even had to pull my gun to get Sweet Pea backed up against the wall. It was a real ugly show."

"Go on," she urged, "tell me the rest."

Dan shrugged, but the movement was strained. "Not much to tell. Washington never carried a piece—a gun," he added, "so the boys, when they got their heads straight, got real scared. They stood in that cold warehouse and concocted the story that they found Washington already beaten up when they arrived."

"And Harry went along with it?"

"He had to," Dan said. "He was as guilty as the other two because he had stood there and done nothing. It's called complicity."

"And you?"

"Me?" Dan laughed grimly. "I just walked out and felt like puking. They figured because I was one of the clan I wouldn't rat on them." He looked at her. "Then, back at the precinct when they were filing their reports, they began to lean on me. 'Say, Danny,'" he mimicked his old partners, "'you never saw nothing, right?' And I kept my mouth shut. *Then.*"

"Why?"

Dan whirled on her abruptly. "Because, damn it, I was one of them, a brother! Harry was my best friend, he'd gotten me on the force, been like a father to me."

"So how did the story come out, then?" she asked, confused.

"I'm getting to it," Dan snapped, and he raked a hand through his hair, grimacing when he touched the bandage. "I did end up ratting on them," he said in self-disgust. "Let's just say I couldn't live with it. Anyway, about a week later I went to my captain, MacMurray. You remember him," Dan said darkly, "the man your *pal* Dutch talked to."

Piper could only nod.

"Anyway," Dan said, "I was very careful of what I told MacMurray. I suppose I was feeling him out. I wanted reassurance, maybe, I don't know. What I did was ask MacMurray if any of us could get into trouble for the Washington thing. By then, the poor slob was in a hospital in a coma, not a very good prognosis, so he wasn't about to give evidence against anybody. MacMurray looked me straight in the eye and told me that no cop under him had ever gotten into trouble for doing his job, and he wasn't about to let it start happening now."

Dan sighed. "He was warning me. He knew the score, he knew what had happened, all right, but he wasn't going to let his boys look bad. The press would have had a field day with it. After that mess a few years back when the cops just about burned down half the city, the press was just looking for an excuse."

"So what did you do?"

"I took a vacation," Dan recalled with a bitter edge to his voice. "Came out West with the ski club for some R and R and met this very lovely lady in a boot shop."

"Did Diana know all this?" Piper had to ask.

He nodded. "Not at first. But she was a smart woman. She knew I had problems. She asked."

"And you told her."

He nodded again, and Piper felt her heart constrict oddly—Dan had confided in Diana from the start. But Dan had never once mentioned his past to Piper, not a word. But then, why would he? They were nothing to each other.

"Anyway," Dan was telling her, "I got back from Steamboat Springs and everything was the same. The books were closed. Internal Affairs never even got wind of the whole deal."

"How can that be?" she asked.

"Simple. Like I said, there were no witnesses to any crime."

"There was you, Dan."

"Right," he said, "there was me. But unless I was willing to take it the whole nine yards to Internal Affairs the case was over. The trouble was," he went on, "right down to the greenest rookie on the force, they all knew I'd gone to MacMurray."

"They must have made it hard on you," she said.

"That, kid, is an understatement. I held on as long as I could," he said, "but I was fooling myself. I was through the minute I walked into MacMurray's office."

"And then there was Diana," Piper put in.

"Yes, Diana. She was pretty...persuasive."

"I knew her," Piper said softly. And then she held his eyes. "So you quit and moved here and got married. I know all that. But what about Diana's accident? How does all this fit?"

"It fits," Dan said, still holding her eyes with his, "because Joey Washington died in December."

"December," Piper whispered, "the same time Diana..."

"Not the same time. Diana died a week later."

Piper held her breath, waiting, a sick knowledge beginning to seep into her.

"When Washington died," Dan told her, his voice now carefully low, "the stakes were raised for Harry, Sweet Pea and Frank. It wasn't assault any longer, it was murder. They came after me."

"You."

"Yes. I was the loose end. I was the only one alive who knew the truth. I guess they decided it was too risky to let me live."

Piper sat back and felt goose bumps rise all over her as the truth of what had happened to Diana finally dawned on her. Her stomach knotted and turned over sickeningly. They'd come for Dan…Diana had taken Dan's truck….

Her eyes flew up to his. He nodded slowly.

"Oh, God," Piper moaned. "Oh, my God."

"I'm … sorry," he said quietly.

But she was biting her lip, fighting a sudden wave of nausea. They'd thought they'd gotten Dan….

"Listen," he said, "Piper, *listen* to me. They're going to pay. Do you hear me? They *are* going to pay."

"Sure," she muttered, and looked up into his face. "Dan," she breathed, "why…why didn't you do something then? Why now? What's going on?"

Dan's expression darkened. "I never made the connection," he said. "I guess I was too involved in my own pain when Diana was killed. I never *would* have made it, either, if you hadn't started asking me questions about Six Mile Curve. That's the irony of it. By coming after me, by killing my wife, they tipped their hands. But not to me. No. I was too hung up in my own problems to see it. They tipped *you* off, Piper."

Piper sighed shakily in comprehension. "So why," she said then, "didn't they come back and do the job right?"

Dan shrugged. "I figure that first of all two accidents in a row would have looked pretty suspicious to

even your average Dutch Radowsky. But mostly, I
suppose, it was because I never made a move against
them. They figured they'd botched the job and it was
better to let sleeping dogs lie."

"You being the sleeping dog."

"Oh, yeah, you got that straight."

"And now," she said, "you blame yourself."

"Of course I blame myself!" he thundered
abruptly. "Even *you* knew there was something wrong
with Diana's accident."

"I did," Piper admitted, "but then I knew her a
whole lot better than you. We grew up together."

"Swell," he said, and he leaned against the sink
again, his arms folded stiffly.

What could she say that wouldn't sound trite?
"Okay," she began again, "so you went back to Philadelphia, and I take it you stirred up the pot."

"Putting it mildly," he stated, still angry with himself, his face twisted into a rictus of self-reproach.

"And now they're back to do the job right."

"If they can."

"Great."

"Isn't it."

"You've set yourself up as bait," she said, the
whole picture becoming clear in her mind. "You *knew*
they'd do this, take a shot at you."

"I figured it was the only option left to them. Plan
A worked," he said, and gave her an offhand smile.

Piper stood abruptly, scraping her chair across the
floor. "It worked. You almost got killed! And then
nobody would've known the truth, no one. They'd
have gotten away with *three* murders!"

"But they didn't kill me, did they?"

"Oh, Dan, why didn't you go to someone back there? Why didn't you go to Internal Affairs, to somebody? You can't do this by yourself."

"Why not? I know those men, I worked with them. I knew they'd come. I can't go to IA. I have no proof, nothing. There's no other way."

Piper could only stare at him. "I can't believe this," she said. "It's crazy. Men shooting at you. Diana..."

"Yes, Diana," he said quietly, pushing himself away from the counter and going to sit in the chair she'd vacated.

Piper watched him. She saw the sag in his shoulders and could almost feel the pain he was suffering. But was the pain born of guilt? Or pain from his loss? "Did you really love her?" she found herself asking.

Dan gave her a sidelong glance, his head bowed. He looked back down at his hands. "I loved her," he managed to say, "but don't ask me to explain it."

"I'm asking," Piper said, knowing what he was thinking, knowing he would totally misunderstand her need to ask. She barely understood it herself. She knew only that if Dan had truly loved her friend, it would make him worthy. But if he'd really loved Diana—that forever kind of love—then how could he conceivably love anyone that way again? "Well?" she said, still standing over her.

"You're a hard woman," Dan said, and he shook his head slowly.

"It matters to me. A lot."

"I *can't* explain it to you," he said. "I only know that I loved my wife, but we both married for the wrong reasons. I can't tell you any more. If I could, I would.''

"The wrong reasons," Piper said thoughtfully.

"Oh, hell," Dan barked. "I guess I was escaping, and Diana, I don't know, she just wanted me to forget my past. She wanted to be in love and get married."

"And you weren't as sure."

"Wrong," he said hoarsely. "I was happy to leave my life behind, to start over with someone I loved."

"Then you *did* love her."

"I *told* you that. It's the truth. The trouble is, if I'd stayed in Philadelphia and cleared things up, Diana would still be alive today."

"She didn't want you in Philadelphia," Piper said. "She wanted you here on any terms."

"Yeah, well," he said, "it was my decision, wasn't it?"

"So you'll go on and on blaming yourself," Piper ventured.

"It's my life, kid," he said broodingly.

The room seemed suddenly too silent. The ticking of the schoolhouse clock on the wall and the off-and-on hum of the refrigerator roared in her ears. There was too much to digest, too many new pieces of knowledge churning around in her brain—murder, love, betrayal, pain, loss. And the dawning of a revelation: Piper had been wrong, so very wrong about Dan. A strange lightness, a release from resentment, from the terrible effort of hating him, replaced the tension she'd felt for months. A gladness. It bewildered her how she could feel this when she'd just learned her best friend had been murdered, that someone had just tried to murder the man sitting in front of her. But it was there, a small kindling in the jumble of thoughts in her brain, and she cherished it, unquestioning for the moment.

She stood there and saw Dan's bowed head and knew despite what Dan believed that Diana was as responsible for what had happened as he was. Diana had known his situation, had known everything. He'd confided in her. Yet she'd ignored it, snatching him before it had been settled, grabbing Dan on the rebound from a tragic event. Oh, yes, Diana had sworn to Piper she hadn't made Dan quit the force, but she'd been there, offering an easy alternative, enticing him deliberately. When Diana wanted something, she went after it and she got it.

Dan hadn't married Diana to take advantage of her. No, it was Di who'd taken advantage of him. Impulsive, headstrong, that was Di. She'd chased her man and she'd caught him. Oh, God, and she'd paid the ultimate price.

Piper finally moved. She walked across the room and leaned on the counter to look between the curtains out into the darkness. Out there were men who wanted to kill Dan. She turned then, leaned back against the Formica and folded her arms. "You're wrong to blame yourself, Dan."

He lifted his head but didn't turn to face her. "Just drop it," he said wearily.

But Piper couldn't, not yet. "Diana was my best friend," she went on, "and, trust me on this one, Dan, she knew exactly what she was doing and who she was marrying."

"I said, let's drop it, okay?"

"All right," Piper said, giving in, "but just remember what I said when you're busy beating yourself up."

"Anything you say," he remarked dryly.

Piper gave a short, nervous laugh. "You know," she said, "I think we've broken a barrier tonight."

"A barrier."

"Yes. I mean, we've barely ever had a conversation before."

"So?"

"So, Dan Bourne, I've decided you aren't as bad as I thought."

"Oh, really?"

"I mean, maybe we could become, well, friends...buddies, you know."

But Dan was regarding her too soberly, his brow drawn into a heavy dark bar above those blue eyes. Piper felt like squirming suddenly, and she could have kicked herself for saying anything. She didn't even know why she'd brought up the subject. This was all too complicated—everything between them had shifted, and maybe she'd liked it the other way, when she'd hated him. This unknown relationship was far too unsettling.

He kept watching her, making her want to crawl away and hide. Why did Dan have that power over her?

"Buddies," he finally said, his expression never changing, "is that what we are?"

And she replied too quickly, smiled too brightly. "Sure, why not?"

That thin, mocking grin touched Dan's lips, but Piper ignored it. "Well," she said, desperate to change the subject, "I guess there's only one thing to do now. We better call Dutch. For all we know..."

"Forget it," Dan said.

"Look, *I'll* talk to him. I'll explain everything. He's going to find your truck sooner or later, anyway. Dutch can even send someone else out here," Piper said briskly, pacing around the room now.

But Dan was laughing. "After that scene tonight?"

"This isn't personal. Dutch *has* to do his job."

Dan gestured with a hand. "Forget it. Radowsky is inept. He'd bungle the whole operation. He'd chase the men away so fast... No, not Dutch Radowsky. Let him take care of traffic tickets."

"He's the sheriff here, Dan. Don't you think he should be told?"

"No. Catching these guys is my responsibility. I got them here, and I'll take care of them."

"What about Harry? Your best friend, Harry?" she pressed.

Dan's face grew taut. "If he's with them, I can't protect him."

She saw the pain that dug its talons into Dan. He'd had hard choices to make, but he'd made them, and he'd stand by them. In retrospect, what she'd gone through that summer seemed so petty, so vastly insignificant. Never in her life had she been forced to make such awful decisions.

"I *am* sorry, Dan," she said abruptly. "I'm sorry I was such a bitch to you. I misjudged you. I apologize."

He smiled wryly. "I accept. Forget it, Piper. You had reason enough."

"Okay, so now, what're you going to do?" she asked. "You're sure your head is okay? You're not dizzy? Nauseous? What else do people feel when they have a concussion?"

"I'm okay, Florence Nightingale," he said.

She sat across from him, her hands on her lap, full of tension, jittery. "I'm a nervous wreck," she said. "I'm not used to dealing with things like this. Shooting at people, murder. I can't get used to it. Dan, when I saw your truck go off the road like that . . . and you in there . . . the blood." She leaned her forehead on her hand. "I can't take it all in."

"I'm sorry you had to be involved. It isn't pretty, I know. Try to forget it," he said.

"Forget it! You were almost killed. . . ."

He said nothing for a time, then turned his gaze on her. "It's hard the first time," he said. "I know." Then he gave a short laugh. "It's hard the second time, too."

"Even so," Piper mused aloud, "I'm glad I was there. You might still be in that truck."

"Maybe," he allowed.

"So what now?" she said. "What do we do now?"

"*We* do nothing. You're staying here for the night to play it safe, then tomorrow I'll drive you home and you pack and get out of Dodge until this is over."

"Dan . . ."

"I'm serious. No arguments, lady. Those men have to assume you know too much already."

"And what about you? You're seriously going to face this alone, after nearly getting killed tonight?"

"That was a slip," he said. "I was off guard after that scene with Radowsky."

"Right."

"Yes, right, Piper. It won't happen again, as long as I'm not distracted."

"And I'm a distraction."

He shot her a smile, and for the first time she got a hint of what Dan could look like if he let loose, went flying free, without a care. His face would be relaxed, his eyes soft, his grin a flash of white teeth and good humor, the double lines on either side of his mouth deepening.

"A distraction," he said. "You could call it that." He got to his feet and left the room. She sat there, though, wondering, questioning, still shaken by all that had happened in the space of an evening. Her world seemed askew; everything was at a different tilt. And she recalled then, suddenly, that strange spark that had shot between her and Dan at the wedding two years ago.

She heard Dan walking through the house, apparently locking up, closing windows, battening down for the storm. She'd have gotten up and helped, but her legs wouldn't move, and her brain began to wrestle with a new, extremely unsettling concept. Oh, yes, it was becoming clearer by the instant. She'd hated Dan, all right, from the very start, and it hadn't just been because of Diana's death.

Then there was Dutch. She'd told herself she'd sworn off men because of his suffocating possessiveness. But those had only been mental sleights of hand, she could now see. All the hatred and anger at Dan, her decision not to seek a relationship with a man... Her mind had been trying to cope, hadn't it? Cope for the past two years with an insane attraction she'd felt for a man she could never have.

Suddenly weary, Piper rose from the table and pushed her hair over a shoulder. She felt like laughing. Or maybe it was crying. The trouble was, nothing had really changed at all, except that now—now she could no longer hate Dan Bourne.

CHAPTER ELEVEN

DAN SWITCHED ON THE LIGHT in the guest room and glanced around. "I guess the maid forgot to come last week," he said wryly. "Sorry about the dust."

"It's fine," Piper said, looking into the room past his shoulder.

"There's a blanket, I think," he said, "on the top shelf in the closet." He nodded in that direction.

"I remember," Piper replied, moving into the room past him. "I've spent a night or two here before."

"Oh, sure, of course you have. Well," he said.

"Your head... *is* it all right? Are you positive you shouldn't see a—"

"No, no," Dan said, "I'm fine."

"Well..." And an uncomfortable moment passed.

"Yeah, well," he said.

"Good night, then," Piper murmured.

"You're sure you'll sleep all right in that old T-shirt?"

"I'll be fine."

"Good night, Piper."

"See you in the morning," she replied, and gave him a faint, brittle smile as he hesitated a moment longer, his expression somber as he closed the door with a snick.

Piper sat on the side of the bed, gratefully let out a long breath, then reclined onto her back, an arm flung over her brow. He'd been so insistent that she stay there for safety's sake, even though he was confident his buddies wouldn't try anything more that night. Still, Dan had been unwilling to let her drive off alone. As he'd put it a few minutes ago, "Yeah, I'm positive they're back in hiding for tonight, too, but I'm not letting you head on into town just to find out I was wrong."

So she'd given in. She was staying. Okay, fine, Piper thought, staring up at the white ceiling, she'd stay in the house with him tonight. Oh, she wasn't going to get a wink of sleep. No way, not with Dan right next door, only a few feet away....

Piper groaned softly to herself.

What was it about Dan that seemed to strip her naked? He was only a man, after all, and certainly not one for her. He was—he'd *been*—her best friend's husband, for God's sake. Yet...yet all he had to do was look at her with those blue eyes and her blood began to pound. *Stripped naked*, she thought, and it was true. Around Dan Bourne none of her defenses worked. She conjured up his face on the blank white ceiling as plain as day, those grooves in his cheeks, the firmness of his square jaw, those eyes....

Piper got to her feet and strode into the bathroom, switched on the light and peeled off her clothes. She pulled back the plastic curtain and reached into the tub, turned on the shower, then twisted her hair into a knot on the back of her neck. Maybe a nice long shower, something relaxing, and she'd get some sleep. It was worth a try.

She stayed in the shower an indecently long time, letting the hot water stream down her neck and back, turning her skin red, her toes pink, her cheeks crimson. It felt good, loosening her muscles, the water almost hypnotic, sensual, coming in pulses out of the shower head. She tried hard not to think about that—about Dan. She tried not to consider anything he'd told her. After all, none of that mattered to her. So what if he'd been through hell? What mattered was that the truth about Diana's death was going to come out at last, and the men responsible for it were going to be caught and punished.

The water ran off her shoulders and swirled down the drain. She wiggled her toes, trying to relax, but found instead that an image of Dan had once more planted itself in her mind: Dan pulling off his clothes only a few feet away from her, stepping out of his pants, unbuttoning his shirt, shedding it, sliding into his bed between the cool sheets, his dark head lying on the white pillow. Was Dan hearing the shower? Picturing her... ?

"Forget it!" Piper whispered, angry at herself as she turned off the water and stepped out onto the bath mat, reaching for the towel. Still, despite her desperate urge to put him out of her thoughts, Piper couldn't help a sudden quickening of her heart when she glanced at the bathroom door, left slightly ajar, and wondered what she'd do if he were to put his hand out and pull the door toward him and...

Wearing one of Dan's old T-shirts as a nightgown, Piper slid into bed and pulled the sheets up under her chin. She was wide awake, darn it all, even after the shower. She wished she was in her own bed, at home, where everything was familiar. Though, she remembered, she sure wouldn't put it past Dutch—especially after that scene at the tavern tonight—to be watching the Hilyard house. So she guessed she'd be just as restless at home. And now, to make things worse, Dutch would see that her car wasn't there.

She rolled over, punching the pillow, and was wondering if Dan was asleep when she heard it, a creaking on the stairs.

Piper sat bolt upright, her heart pounding in her ears. It couldn't be . . . Those men wouldn't come into the house. . . .

She climbed out of bed. Had Dan heard the noise? Was he asleep?

She went to the door, her heart still beating too furiously. Had he locked up? But that wouldn't matter. Anyone could get into this place if he really wanted to.

Piper opened the door a crack, holding her breath, praying it was only Dan on the prowl. He'd said they wouldn't try anything else that night. Surely Dan knew.

A step into the hall. She could see the darkened staircase ahead. . . .

"Piper?"

She gasped, grabbing her chest, stumbling back against the wall even though she recognized Dan's voice. "Dan," she breathed, "where . . . where are you?"

A light in the hall snapped on. "I'm down at the bottom of the steps," he said. "You all right?"

"I'm fine. I just heard a noise."

"It's only me. Go back to bed."

She moved to the top of the stairs and peered down. He was standing with one foot on the first step, his hand on the rail. "Aren't you coming up?" she asked.

But he shook his head. "I will, in a while. Go on back to your room."

"Okay," Piper said, and she became aware of his gaze on her long bare legs. The T-shirt only just covered her hips, as it was. She took a step back, ridiculously embarrassed. "I'll see you in the morning," she said, and beat a hasty retreat.

PIPER'S EYES FLEW OPEN just before dawn lit the Elk River Valley. She remembered closing them, and pulling the soft pillow up over her ears to muffle the sound of Dan on his watch. Had he stayed up all night?

She sat up in bed in the inky, predawn blackness. Was he still downstairs, alone, keeping watch? He was all right, wasn't he?

Piper dressed and quietly descended the stairs, finding the living room light on but no Dan. He wasn't in the kitchen, either. She peeked into the office. It was dark. But there he was, lying on the leather couch, breathing softly. She stood for a moment longer and gazed at his sleeping form, then quietly pulled the door closed.

It was only six-thirty when she finished a cup of coffee and decided it was light enough to head over to the barn and at least see to a couple of chores. Luis and Rick would be there by eight and could take over, although if Dan's scheme came about and she was persuaded to leave Steamboat Springs for a few days, the two helpers were going to have their hands full. Too full.

Piper crossed the yard in the quickening light of morning. Except for the yearlings stirring in the fields and the trickle of water from the river below the house, it was breathlessly still that early morning, and she stopped once, in midstride, and listened.

What if Dan was wrong and his friends from Philadelphia *were* on the ranch somewhere, waiting, watching the house? But Dan had seemed so positive they'd wait to make another move.

She shrugged and walked on, unlatched the barn doors and swung them open, the familiar scent of dust and hay and leather assailing her, reassuring her that all was normal. Chirping rose from a nest of barn swallows, a calming chatter. Everything was okay. Besides, Piper thought, Dan knew exactly how these men operated. And on the ranch the chores never waited, anyway.

She scooped oats into pails and laid out some tack, thinking that surely she could accomplish a few tasks that day before Dan made her leave. And on *that* subject, Piper was thinking, maybe he was wrong about the danger to her. In the light of day, in fact, his idea that she leave town was starting to seem like overkill. No one was stalking *her,* after all.

Piper stood on tiptoe in the tack room reaching for the can of saddle soap on a shelf, thinking about discussing Dan's plan. This morning it did seem an unnecessary precaution. It was merely a hangover from his days as a cop in the big city. Out here, in God's country, things were simpler. Diana—that had been an accident, a murder, yes, but a case of mistaken identity. Piper wasn't going to take chances. And another thing, she mused, Westerners were a different breed.

Her great-grandparents had come to this valley to farm. They'd been a hardened lot, never ran from a fight. How dead wrong all those old Western movies were portraying the townsfolk hiding behind closed doors when trouble came to their communities. The truth was, they were all fighters, tough as nails. And so was she.

Maybe over coffee with Dan she'd explain that to him. Surely he'd see her point.

Piper would never know how she missed his approach. All she knew was that one minute she was alone, and the next a hand was clamped over her mouth, and she was wrenched around before she could even put up a struggle.

Her heart flew into her throat, and adrenaline raced through her veins as she was brought up against a rock-hard barrel of a chest. She tried to fight then, shock making her panic, but he was so strong, too strong.

"Shh," came his voice, over and over, "shh, Piper, take it easy."

She kicked out, and the man had to lift her, struggling, off her feet to protect himself.

"Shh," he said again, "it's me, Harry, shh."

Harry. Her mind reeled, trying to grasp at reality. *Harry...*

"Quiet, Piper, I'm not going to hurt you. Quiet." Then a moment later he said, "There, there, that's better, take it easy. I'm going to move my hand away from your mouth. You won't scream, will you?"

Harry, she thought, still frantic, Harry Tegmeier. He was Dan's friend, he wouldn't hurt her. It was Harry....

"Calm down, girl," he was saying. "I gotta talk to you. Will you settle down and listen?" Carefully, slowly, he took his hand from her mouth.

Piper gulped air and fought to control her heartbeat. He wasn't going to hurt her. . . .

"Okay," he whispered, letting her loose, though one big hand still held her arm. "Okay. You gotta give Dan a message, honey. Can you do that?"

Piper kept sucking in air, and stared at him in the close room. "What're you—" she began.

"Just *listen*," he said, his voice low and urgent. "I haven't got much time. Can you remember what I'm gonna tell you?"

"Sure, yes," she whispered, staring hard at his red, jowly face in the glowing light. She recalled him well then, the dance they'd had at the wedding, his sweat, the tight collar at his reddened throat, his good humor. Harry, Dan's partner, his best friend. Even in the dimness of the barn she could see a bead of sweat running down his temple. "Yes," Piper said more clearly, "I'll tell Dan whatever you want. But . . . but, Harry, you weren't . . . there last night. . . ."

He looked at her gravely, his eyes red-rimmed and darkly circled in the poor light. She was aware of his clothes then, a brown hunter's jacket, wrinkled, baggy khaki trousers—he smelled of perspiration and wood smoke. "Listen," he was saying, "you gotta tell Dan to get the hell out of here. He has to go today. Tell him I can't stop the others."

"They're both here with you?"

"Yeah, Sweet Pea and Frank," he said, "and they mean business. We're camped at a cabin up the valley here. It's called Hahn's Peak. I'm supposed to be getting supplies. You tell Dan I can't stop them. Last night they... Never mind that," he said. "You just get Danny-boy away from here. Can you do that?" His grip tightened on her arm.

"I...sure," Piper said, "I'll try. But he's—he's very stubborn, Harry, and I..."

Harry gave a short, humorless laugh. "I know it'll be hard. But you tell him old Harry here means it. They'll kill him, honey, they honest to God will do it. They tried before and—" Harry stopped abruptly. "I'm really sorry, honey," he said. "You tell Dan that." She could have sworn his voice broke.

"Diana," Piper whispered, her eyes roaming his face accusingly. "You..."

But he was leaving, poking his head out the tack room door and looking around furtively. He turned back to her. "Just tell Dan to go," he said once more, his tone more urgent. Then his eyes held hers for one last moment. "I'm so sorry," he said, "I'm so god-damned sorry," and he was gone. For a full minute she could only stare at the door, her knees shaking like jelly, remembering what Harry had said. Had he meant he was sorry about the others, about them forcing Diana from the road that cold winter's night, or had Harry Tegmeier meant he was sorry for him-self, sorry he'd been in on the murder of her best friend? And now, now Harry was here again—only this time it was for Dan....

"WHAT?" DAN SAID, his coffee mug suspended mid-way to his mouth.

She said it again. "*Harry* was in the tack room, just now, a couple of minutes ago."

"Here?" Dan's expression turned to stone.

"Yes," Piper said softly, "he's in Steamboat Springs with the other two. He gave me a message, Dan, for you. He said..."

But Dan was swearing.

Piper crossed the kitchen and quietly put a hand on his arm. "Listen," she said, "I know how you must be feeling."

"Like hell you do," he growled.

"I lost a friend, too," she reminded him.

"I lost my *wife,*" Dan said, and the pain in his voice lashed out at Piper like a fist. "And then Harry... Harry, too. Goddamn it, why?" He turned and leaned over the sink, grasping the edges of it with white knuckles, his head bowed. The muscles in his shoulders and arms swelled, bulged, stretching his shirt. Pain and rage shook his body, and she averted her eyes. This was too private an agony for her to witness.

Piper waited. She backed off and waited for the fury to pass. The pain, she knew, would not go—it never would—but Dan Bourne was too disciplined to let his anger cloud his judgment. She stood close by, watching him carefully, and waited, waited for the storm to abate. It took several minutes, several long minutes before his fists finally unclenched and his shoulders gave a little, sagging slightly. As if bone weary, he reached up and pulled the bandage off his head, letting it drop into the sink.

Piper took a breath. "You want to hear the rest?" she asked cautiously.

He came back around to her, folding his arms across his chest, his eyes still on fire. "Go ahead," he said tonelessly.

She told him. She told him everything Harry had said, word for word. He listened grimly, a muscle moving inexorably in his jaw, the veins in his arms still pumped up. "I think we better call Dutch now," Piper finished, trying to sound matter-of-fact, hoping he'd see the sense of it.

But not Dan. She should have known. "Dutch?" he said, and laughed mercilessly. "You refuse to get it. They'd sidestep Dutch like a bum asleep in an alley. They're pros, lady, *pros*."

Piper sighed. "Okay," she said, and she felt tears fill her eyes. "So what, then? You're so good you can deal with three of them? Right, Dan, oh, sure," she said, losing control herself. "The great Dan Bourne can handle them all by himself. Are you out of your mind?"

Dan watched her with a dangerous look flashing in his eyes. "You're out of your element," he stated flatly. "I can, and I *will* handle them. But not with you here, Piper." He shook his head as if daring her to defy him. "Don't push me on this one. You, lady, are out of here."

Piper clamped her mouth shut, frustrated. She, too, folded her arms stiffly. "I won't leave you alone," she stated. "You *can't* go this alone. I owe them, too, you know, for Diana."

"You *are* leaving," he said, "and if you give me one more word of argument, I'll . . ."

"You'll *what?*"

"I'll haul you into town over my shoulder if I have to and pack your suitcase for you. You're going, Piper, and you're going today."

She gave a short, brave laugh. "Big tough guy," she said, "just like all cops."

"I'm not a cop any longer," he said harshly, "or did you forget that?"

She knew from the way he said it that the words were wrenched from him. "I didn't forget," she said. "It's just that you're still trying to act like one, as if getting these men was still your job. It isn't, Dan, don't you see that?"

He set his jaw and made an impatient gesture. "For God's sake, Piper, I've been a cop all my adult life! You think you give it up so easily?" He put a fist against his chest. "In here I'm still responsible. I always will be. Nothing can ever change that."

She watched him with dawning realization. For two years Dan Bourne had been pretending to be a civilian, but he wasn't, he couldn't be. All he'd ever wanted, despite what he had told Diana, despite what he'd told himself when he quit, was to be a policeman. She didn't claim to understand it, but it was unquestionably clear, and she felt a rush of pity for Dan. It would be that way for her if she could never touch a horse again, or ride, or look at them. It would kill her.

"Dan," she said, hurting for him, "please, can we call Dutch?"

He turned on her angrily. "I said no, Piper. It's a closed subject."

"You're a fool, then!" she cried, getting angry, too. "You'll get yourself killed! Stubborn idiot! What's the point? What're you trying to prove?"

"I'm not trying to prove anything. I'm doing my job. I should never have quit the force, and I should have taken care of this two years ago. I made a mistake, I got my wife killed, and now I'm just trying to rectify it," he said coldly. "I've flushed them out and they're desperate. They'll make a mistake and I'll have them dead to rights this time."

Piper shook her head. "It's not that simple, Dan. There are other people involved now. It isn't your city. It isn't your job. You're making a terrible mistake."

"Then it'll be *my* mistake, but it's something I have to do."

She couldn't reach him. He was hard, as impenetrable as rock. She cast wildly for some way to find a chink in his armor, change his mind, some way to get to him. "Don't play this holier-than-thou role, Dan. It isn't you. I have a feeling you have other reasons for not calling Dutch," she blurted out.

Dan grunted. "And just what's that supposed to mean?"

"Go ahead, deny it," she challenged. "You hate Dutch. You're . . . you're jealous."

He gave a short laugh, but she saw that she'd pricked him. She'd found that chink.

"You wouldn't ask him for help, would you? You couldn't handle it. It would hurt your ego, wouldn't it, Dan?" she dared to ask him.

"You're stalling," Dan said roughly, brushing aside her words.

"No," Piper said, "I'm serious. That's why you won't go over there and pick up the phone and call the sheriff." She knew she was treading a razor's edge. She knew her timing was awful and that he was right, she *was* stalling, afraid to leave him, worried sick he'd get himself killed. But Piper also knew she had to hear the truth. If Dan was going to go through with whatever his ridiculous plans were, she had to know: *Was* he jealous of Dutch? Did he care? Had he given one thought to how she'd feel if he got himself murdered?

And then, too, just how *would* she feel if suddenly Dan was gone?

"This isn't the time," Dan was saying, and he came up to her, tall and strong and in command, took her arm and steered her unwillingly toward the living room and the door.

But Piper had to know. She felt as if she were at the brink of forbidden knowledge. She wanted to turn back, to flee to safety, but, contrarily, she knew she couldn't. She'd come too far; she was ready to leap into the abyss despite the outcome.

She wrenched her arm free from his grasp and pivoted, facing him, her chest heaving. "*Are* you jealous?" she dared to ask, deathly afraid of the truth.

But Dan only studied her for a horrible few seconds, and she was jolted by the knowledge that she'd been wrong—he didn't care one bit about her. He never had and he never would. What a fool she was, a blind, stupid—

It happened so suddenly, with such an explosion of emotion, that Piper never had a moment to finish the thought. One second she was beating herself up mentally, writhing inwardly with guilt for secretly coveting Diana's man, a man who didn't want her, then the next second she was crushed to the hard swell of his chest, and he was saying in a husky voice, "Does this answer your question?" and his mouth was covering hers, grinding her lips to his, his arms a steel-like band around her waist, lifting her, carrying her, pressing her against him.

She was lost. That it was broad daylight, that there were three men out there somewhere who wanted to kill them, that this was all wrong between them, a passion born of tragedy, meant nothing to either one as Dan embraced her, his lips claiming hers with an urgent hunger, his tongue probing her mouth, their quick, panting breaths mingling, hands on fire, stroking, craving, touching.

After what seemed an eternity Piper freed her lips from his. She was still suspended in his arms, pressed to him, gasping for breath, her blood ablaze. "Oh, God," she breathed, "Dan..."

"I know," he muttered. Abruptly he swung her into his arms, kicked open the door to the office, and they both fell, locked together, onto the couch.

From that moment there was no turning back. Crazy with fever, they tore at each other's clothes, their hands moving swiftly and desperately over each other's flesh, kneading, grasping, deliciously soft and hard and warm.

Kneeling beside the couch, Dan took her face in his hands and kissed her thoroughly, then moved his mouth to her neck, along her collarbone, his tongue warm and wet, sliding across her, tasting her. Piper moaned, her fingers twisting in his black hair as he found her breasts with his lips and, cupping them in his hands, teased her until she was writhing beneath him, murmuring, wanting him, wanting him so badly her belly was clenching.

Neither asked if the other was sure. There were no words spoken whatsoever when Dan stood and looked down at her, his body a beautiful statue of rippling muscles, hard cords and sinews, a man's body, a body carved by an expert's hand to give a woman pure pleasure. Piper took his hand in hers, her fingers trembling with need, and guided him down on top of her, her knees parting as he slipped his hands beneath her hips and raised her to him. And then he was inside her, filling her until she cried out, her back arching, her hips rising to meet his thrusts, heat held within heat, released, held again, over and over, with more desperation as the seconds fled unnoticed, until Piper's fingers grasped the hard muscles of his back and she moaned aloud and then Dan did, too, plunging into her, faster, faster, and together, their sweat-slick bellies gripped to each other, they quivered and groaned and finally sighed with the wild release.

CHAPTER TWELVE

LATER THEY SAT next to each other on the couch, almost primly. Piper had pulled a woolen throw around her shoulders, and Dan wore his jeans. There wasn't a sound in the office. The silence was so thick it pressed on her suffocatingly. The lemon yellow brightness of morning filled the room.

A million things came to her mind to say to him, but nothing would come to her lips. And Dan... he only sat close to her on the couch, hanging his head, his hands clasped between his knees.

She swallowed. "A penny for your thoughts," she said, feeling old and young and weary and vibrant all at once.

"Um" was all he said, reaching a hand up to touch the cut on his head.

She swallowed again. "Dan, tell me what you're thinking."

He turned and glanced at her for a moment, then looked back at his hands. "I'm thinking that you didn't really want to do that," he said.

"You're kidding, of course," she said, giving a short laugh. "We did it *together*."

"Maybe," he allowed. "And maybe not. But you were right about one thing," he said. "I was jealous of Dutch."

"Dutch," she said then. "Don't you think that now, well, now that we've gotten your feelings about him aired out, you could give him a call? I mean, you're still in—"

"No," he said. "My reasons for handling this myself haven't changed."

"I'm . . . I'm afraid for you," she breathed.

"Look," he said, surprisingly gentle, "you should be more afraid for me if I didn't do this. You understand?"

"I don't know. I guess. But I could never feel that way. I could never do something like that," she said.

"You did your part. You kept pushing until the truth came out. If you don't think that was pretty brave, you're crazier than I am."

Piper hung her head, too. He was talking about her being brave, but he didn't know . . . he didn't know what she'd done. "I—I have to tell you something," she said, averting her eyes.

"Okay."

"I, uh, well, you know we called your captain, MacMurray. It was all my idea. I made Dutch do it," she said, playing with the fringe on the throw.

"Nice stunt, Piper," he said.

"I had to find out. I was desperate to know everything. I couldn't figure out what else to do. Please, Dan, don't get mad all over again."

"All right, it's over. And MacMurray wouldn't have told you anything, anyway," he said tightly.

"He didn't, but . . ." She turned to gaze at him. "I made Dutch call someone else. A reporter on the *Philadelphia Inquirer* who'd covered the Joey Washington case."

"Well, well," Dan said, looking straight ahead, his profile severe. "And what did you find out?"

"All about Joey Washington, but he didn't really know why you'd resigned. He said the rumor was police brutality," she replied. "But, Dan, I—"

"And it looked bad, didn't it?" he interrupted. "You figured I was forced to resign because I was in trouble."

"Yes," she whispered.

He was quiet for a time, staring straight ahead, then said, "I guess you had a right to think that."

"I'm so sorry, Dan, but I had to find out—for Diana. I knew...I knew there was some connection, and I couldn't ask you. You know I couldn't."

"You're right. I wouldn't have told you."

"I wish you had. I wish you'd trusted me," Piper said.

Dan turned to her and smiled grimly. "Trust the person who was practically accusing me of doing in my own wife? Right, Piper. You hated my guts."

She buried her face in her hands. "I said I was sorry. Oh, Dan, I'm so ashamed. I had everything wrong." Flushed, she raised her eyes to his. "But I didn't hate you. I tried, oh, how I tried, but I didn't, I couldn't."

"It's over now, okay?" he said. "Forget it. I'll take you on home, and it'll be history for you, kid, ancient history." He shrugged, that all-too-familiar body language of his that was meant to close her out.

"Don't," she said. "Please don't shut me out."

"I'm not" was all she got in reply.

They ate an early lunch at the kitchen table. The relationship between them had shifted so abruptly and so irreversibly that Piper wasn't sure how to act or what to do. Her normal quick temper had been burned out; nothing remained but cold, gray ashes. She hadn't had time to examine her feelings, to let the significance of what had happened between them sink in. She was working on raw instinct.

She'd fixed sandwiches, and they were both trying to eat, trying to pretend things were normal, that the earth was still rotating calmly on its axis. She wondered if Dan was as shaken as she was.

"What will you do now?" she asked, pulling a piece of lettuce out of her sandwich.

"Wait." He took a bite and chewed.

"What if they come for you now?"

"They won't. It'll have to look like an accident. No hint of a fight, and besides, they won't come till dark."

"How will you—" she swallowed "—how will you protect yourself?"

"I have my service revolver. I hope not to use it, but you never know."

"But, Dan, three against one?"

"They won't have the benefit of surprise, Piper. That's worth a lot." He was looking past her shoulder, avoiding eye contact.

She nibbled on the bread crust, her stomach in her throat. "And I'm just to leave? Leave town?"

"You understand," he said soberly, "that if you're here, you're a liability to me. You'd make my job harder."

"It's *not* your job," she said.

But he glanced at her impassively, refusing to be goaded into an argument, calm and sure of himself.

"It's the only job I ever had or ever wanted, Piper. Leave me that, at least."

Piper gave up trying to eat. She rose from the table, tossed her sandwich down the garbage disposal and started washing the dishes. Over the running water, she said, "This was all my fault."

"What?"

She shut the water off and turned to face him, her hands dripping. "It's my fault, all my fault. I shouldn't have come out here when I got home. I let my folks convince me you needed help, but it was wrong." Slowly she rubbed her hands on her jeans to dry them, up and down, up and down.

"I let you stay."

"For a year and a half I'd put you out of my mind. And after Diana died I told myself I hated you. But—" she took a quavering breath "—I never hated you. At the wedding..." Piper stopping talking and begged him with her eyes, but he only looked at her. "Didn't you feel it, too?" she whispered. "Or was it just me? It was so wrong, unholy, awful. My best friend's husband..."

"Stop it, Piper," he said harshly. "Don't beat yourself up over something that never happened."

"Tell me you didn't *feel* it," she said.

He looked away.

"Dan," she said, her voice cracking, "tell me you didn't feel it, too."

He let out a sigh, a groan. "I felt it, okay?"

"No, it's not okay. What...what happened to us?"

"Nothing. Not a damn thing happened."

"*Something* did."

"It doesn't matter," he said bitterly. "I was happy, Diana was happy, we'd still be happy. I don't know what happened that day between you and me. I'll never know."

She let it go; she had to. Whatever had passed between them two years ago was never going to be explained. No one had been injured by it, and if Diana were still alive the unaccountable incident would have been long since forgotten.

After the awkward meal Dan sent Rick and Luis home, telling them he only needed them for a few hours each morning, just for the heavy work. Otherwise, he was shutting operations down to the minimum. "Money trouble," he told them.

To Piper he said, "I want them out of the way."

"But the horses," she protested.

"For a few days, a week, maybe, they'll be fine. They'll be fed and watered and doctored."

"And then?" she asked.

"We'll see," he said carefully.

They did some chores together, driving hay to the horses in the outer fields, checking on Pearl, who had an eye infection, and one of the yearlings who'd cut his leg. Dan was hurried, almost brusque, wanting to get the work done and Piper out of the way. But she lingered, running her hand over a horse's flank, scratching another behind the ears. When would she see them again? *Would* she ever see them again? What would happen if...? But she was afraid to ask Dan, afraid of his answers.

The sun was very hot, the sky a deep, perfect bowl of blue from horizon to horizon. The grass crunched under their feet, dead and brown. Puffs of dust rose from every footstep. "There's enough hay, isn't there?" Piper asked.

"For at least a month," he said. "Then I'll have to buy more."

A month. What would the situation be in a month? Who would be feeding the horses in a month?

Dan was in the back of Rick's old wreck of a pickup cutting the string on a bale, pushing it off the tailgate. He straightened and looked around, scanning the line of trees that bordered the field. Alert, careful. "Let's go," he said. "We're done."

They bumped over the fields toward the barn, Dan driving, Piper getting out to open and close the gates. She felt enervated by the heat and by the events of the past day, afraid, scared of what Dan would do, of how she felt, of how completely her world had spun off course.

Dan parked Rick's truck and got out, walked around to her side and leaned against the door. "Time to go," he said.

"Come with me," Piper said suddenly. "Let's go to Denver together. There's an FBI office there. We'll tell them. They'd have to look into it now that those men have crossed state lines."

"No," he said stolidly.

"Please, Dan."

"Piper, let's go. Where're your keys? I'm driving you home. Then either I take you to the airport or you drive to Denver. I'll need your Jeep, so if you have a car at home you can use, you can drive, otherwise..."

"I can use my folks' Cherokee," she said. "I'd rather have a car. I'll probably stay at a motel. Can I call you when I get there? I'll give you my number, and you can keep in touch. You'll keep in touch, won't you? I'll go out of my mind if you don't.''

"Sure,'' he said, but his attention was elsewhere.

"My keys are inside,'' she offered.

It was much cooler in the house. Piper found her keys and went into the kitchen, where Dan was gulping a glass of water. "Hot out,'' he said when he put it down empty.

"Yes, it's hot,'' she agreed.

"Got your keys?'' he asked.

Piper felt the words rise in her and choke her. They came spilling out, words of fear and desperation. "Dan, you've got to promise me that you'll be careful. You'll call, you'll call me, won't you? I swear if you don't I'll get the police. I'll scream bloody murder! If I don't hear from you, do you understand, I'll have to do something!''

Dan came to her then, angrily, and held her arms with his strong hands, one above each elbow, hard. "Piper, you are not to contact anyone—no cops, no sheriff, no FBI. These guys were my *buddies*. That makes them *my* responsibility.'' His brows were drawn, his eyes stormy, his mouth a hard line. "Do you understand me? You *will* do what I say. I'm not begging, I'm not asking. I'm giving you no choice.''

She clamped her teeth together and gave a short nod. *No,* her mind screamed, *no!*

"Okay, let's go,'' he said, dropping his hands.

But Piper didn't move. She couldn't make herself pick up her feet and walk out of Dan Bourne's life, leaving him to fight and maybe die alone. "I—I can't,'' she said. "I can't, Dan. I won't leave you.''

"Let's go, Piper," he repeated.

"God help me," she said, "but if anything happens to you I'd never forgive myself. I can't, don't you see?"

He studied her for a long moment, his dark brows still drawn, and then something seemed to give inside him. His face relaxed, and he shook his head at her.

"I don't want to leave you alone," she whispered.

Dan raised his hand then and touched her cheek with a finger, ran it down to the corner of her mouth and across her lip while she stood there, her eyes closed, trembling. "Brave girl," he said, "but you can't help me."

"I can," she said. "I can! Let me help you!"

His hand slid around to the back of her neck, under her hair. His expression was still soft, and when Piper opened her eyes she saw the two cynical lines on either side of his mouth, the arrogantly curved nose, the blue eyes fringed with dark lashes, the thick, dark brows and fine black hair, and she couldn't stop. She put her hands up to cup his face and slowly, inexorably, pulled it down to hers. "Make love to me," she said against his lips, "and then maybe I'll be able to go."

Her lips tasted of sunshine and honey. It took Dan a moment to recover his equilibrium, to comprehend what he felt, but when he did his blood surged with heat, and he took her mouth with his. She moaned, and passion flared even higher in him, a flame burning, consuming. For a moment it didn't matter that there were men waiting to kill him, that Harry was out there, that he was in danger and had a job to do, his duty to perform. For a moment he was lost in the sensations awakened by this woman, the confusion of senses, the opium of desire.

And then reality intruded, and he tore his lips from hers and put his hands up, to enclose hers where they held his face. "We have to leave," he said.

Tears glistened in Piper's eyes. Mutely she shook her head and mouthed the word *no,* her lips trembling.

"Look," he started to say, trying to pull himself together, but she was standing there so close, the taste of her lips still on his, and he felt his resolve begin to weaken. "Look," he tried again, unable to meet her eyes, "it's not going to be daylight forever, we should—"

"There's time," Piper whispered. "You know there's still time. Love me," she said, "just make love to me, Dan," and his last obstruction shattered.

Hand in hand they climbed the stairs and went, without even speaking, not to the master bedroom but to the guest room where Piper had slept, a place where neither of them had memories of Diana, a neutral place.

She unbuttoned his shirt, the same yellow shirt she'd helped him button up last night. Her hands, fingers splayed, roamed his chest, his back, touching him delicately, exploring. Her eyes held his, and he bent to kiss her, to taste the nectar of her mouth. He ran his hands up through her hair, lacing his fingers through the wild tangles of chestnut brown, holding her immobile while he kissed her.

Nothing existed but the two of them, alone in a universe of gentle touch and sweet aroma and low murmurs. Not frenzied this time, more patient, they were both willing to wait and absorb and learn each other's bodies.

Piper pulled her T-shirt over her head. She wore no bra; her breasts were small and perfect, her waist narrow. She kicked off her boots, unzipped her jeans and stepped out of them. Her stomach was flat, her hips round and womanly, her legs long and slender. She smiled tremulously and stood there for him to see, endowing him with her beauty.

He shrugged off his shirt and jeans, too, and her dark eyes roamed his body, their expression so very serious, intent, as if she'd never seen a man before. And then she stepped up to him, and he took her in his arms, bare skin to bare skin, the heat kindling between them, and Piper sighed deeply, her breath warming his cheek. "Yes," she whispered, and he knew what she meant, that this was good between them, right.

Dan was careful with her this time, more gentle, the passion growing slowly and steadily, building as he caressed her smooth skin, felt the long muscles in her arms and legs, the strength from her years of riding. He stroked the muscles in her thighs, in her arms and shoulders, loving the strength and softness and slenderness all on one body. He kissed her breasts and her neck, felt her shudder with sensation, heard her breath quicken.

And inside his own belly the need grew, the ache coiled in upon itself, making him hard and ready. Piper rose over him, her face flushed and beautiful, and he pulled her down onto him, thrusting, filling her. He gasped and heard her moan, and she leaned forward, her hair falling around her, supported on her arms. She rode him, her eyes closed, her breath quick, and he held her hips, guiding her in a quickening cadence, faster and faster.

Then Piper cried out and arched her back, and Dan felt his loins convulse, and he spent himself in her over and over again, endlessly, forever.

He didn't know how long they lay there, sated, exhausted, but he became aware in small increments that her hair tickled his face and that there was something, something important that he had to do, and that the sun was hot and bright and moving relentlessly toward the western horizon. He stirred, and Piper murmured something.

"Kid," he said softly. "Piper, hey."

"Um?"

He couldn't help running his hand along her backbone, feeling the bumps and hollows, the delicious curve and swell of her bottom. "We have to go," he said.

She moved then, turned her face to him, holding her hair back with a hand. "You haven't changed your mind," she said.

He smiled a little then. "Is that what you were trying to do? Change my mind?"

She stared at him with absolute solemnity. "Maybe," she replied.

"Piper..."

"I'd do anything, you know," she said gravely, "to keep you safe."

He studied her face, and her eyes never wavered from his. He felt a rush of some emotion, unwanted, unasked for, unidentified. "Sorry," he said, a little too quickly. "Nothing's changed."

"You're so damn stubborn," she whispered.

They dressed slowly, drained, moving in a kind of viscous fog. But now, this time, there was none of the shyness and uncertainty of the morning. Instead there was acceptance, not agreement but a knowing, a coming to terms with each other, a sweet, melancholy closeness, made excruciatingly poignant by what had to happen.

Dan took her keys and drove her to her house in the Jeep. They said nothing, nothing, at least, that he could remember, nothing of any consequence, but he felt her anguish as if she spoke of nothing else. Yet he couldn't give in to her, not even after what had occurred between them. He couldn't give up what he had to do for the comfort Piper could give him. He'd done that once, and tragedy had been the result. No, this time he'd do it right.

He pulled up in her driveway, under the big willow tree and its long afternoon shadows, switched the engine off and turned to her.

"Promise me you'll pack a bag and get out of here right away," he said.

She nodded, biting her lip, looking down.

"You'll go right to Denver, stay there until this is over?"

Again, a silent nod.

"You understand, Piper, I can't be worrying about you." He hesitated. "I'll try to call you, but I can't promise...."

Her eyes flew up to his, full of torment, but she said nothing. Then she leaned close and pressed her lips to his, tenderly, and he could taste the salt of her tears.

"What's going to happen to us?" she asked then. "Dan, what's going to become of us?"

He turned his head away, hating to hurt her yet knowing he couldn't promise anything, knowing he had to harden his heart against her, against anything that could distract him.

"I have no future right now," he said evenly. "Not until justice is done."

"Oh, God, don't say that."

He shrugged. He couldn't have her around him, another innocent victim, until this mess was resolved. It was too important, too dangerous, and it stood between them like a wall, endlessly high, unthinkably thick, a barrier between Dan and life.

"Dan," she was saying brokenly, "I—I think I love you."

But he only moved away from her and shook his head, his eyes dark, his mouth a taut line. "Look," he said, "you're way off base. We had an affair, that's all. It's over now, finished." She refused to look at him as she climbed out of the Jeep. He slammed it into gear and headed down the road. The whole time he was thinking bitterly, *Like Harry always said, you do what you have to.*

CHAPTER THIRTEEN

IT WAS AN HOUR OUT OF Steamboat Springs, on the serpentine, mountainous road to the Front Range and Denver, that Piper suddenly pulled off onto the shoulder of the highway and jammed on the brakes.

Dan was lying.

Here she'd been driving along for the past hour, her heart breaking, and she'd never even considered that he'd calculatingly deceived her! No man could have made love to a woman like that and then turned as hard as stone at the drop of a hat.

Oh, Dan, she thought. What a fool she'd been to buy into his act! If she'd been herself, instead of a love-drowsy idiot, she'd have seen through his ploy instantly.

She mentally rewound their last few minutes together and played the tape back in her head—everything he'd said, his facial expressions, his body language. It had all been a big lie, a smoke screen he'd set up out of a misguided sense of honor, for what he'd considered her safety.

Of course he'd been lying!

Piper checked the rearview mirror and pulled a fast U-turn, pressing the gas pedal to the floor. She had no idea what the future held; she knew only that she wasn't going to leave Dan alone to face those murderers. Later, when the danger was past, well, they'd just have to confront that nebulous future together. But for now Dan needed help, and she'd be darned if she was going to turn tail and run.

She drove back toward Steamboat Springs like a demon, pushing the Cherokee too hard, passing campers and motorcycles and gawking tourists who were doing the speed limit.

The road rose and fell and wound through the wide valleys of northwestern Colorado, the Continental Divide peaks jutting up from deep gorges, delineating the summer blue sky. The fields were brown, though, sucked dry of all their moisture—what a hellish summer it had been. No farmers or ranchers, she saw, were irrigating any longer, like Dan, they'd . . .

Dan. Her mind halted, and she let up on the gas in the middle of passing an RV, just as an eighteen-wheeler was barreling down the passing lane toward her. Suddenly she snapped to and shoved the pedal to the floor, only just making it around the camper. The driver sat on the horn and shook his fist at her.

Phew, Piper breathed, but when she remembered the danger Dan had put himself in, speeding down the highway seemed positively safe by comparison.

She was flying along the darkening Yampa Valley, only a few miles out of Steamboat Springs, when suddenly she knew what she had to do.

Dutch. He was the only one who could help Dan now, the only one who even had a clue as to what was really going on. Dutch was going to have to come down off his high horse and help. It was his job, for Lord's sake; even he wouldn't ignore Dan in this situation. He wouldn't dare. The most important thing on earth to Dutch was his position as sheriff, and if anything happened to Dan, especially if Dutch didn't give it his all, the voters of Routt County would have a heyday come election time.

Of course Dutch was going to come through.

She found him not at the office but across the street in a café, having an evening coffee break.

She slid onto the stool next to him, shaking off the waitress's offer of coffee.

"Thank God I found you," Piper breathed. "I'll tell you all about it on the way to the ranch, but, Dutch, you have to come with me right now. We have to—"

"Whoa, there," he said, turning on his stool. "What in the devil are you talking about?" He took a drink of his coffee, purposely unruffled.

"Oh, God." Piper squeezed his arm with her hand. "It's Dan...he's in bad trouble. Look, we don't have time to go through the whole thing right now. I'll fill you in on the way to—"

"I got all the time in the world," he said, and glanced at his watch. "Yep," he went on, "I'm off for the night in about forty minutes, in fact."

"*Dutch,*" she said, "stop playing games. You're the sheriff! There're three men, cops from Philadelphia, after Dan with guns right this second. *And,*" she added, positive he'd drop his act immediately, "they're the *same* ones who forced Diana off the road. Dutch, they're murderers. They even murdered a man in Philadelphia. Oh, it's all tied together. I'll tell you every—"

But Dutch was shaking his head, bored. "Forget it," he said. "Sounds like some wild tale Bourne's dreamed up to snow you."

"Snow me?"

"Sure, babe," he said with bitterness. "The guy wants you to think he's this real macho man, out there in a standoff against three big-city killer cops. What a bunch of crap. And you fell for it."

"It's *true*," Piper breathed. "You can even check Dan's truck. It's in the ditch just past—"

"I saw it this morning." Dutch shrugged. "So Bourne ran off the road last night. Guess he'd had a few beers. Big deal."

"For God's sake, Dutch," she whispered urgently, "there's a bullet hole in the windshield!"

"I didn't see any bullet hole."

"Then go back and look again!"

"In the morning."

"*Now.*"

Again he shook his head. "I got paperwork, babe. I don't want to get hung up all night long."

"You're...you're crazy," Piper sputtered, and she clutched at his arm again. "Dutch, you can't do this. You know something's happening out at the ranch. You *know* it's true. You've got to put your personal feelings aside and do your job. We'll iron everything out later, I promise, but..."

"You know," he said as he threw some coins on the white countertop, "I wouldn't lift a finger to help you or Bourne if your lives depended on it." He put on his gray Stetson and stood. "By the way," he added, "I saw your Jeep at the ranch. I take it you spent the night."

Speechless, Piper watched him head to the door and give the waitress a flashing grin. "Dutch," she whispered, frantic, "don't you realize this will mean the end of your career? You can't, you *can't* do this!"

But all he said was, "Have a nice night, Piper," and he headed out the door into the late-evening shadows.

The decision, of course, was easy. In fact, Piper thought as she headed out of town toward the Elk River Ranch turnoff, there *was* no decision. Dan was one man against three. Well, maybe she could make it two against three.

It had occurred to her when she'd hurried back to the Cherokee that she should try to persuade one of Dutch's deputies to help. But the brainstorm had passed quickly. Not one of them would dare defy his lord and master, Sheriff Dutch Radowsky.

Okay, Piper thought as she steered along the dark road, trying to press down her fear, *so it's two of us to three of them.* She wondered then if Diana's .22-caliber rifle was still in the hall closet. It wasn't much against powerful handguns or the high-powered rifle they'd used ambushing Dan in his truck, but it was better than nothing, and Piper, years ago, had done some target shooting with it. Diana had kept it around to shoo off pesky skunks and raccoons, but it might just do for three city cops.

She drove the narrow winding road and wondered if she could fire a gun at a man. Of course, in the dark, maybe it was enough just to fire into the night, to scare them off. Dan, on the other hand, would mean business.

What *was* she thinking? Nothing had happened yet. Maybe, after last night's miss, they'd gone back to...but no. It was just that morning that Harry had come to her in the tack room. They weren't going anywhere. Not until the job was done.

Oh, God, Piper thought, heaven help Dan and her, because sure as heck no one else was going to.

She was imagining Dan's furious reaction when she got to the ranch in a couple more minutes, and she was wondering just how to deal with him, when she first noticed the set of headlights moving quickly up from behind. Well, she wasn't about to slow up and let the fool pass; the road would be his, anyway, as soon as she turned into the driveway to the ranch, just up there, around this last curve.

She went back to thinking about Dan, trying to dismiss the notion that Harry and this Sweet Pea and Frank might, at that very moment, be moving up to the ranch house under the cloak of darkness.

No, Piper decided, they'd go for Dan later, wait for him to wear down, wait for his nerves to be raw and for exhaustion to make him more apt to make a mistake. Sure. But what those three cowards didn't know was she'd be there, too. Piper Hilyard to the rescue, she thought grimly.

The vehicle behind her was tailgating now, the headlights blinding her. She reached up and was snapping the night rearview mirror into place when suddenly the lights were gone, swinging to her left as the driver attempted to pass. On a curve!

"Idiot," Piper said, moving the Cherokee as close to the right edge of the road as was safe. "Stupid drunken tourists—"

It happened in a heartbeat. One second she was cautiously steering along the unlined right edge of the road, the next second her parents' car was skidding into the drainage ditch, nudged right off the road. It came to rest, precariously tilted, the right-side tires sinking into the soft ground.

Piper tried to contain her shock, and took several fast, panting breaths, her knuckles gripping the steering wheel whitely. "You stupid...dumb, stupid..." She was gasping, furious, shaken, when abruptly her door was yanked open. "Now, just you listen here," she began, startled, her pulse racing.

"Shut up," a voice commanded, "and get out."

She felt her whole body go numb. She stared at the face confronting her, and no words would make it past her constricted throat. "Get out!" the stranger said again, and he grabbed her arm, pulling her up onto the embankment, where she stumbled.

It was then she saw another man. Through her horror and confusion she saw him standing behind the stranger. It was Harry Tegmeier.

"BUTTON IT UP, HARRY," said the driver, who Piper soon learned was Sweet Pea. "No more unnecessary talking to her."

From where she was sitting, handcuffed in the back seat of the Ford Bronco, Piper could see the backs of two heads, Harry in the passenger seat, Sweet Pea doing the driving. Next to her, keeping a close eye on her, was the man called Frank.

"Go ahead and talk to me," Piper said to Harry. "He's not your boss."

"Shut up," Sweet Pea growled. "Shut up or we'll stuff a gag in that trap of yours."

"Hey, Sweet Pea," Harry tried, his face ashen, "there's no need to get on the lady like that."

Piper saw Sweet Pea's pockmarked face in the rear-view mirror. His eyes were on her, black stones swimming in oil.

As they drove up the long Elk River Valley road to where Steamboat Lake sat below Hahn's Peak, Frank said almost nothing. He checked her handcuffs once, giving them a tug, then straightened back up in his seat. It was Harry who talked. Almost incessantly. He talked about nothing, remarking on the density of the forest, a deer that was caught, mesmerized, in the headlights. He talked as if he was on an ordinary camper's outing, as if he could make everything okay if he just kept talking.

But everything wasn't okay.

Piper's brain churned. She had no idea where they were taking her, or, for that matter, why they'd kidnapped her. She kept thinking over and over that Dan must still be alive. Maybe they'd caught him, too, and they were taking her to the same place they'd stowed him. Then, oh, yes, *then* they'd do away with them both. Far from civilization. Nice and clean. They could bury their two bodies and no one, ever, would find them.

"I'd like to fish that lake someday," Harry was musing. "They got trout in that lake, Piper?"

"Shut the hell up!" Sweet Pea, fed up, pounded his arm against the door.

"Yes," Piper said defiantly, "rainbow trout. You'd like it, Harry." If she could keep Harry going, Piper began to think, keep him talking, maybe they'd be distracted, maybe she could somehow get away. But how? And where? "The river's good fishing, too," she said, leaning forward, aware of Sweet Pea's eyes flickering onto her in the mirror, "but you catch brookies there, brook trout."

Frank put an arm over and forced her back. "Be quiet," he said, his voice strained, his hatchetlike features tensed.

But Piper kept at it. "Where are we going? Is Dan there?" No one spoke.

Sweet Pea headed straight past Steamboat Lake and continued on up to the smaller lake at the foot of Hahn's Peak. "That's called Hahn's Peak Lake, Harry," Piper said. "Is that where we're going?"

"Please," Frank said, warning her.

"Is Dan there?" Piper tried again, and she felt her nerves scrape one another, chafing her whole body. "*Is* he?"

"Take it easy, Piper," Harry said, turning in his seat.

Sweet Pea, for the moment, seemed to have given in. In silence he drove on through the black night.

Just past the smaller lake they made a right onto County Road 488. It was a graded dirt road. Piper knew it well. In a few minutes they'd come to the tiny village of Trilby Park, open to tourists in the summer, providing the bare minimum of necessities: some food, fishing worms and tackle. Were they holed up in a cabin there? Harry had said a cabin near Hahn's Peak, Piper recalled from his morning visit, but there were dozens of mountain cabins in the area—hundreds near the peak that was surrounded by millions of acres of prime national forest and wilderness area. In fact, she realized, there was nothing between them and the Wyoming border *but* forest.

They drove through the tiny village and bumped on up the dirt road, coming to the foot of Iron Mountain. And there, finally, Sweet Pea pulled off the road, hiding the Bronco behind some underbrush.

Piper was hauled out of the back of the Bronco by Sweet Pea and shoved in front of him, his beefy hand gripping her arm. She cast around, trying to peer into the darkness. She couldn't remember a cabin around here, though. Only a trailhead leading up along a ridge of Iron Mountain, five, maybe only four miles by foot. But, yes, Piper recalled, there *was* a hiker's cabin up there somewhere. She'd ridden past it on horseback once. With Diana. Was that where they were headed? It was remote—no one was apt to stop at the cabin, either, because it wasn't located along the trail far enough for even a day hike. Just far enough from civilization, but not too far. Ideal. Was *that* where Dan was? Or was he still at the ranch? Were they going after him next?

They started up the darkened trail, Frank leading the way with a heavy-duty flashlight, Harry walking next and then Sweet Pea, with Piper handcuffed and safely in tow. The trail rose dramatically for the first mile, and Sweet Pea was breathing up a storm at her back. She could smell the sweat on his big body, and his hand was sticky and hot when he shoved her along.

"It's not too far," Harry turned once to tell her, trying to be kind, she thought derisively, hating him for what he was doing.

"Be quiet," Frank said, swinging the beam of the flashlight into their faces.

Piper trudged on, still wondering if she was going to find Dan at the end of their trek. She hoped so. But then she realized it was better if he wasn't there, because if he was, they were both goners.

"Goddamn it," Sweet Pea said after the second mile, "hold up. I gotta get my breath. It's too hot out for this stuff."

Frank stopped ahead. Harry, too. "If you'd lay off all that bourbon," Frank said, irritated, "we'd be there by now."

Sweet Pea swore at him. "Yeah, and if we'd all quit smoking we'd live longer." He swore again, panting.

"You all right?" Harry asked her.

But Sweet Pea answered. "Who gives a hoot how she is?"

Piper whirled around. "You're a real nice guy," she said, "and I hope a bear comes screaming out of these woods and chows down on you."

"Button it up," he rasped.

"Bears," Frank said. "There aren't bears here."

"Oh, yeah?" Piper retorted. "There are most definitely bears and wildcats, and they're night feeders, boys."

"You're lying," Frank said, swinging the light into her eyes and then beyond her, into the dense forest where the trees stood like tall black sentinels, ghostly in the night. The light pierced the darkness in front of them and then faded, dispersed into the thick growth beyond. For a moment it was too still, hot and breathlessly silent, and then deep in the black forest a twig snapped somewhere, and even Piper's heart gave a knock against her ribs.

"There's no bears," Frank murmured. "You're lying."

"Am I?" Piper whispered.

They went on, all of them tripping several times, and everyone but Piper suffered from the altitude. Still, they pushed forward along the trodden path, through stands of evergreens and aspen trees, across a few meadows and one boulder field, up, up into the blackness, the hot, dry air sucked into straining lungs.

"Christ!" Frank yelled, and stopped, swinging the flashlight beam wildly across the trail ahead. "What the hell was that!"

"Hope it isn't a bear," Piper said snidely, and Sweet Pea gave her a brutal tug on the handcuffs.

"What?" Harry was saying, catching up to Frank. "What'd you see?"

"I don't know." Frank's voice was shaking.

"Give me that," Harry said, and snatched the flashlight, training it on the trail with a calmer hand.

Of course, Piper knew it had to be a skunk or porcupine—at worst, a cow having strayed from some high-country federal grazing land. No bear in his right mind would be within a hundred yards of four humans. God, she thought, these guys were dumb.

It turned out to be a porcupine, waddling his slow way along the trail, occasionally stopping, looking behind, moving on, utterly unafraid.

"Kick him off the trail," Sweet Pea called.

"*You* kick him off," Frank yelled back.

"Their quills are poisonous," Piper lied easily.

Her wrists were really starting to hurt by the time they reached more level ground. Her legs and lungs and stamina were fine, but Sweet Pea was sure getting a charge out of yanking on those handcuffs. A cruel man, Piper was learning, and she recalled Dan's vividly detailed story of Joey Washington's beating in that warehouse. A real nice guy, Sweet Pea.

She fought her fear the whole way. Fear, Piper was finding out, had sharp claws, and once they dug in, they stuck. No, she had to stay calm, clearheaded—if not for herself, then for Dan. If they were going to...die, she wanted to be brave for him. It was tough, though. God, but it was tough.

They reached the cabin—the same one Piper recalled—in a little over three miles, not the four or five she'd thought. There was no light, no sound, but then, if Dan was being held in there, they wouldn't have left him with any creature comforts—not a man they intended to kill.

Frank pushed open the creaking door, and Piper held her breath. *Please, Lord,* she prayed, *don't let Dan be here.* And yet, just to look at him once more, to gaze into those eyes and smell his smell, to feel the strength of his hand in hers . . .

"He's not here," Harry said at her side.

"Thanks," Piper breathed.

Inside, Frank switched on a battery-packed lantern that cast long shadows on the bare plank walls. The cabin was at the most twelve by fifteen feet, a rough-hewn shelter with a couple of logs as chairs and a crude, scarred table. Three sleeping bags were rolled up and tossed in a corner. There was a brand-new rucksack stacked behind the bedrolls, half shielding a high-powered rifle. They had their handguns on them, though, because she could see the bulge of Frank's beneath his shirt.

"Over there—" Sweet Pea nodded at her "—on the floor, and keep that mouth shut for once."

Piper did as she was told and sat with the sleeping bags to her back, the hard earthen floor as a seat. It was hot and stuffy in the cabin. Sweat broke out all over her body, a sick, clammy sweat of fear. She tried to ignore it, and concentrated on controlling her emotions instead.

At least, she thought, watching the men, Dan was safe for now. But surely they must plan on taking him tonight. So why, then, she asked herself, hadn't they stayed in the valley? Why this climb to the cabin? They could have killed her, as well, hours ago. Why hadn't they?

A plan. They had to have a plan all along, something they thought was foolproof. But what?

They ate some beef jerky and drank from thermoses, Harry offering Piper some despite Sweet Pea's growl. "A last supper?" she asked flippantly, but astutely drank some water.

"No one's hurt you," Harry said, but he couldn't look her in the eye.

Frank and Sweet Pea were standing near the door, their heads bent, talking. Piper was sure now that they had a plan, but just how she fit in was a mystery.

It didn't remain a mystery for long.

About ten minutes after they'd arrived at the cabin Sweet Pea strode over to her, thrusting his boxer's face into hers as he stooped. "You figured it out yet, lady?" he asked.

Slowly Piper shook her head.

"It's you, honey, in trade for Danny."

It took a moment, but finally Piper got it—they were holding her as a hostage to lure Dan.

"He'll never fall for that," Piper said coolly in spite of the leap of her heart. "Dan will know the same thing I do."

"And what's that?" Sweet Pea said.

"That you can't leave either of us alive now."

He smiled thinly. "You been watching too much TV, lady."

Piper said nothing. He was lying through his teeth.

Shortly, both Sweet Pea and Frank left for the valley once more, telling Harry they were going to phone Dan and give him the scoop about his girlfriend. "Keep her quiet," Frank warned Harry, "and don't let her fool you with no female stuff."

"I know what I'm doing," Harry said.

Sweet Pea turned to Piper before he closed the door behind them. "You know," he said, "this is going to work just fine. Dan'll come for you, all right."

"He won't," Piper retorted.

"Oh, yeah? Dan always was a chump," Frank put in, and the two men left, giving the door a good shove to close it. And then, just outside, Piper could hear Sweet Pea launch into a tune, a surprisingly on-key rendition of the old Irish ballad. "Oh Danny-boy, the pipes, the pipes are calling," sang Sweet Pea. "From glen to glen and down the mountainside." Then the men laughed, and the last thing Piper heard before the forest swallowed his voice was, "The summer's gone and all the flowers are dying..."

Harry swore softly.

It was unbelievable, Piper thought, swallowing, but these men who were once partners of Dan's—his brothers—were now his deadliest enemies. Simply because Dan had done his duty, tried to be just and honest, in their view he deserved to die.

Piper glanced at Harry, who was standing by the door, peering out the tiny window next to it as if he could see into the night, or maybe into the future. Sweat glistened on his red face.

Okay, she thought, Sweet Pea and Frank had not been as close to Dan as Harry—maybe their turn-around from friend to foe could be understood. But Harry Tegmeier, the man whom Dan referred to as the closest thing to a father in his life... Then again, she mused, perhaps Harry wasn't so committed to killing. Maybe not...

"Harry," she said, her voice far more controlled than she was feeling, "Dan won't come for me. I *know* he won't fall into such an obvious trap."

Harry looked at her and leaned against the door. "Dan'll know it's a trap," he said, "but he won't have a choice." And then he stared down at the floor.

"There are always choices," Piper said.

"Not many in this situation," he replied. "Not for Danny. He's too predictable."

"Maybe he's tougher than you think," she said. "Would you like that, Harry, would you be glad if Dan plays it smart and *doesn't* try to rescue me?"

"I don't know..." he began and suddenly fell silent.

"Come on, Harry," she argued, "you don't want to hurt Dan or me."

"Look," he said, his tone suddenly harsh, "I got a family to protect. I don't care what happens to me as long as my wife and kids aren't left without a cent."

"Your pension."

"You're goddamned right, my pension!"

"Well," Piper said, "two people are already dead—Joey Washington and my friend Diana. I guess," she put in bitterly, "two more won't really matter."

He turned his face away. "Be quiet," he said. "Get some rest. Whatever. Just be quiet, will ya?"

"Maybe Dan won't come," she pressed on. "Maybe you'll just have to deal with me alone. Then what? Then what, Harry?"

He pulled open the cabin door, still not looking at her. "He'll come," he whispered hoarsely. "Dan will come." And with that he closed the door behind him. Piper stared at the door, praying she'd made a dent in his resolve, praying, mostly, that Dan would think of some other way to save them—there *had* to be another way.

The light in the lamp flickered, the batteries weakening. Piper sighed, fighting her sick fear, alone, waiting in the close dimness with the strong beat of her heart.

CHAPTER FOURTEEN

DAN SAT on the living room couch and tried to eat a cold piece of pizza he'd found in the refrigerator. He had to force himself; his appetite was gone. It was a familiar feeling, the same one he'd always had before a big operation when he'd been a detective. His body was suffused with a taut and deadly calm.

Frankly, he couldn't figure out why Harry, Frank and Sweet Pea hadn't made a move yet. It had been a full twenty-four hours since they'd shot at him. They'd had lots of opportunities. Hell, they could have tried something when he'd driven back out here after dropping Piper off. Why hadn't they? Or when he'd gone out to feed the horses tonight, or when he'd driven, deliberately slowly, into Clark to the Timber Parrot to have a beer. Harry had told Piper they were staying around Hahn's Peak somewhere, so he'd even driven up there, nosing around, looking, scenting the air, waiting for it to happen, for the shot or the car coming up behind him or the menacing rustle from a dark shadow.

He was ready, but there hadn't been a hint of the men from Philadelphia. He couldn't believe they'd given up and gone home. No way. He could only assume they'd come, under the cover of darkness most likely, that they were waiting for exhaustion to over-come him.

His eyes strayed to the gun lying on the table next to him. He put his hand on the smooth, cold, oily metal, closed his fingers around it, hefted it in his hand. Familiar, comforting. Memories nudged his consciousness, fleeting images of when he'd held this same gun before, both hands gripping it chest high, his nerves spurting liquid fire into his fingers. He'd shot a suspect only once—in the thigh. All that shoot-'em-up garbage they filmed for TV and the movies was bunk. But firing at a man once had been enough. Aiming it at a suspect was another thing, producing the desired effect. And Dan sure hoped that was all he'd have to do tonight, although he wondered just how he was going to get the drop on three men at once. If he could get them into the darkened house, lure them in. Dan knew every inch of the place. They didn't. It was possible. . . .

Of course he *could* get killed. In that event Piper would go to the authorities. Even that dolt Dutch knew some of the score. And as for the ranch, well, when Diana had died he'd had a new will drawn up by her lawyer, and Piper had been named heir. Dan had always known Diana would have wanted it that way.

He sat in the dark room listening to the familiar night sounds through an open window behind him. He still held the gun in his hand, gripping it lightly. *Come on, guys,* he thought, *let's get it over with.*

Ten more minutes passed. Time seemed out of kilter. The minutes sped by. Seconds were dragging. Where were they?

Ten minutes more. If they were counting on him to get edgy, it was working. But when the time came he'd be ready. He could see their faces, even Harry's, and his blood heated. Oh, he'd be ready.

It must have been another hour before Dan stood and stretched, peering cautiously out the window. The moon was a sliver shy of being full, a huge round orb in the eastern sky, so big, so close it seemed as if he could touch it. Bright, golden yellow with facelike smudges. Its brilliance threw shadows on the land. So much the worse for his buddies if they planned a night assault.

Piper should be in Denver by now, he thought out of the blue. In the city, with its lights and traffic, an anonymous stranger among thousands. Safe. Dan moved around the house then, peering out the windows, looking for anything out of place on the familiar landscape. The refrigerator hummed calmly, his footsteps not even puncturing the stillness.

She probably hated him. You couldn't use a woman like that and then cast her off like an old shoe. But Piper—she was so full of emotion, all sorts of emotions, and her loyalties were so strong he'd had to do something to make her leave. And it had to have been something hurtful or she'd have argued endlessly, maybe even called Radowsky despite Dan's forbidding it. So he'd done what he had to. *That's what you do in life,* he thought again, *what you have to.*

Harry had told him that, and now Harry was doing what *he* had to do. He had to protect his job, his reputation, his family. He was due to retire soon, in two years or so, Dan figured, and he had to have that pension. Otherwise all those years meant less than nothing. All those years of putting himself in danger, standing on that thin blue line between order and anarchy, would be wasted. Oh, Harry had plenty at stake. So did Frank and Sweet Pea.

So did Dan.

He went back into the living room and checked the windows again. Outside, the moon was illuminating the yard in front of the barn, its pale white light shining on the hood of Piper's Jeep. Nothing moved. No shadows shifted. Where *were* they?

Dan stuck the gun under the waistband at the back of his blue jeans and rubbed the stubble on his chin with a steady hand. It was promising to be a long night. They were most likely going to come for him just before dawn. Sure. Dan would have played it that way himself. Dawn. The time when men's blood ran slower. The time when the sick and the old let go and slipped away. The time when Dan's eyes would be closing despite all his efforts to—

The phone rang abruptly, splitting the air like a banshee's cry. Dan's muscles spasmed involuntarily for a split second, then loosened. It was Piper. She was in Denver; she was calling. His heart swelled with gladness and an equal measure of irritation. *Damn it, Piper,* he was going to say.

He reached for the receiver, picked it up, held it to his ear. "Hello," he said quietly.

"Danny," came a voice. Not Piper's—a man's voice, a familiar voice. For a moment he couldn't place it, then his heart froze. "Hey, Dan, it's Frank."

Dan's hand gripped the receiver. "Yeah, I'm here, Frank."

"Okay, Dan, we got a deal for you."

"Uh-huh," he said noncommittally.

"It's like this, a simple trade. We've got that chick, Piper. It's you for her."

Dan's whole body was seized by paralysis, a horrible, choking numbness, then overpowering fear, then tearing rage. *"What?"* he choked out.

"You heard me. We have Piper. It's a trade. We let her go when you show up."

Dan stood there, his head bowed, shoulders hunched, hand white-knuckled on the receiver. His mind raced like an insane demolition derby. "You're lying," he said to gain time.

"Sure, pal, we're lying, and you're going to hang up," Frank said mockingly.

Piper. They had *Piper.* He'd done it again! They'd kill her, and then he'd be responsible for her, too! A man couldn't live with that, couldn't survive...not twice.

"Okay," Dan said, forcing himself to think, "so how do I know you have her? You're bluffing."

"Dan, Dan, I went through the same training you did," Frank said mildly. "Who do you think you're kidding? We got her on the road to your ranch, about eight-thirty tonight. Driving a red Cherokee. She was wearing jeans and a green T-shirt and she was mad as hell. Regular spitfire you got there, Dan."

Eight-thirty? On Elk River Road? She should have been halfway to Denver, was all Dan could think. What the hell? What the...? But there was no time for that now. They had her, all right. And if she'd been mad, that meant she wasn't hurt. So far.

"Okay," he said, stalling, "so maybe you have her. So what? What makes you think I'll trade myself for her?"

Frank laughed. "I'll tell you what makes us think that, you idiot. We saw her Jeep there last night. And, besides, you always were a sucker. You wouldn't let another poor girl get hurt, not after you already lost one, now, would you?"

Dan clenched his fist and felt a knot of sick rage lurch in his belly. He swore at Frank, used every word he knew, cursed him. And Frank only laughed. Dan shut up finally, drained, his fury dying to a dull hate.

"Finished?"

"Where are you?" Dan asked in a hard voice.

"I'll tell you, but I gotta warn you first, Dan, no cops, nobody else. You alone. We see any hint of anything like that, she's dead. Got it?"

"Yeah, sure, right, I know that line. Just tell me when and where," he said impatiently.

"Okay, we're in a cabin past Hahn's Peak. Go up Elk River Road to 488, take a right, two miles on the right you'll find our Bronco behind some bushes. There's a trailhead to Iron Mountain there, a sign. Follow it, three miles. Just stay on the same trail. Can't miss it. You have till morning."

"For God's sake, Frank, what if I get lost? What if it takes me longer? Give me till noon," Dan said.

"No. Morning, say nine o'clock. That's it. Be there. Alone."

Dan held the receiver so tightly his hand hurt. He raised his head and looked up, thinking, figuring, scheming. But he came up with only one possibility at every dead end. "All right," he said coldly, his voice like a steel blade. "I'll be there, Frank. I'll see you in the morning."

"Okay, Dan, it's a deal." And Frank hung up.

Dan put the receiver down very carefully, very deliberately, as if rough handling of it would harm Piper in some indefinable way. He stood there, head down, arms folded, staring at the phone as if it were a poisonous serpent. Hate filled him, squeezing his guts in its fierce grip. And fear for Piper. Hopelessness swept him momentarily, inundating, heavy, then resolve took its place, cleansing his mind, strengthening his body.

He knew what he had to do. He'd known from the moment Frank had spoken. But how? How to get Piper away from them safely?

He'd go now, right now. No sense waiting for morning, even if he could stand to sit there twiddling his thumbs the whole goddamn night. He grabbed a jacket, found a flashlight that worked, stuck an extra ammo clip in his pocket and strode out the door. And all the time his mouth was dry, his heart hammering. *Piper,* his mind repeated endlessly, sickeningly, *Piper's in danger. Got to save her, Piper....*

Why wasn't she in Denver? How did they get her? Was she scared, hurt? Was she terrified?

He knew one thing with utter certainty. Frank was lying through his teeth. They'd never trade Piper for him. She knew what they'd done, she knew who they were. They wouldn't let her loose in a million years. They couldn't. They'd use her to lure Dan there, then they'd kill them both.

And they knew Dan, knew him only too well, the way one cop knows another, deep down inside, all the way to the guts. Oh, yes, they knew that Dan realized they'd kill him and Piper both, but they were counting on his honor—his damn honor.

DAN DROVE NORTH up the Elk River Road too fast, careering around the corners in Piper's Jeep. His mind worked spasmodically, now concentrating on driving, now on Piper, his previous deadly calm replaced by seething anxiety. He sped past Clark and Glen Eden, scattered lights in the night, past Steamboat Lake and Hahn's Peak, up into the mountain wilderness that stretched ahead, unbroken for hundreds of miles west and north and east. His headlights swung wildly across the wall of black trees that bordered the narrowing road, closing in on him, then he started watching for the right turn to Iron Mountain. He jerked the wheel around when he saw the sign and sped on, slithering on gravel corners. A couple of miles, Frank had said, their car hidden behind bushes. Dan strained his eyes in the darkness for the trailhead sign, slowing, his high beams picking out the twin glare of animals' eyes in the forest, and the faint pungent smell of skunk came to his nose.

There, he saw it, a sign. He pulled off onto the side of the road. Yes, that was it. He turned the Jeep off, put the keys under the seat and clicked the flashlight on.

It was eerily quiet, very warm and dry for the mountains at night, the air like a fine effervescent wine. He tied his jacket sleeves around his waist, readjusted his gun and looked for the hidden car—a Bronco, Frank had said. The flashlight beam glinted off something—chrome. It was there, all right, a blue-and-silver Bronco with rental plates. Okay.

Dan's watch said nearly midnight when he started up the trail, his flashlight trained ahead of him. He didn't feel tired, although he should have. Adrenaline coursed through every vein in his body, pumped to each cell with his heartbeat. He set out at a steady pace, and the moonlight streaked the trail where it wasn't shaded by trees, brighter than his puny flashlight beam. The world was warm for this altitude at night, dry as a barnful of hay. The drought, Dan thought as his forehead beaded with sweat, and his underarms and waistband grew damp. A hot night in the Rockies. Weird. He walked and wondered about that. He'd always thought he'd buy it on a cold night. It was just one of those things you got in your head when you worked a dangerous job. So it was warm out. Maybe he wasn't going to die, after all. Or maybe he'd always been wrong about the cold.

Plans ran through his mind as he climbed. Creep up and somehow release Piper while they were asleep. No, they'd have a sentry awake. Start shooting in the window, but he could hit Piper. Lure them outside somehow. A million plans scrambled for legitimacy, but none of them would work. This was a hostage situation, the worst kind of dilemma. He had no psychologist to talk them out of the cabin, no SWAT team to surround them. He had only himself. It was a huge risk, even riskier to call for backup. The statistics on hostage situations were clear in his mind. All cops knew them. In most cases someone, usually an innocent person, got killed. Oh, yeah, he knew those damn statistics.

His flashlight gave out after an hour, and he made his way by moonlight then, slower, more wary. His shirt was damp with sweat and he was breathing hard. He thought for a moment of Harry wheezing his way up this trail. Harry... God, how could Harry have been involved in this? Was he forced by Frank and Sweet Pea? No, damn it, that was too easy, an excuse. Because Harry had helped kill Diana, or at least had known about it, and that Dan could never forgive.

His mind went back to setting up scenarios. He'd climb on the roof and drop a burning branch down the chimney, smoke them out. If there *was* a chimney, and if he had matches, which he didn't. He'd offer money, a safe-conduct. Hell, they'd laugh in his face.

Dan trudged on steadily, trying to see the roots and rocks and holes in the path, thinking, weighing possibilities. The forest around him was warm and striped with silver where the moonlight shone through. Shadows were black velvet, and tree trunks were picked out with the perfect delicacy of a black-and-white lithograph. Above, when he could see it, the sky was immeasurable and filled with stars, and the moon hung there, gazing with ironic benevolence down on him.

When his watch told him he'd traveled an hour and a half, he slowed up and turned off the path, slipping like a wraith into the forest, paralleling it. Luckily, at this altitude, the trees were pine and spruce, set well apart with little undergrowth, so it was easy to move. He watched carefully, because he could stumble on the cabin and give himself away. He had to keep the element of surprise in his favor; it was all he had. They expected him in the morning. Nine, Frank had said.

Maybe they'd all be asleep. Maybe, but he sure couldn't count on it. Would the cabin have lights on? A fire? Probably not—it was too hot for a fire tonight. If they had a fire going he'd be able to smell the smoke long before he reached it. Too bad it was so warm out.

He crept silently, hugging the shadows, placing his feet carefully. He felt his waistband for the gun, a nervous habit. It was there, heavy and reassuring.

And then he saw it, a blot of blackness darker than the night. He stopped short, held his breath, stood like a statue. The cabin—a small, square wooden building, no lights, no smoke, no movement. He slipped behind a tree and watched it for a time, noting the position of the door and windows, of the clearing in front.

Piper was in there, tied up maybe, scared to death, wondering what was going to happen to her. Had they told her about the trade? Maybe, probably. Did she believe it, or did she realize they'd have to kill her, too? He hoped she believed it, because then, at least, she wouldn't be frightened for her life.

He found a tree he could lean his back against, and squatted down, watching the cabin. He went over a dozen new plans in his head, running through them as if a filmstrip were unrolling before him. No good, no good, none of them were any good. He'd get Piper killed in every one of them.

No, there was only one slim possibility of getting her safely out of there. In his heart he knew it, had known it from the beginning. There was only one way to do it without getting her killed along with him.

Dan stood and circled the cabin, looking for something in the chiaroscuro landscape. He found it finally, on the east side of the cabin—a depression in the ground and a fallen log for cover. It would do. He stood there for a minute more, eyeing angles, doors, windows, cover between his position and the door, distances. Finally he nodded to himself. It might work. It might give Piper a fifty-fifty chance to survive, which was sure better than her chances now.

He took a deep breath then pulled the gun out of his damp waistband and moved into the shadows. He swallowed, took another breath and then called, "Frank! Sweet Pea! I'm out here!" He waited. He stood there motionless, his gun held in both hands in front of his chest and realized he hadn't spoken Harry's name aloud. He couldn't. "Come on," he called again, "you've waited a long time for this. Just send the girl out, and when she's safe I'm yours!" He waited another moment, then, "No games, boys. Send her out and I won't give you any trouble!" *The hell I won't,* Dan thought.

He waited again. What was going on? But then he heard it—voices, scuffles, bumping, men moving in the dark interior of the cabin.

"Come on!" he called one last time.

"Dan!" he heard from the cabin. Piper's voice. "Dan!" she cried. "Don't come! They're going to—" And her voice was cut off abruptly with a curse and a thump, and Dan's blood froze in his veins, then spurted with hot fury. He stood there, shaking with anger, waiting, waiting, forced to be quiet when he wanted to attack like a berserker.

"Send her out!" he shouted.

Murmurs, voices, men moving, a fleeting shadow across a window. Then, at last, the door squeaked open, the moonlight moving across the old, silvered wood. He could see dark shadows, figures, detaching themselves from the cabin, moving slowly, stealthily, away from the door. Brush cracked under someone's foot, and he swore he could hear someone panting.

Then he saw their plan. One man held Piper in front of him, a human shield, their bodies a combined blob of darkness. The other two were fanning out on either side to cover Piper and her captor. Sure, they knew the rules as well as he did—get as far apart as possible, shoot at the perpetrator from as many angles as they could, while Dan couldn't get all of them at once. Damn.

"Let her walk toward me," Dan said. "Alone." Quickly, crouching now, he moved deeper into the shadows.

"Sure, Danny, take it easy," came Sweet Pea's voice. "You're a little early. We didn't expect you till morning."

"Dan," Piper said, "don't! Don't let them—" But Sweet Pea jerked her back roughly, cutting her off.

Dan stiffened, had to take a breath and close his eyes for a split second. *Don't lose your cool, man,* he told himself. His one chance now at getting Piper in the clear for a few moments meant keeping his calm, trying to pick off one of the men flanking Sweet Pea and Piper, and then, hopefully, Sweet Pea would have to put his shield aside for a second to get off a shot at Dan. If it worked, Piper would have a moment to—

But he never finished the thought. Before he could think or judge or see exactly what had happened, he

heard Harry yell, "Run! Run, Piper!" And then the
shadows were scrambling wildly, moving too fast, all
jumbled together, and Dan couldn't see—damn the
darkness!—and he heard Harry yell again, and there
was a shot exploding in the night like a bomb, a flash
and a deafening boom.

Then he made out Harry, head down like a charg-
ing bull, running, dragging Piper.

"Here!" Dan yelled, taking aim at the two men behind Harry: standard position, legs straddled, two-
handed grip. "Here! Harry, over here!"

Another shot, crashing in the forest, echoing, and
Dan knelt and squeezed the trigger, unable to see very
well, hoping to force Frank and Sweet Pea to take
cover while Harry got away.

He heard Piper scream. God! Was she hit? But the
two of them were right in front of Dan—red-faced,
overweight Harry, rescuing the maiden. Another shot
from the direction of the cabin. Dan squeezed one off,
a roar and a flash of fire in the night, then he was
grabbing at Piper, who was a shadow ducking down,
and he flung her roughly behind a tree. Harry was
there, too, and he threw himself down alongside Dan.

"Oh, Dan!" Piper was crying. "Oh, my God,
Dan!"

"Okay, it's okay. You're safe," Dan rasped, then,
"Harry?"

Nothing.

"Harry?"

"Dan, I think he's been hit!" Piper breathed, pan-
icky.

It was like a bludgeon, a blow in the gut, taking
Dan's breath away. He said something, a curse, a

groan. A shot whistled past his head, thudding into a tree. Piper was pulling on him, dragging him down, half on top of her, crying and panting.

"Harry?" Dan said.

"He's hit, Dan. Oh, God, Dan, he saved me!" Piper cried.

Another shot, ricocheting off a rock, sparks flying. But Dan knelt by Harry and held the man's head, bending over him. He was scarcely aware of Piper grabbing Harry's gun, lying flat on the ground and firing toward the cabin. He knelt there, Harry's head in his lap, and the moon lit up the dark stain on Harry's shirt. Near him shots were exchanged, and he knew somewhere in his consciousness that soon the gun would be empty and that he and Piper were in mortal danger. But none of that mattered.

"Harry, I'm here, pal, I got you," he said, bending over, his face close to his friend's. "You're going to make it."

Harry was trying to talk, mouthing something, choking, a black line seeping from his mouth. "Danny-boy," he said, "I'm sorry...Diana. Danny, I didn't want...sorry..." And Dan felt the man's body go slack. He was gone. A wild, primitive grief rocked Dan. All the people in the world he loved best, dead because of him! He doubled over in pain.

"Dan!" he heard. Piper, terrified, frantic, her hands on him, shaking him. "Dan, Harry's gun, it's empty. I can't...Dan!"

He straightened and let Harry's head roll lifelessly off his lap. He could smell the hot, coppery odor of blood, and his hands were sticky with it. *Harry!* he cried inwardly.

"Dan! Please, Dan, they're coming," Piper was saying, pulling at him. "Oh, God, Dan!"

Something in Dan righted itself then, an instinct, the need to survive. He crouched, snatched Piper up and retreated farther into the trees, running bent over as bullets chunked into wood around them, and Frank and Sweet Pea shouted at each other and cursed like demons in the darkness.

He could hear Piper's panting, her breath sobbing in her lungs, but she kept up.

"You okay?" he breathed once.

"Yes," she answered, "but these—" she held up her arms to show him handcuffs around her wrists "—make it hard."

He steadied her with a grip on her elbow, and they ran together, leaving the cabin behind, the shots diminishing at their backs, sweating, gasping, dodging trees and branches and tripping over roots. "Hang in there, kid," he said once, his lungs on fire, his chest heaving.

And they kept going, toward the dawn, lost in the immensity of the Colorado Rockies, running, running into the hot, dark night.

CHAPTER FIFTEEN

"IT'LL BE DAWN SOON," Piper said, leaning against a huge fir tree, catching her breath. "Maybe we can make better time."

Dan crouched down on his haunches, resting, a dark shadow at her feet. "Yeah," he said, "we can make good time, but then so can Sweet Pea and Frank. They'll be able to spot us if we don't stick to the trees."

"How close do you think they are?" she asked and turned, trying to peer into the darkness behind them.

"I don't know," Dan replied. "Maybe they got lost. Maybe they're just coming over the ridge." He shrugged. "We better move on. You okay?"

"I'll live," she said, then held out her handcuffs. "But these are a pain. Are you sure we can't risk one single bullet to break them?"

Dan rose and took her hands, turning them over, trying to get a look at her chafed wrists. "They'll hear a shot," he said. "It'd be like sending up a flare to pinpoint us. Besides, one wrong move and I could break your wrists. We better not take the chance."

Piper only nodded. He was right, of course. Hampered as she was by the cuffs, she and Dan still had one big advantage, and that was their stamina. No way could Sweet Pea and Frank keep up this pace for long.

They moved on through the dense, high-country forest, avoiding footpaths and deer trails, sticking to the thick woods for cover. As dawn neared, the heavy stands of trees took on an otherworldly light, a kind of murky haze, though it was still dark. Beneath their feet pine needles crunched softly, and an occasional twig snapped. It was deathly silent in the forest at that hour before dawn—not a branch stirred or an animal scurried, and each snap or crunch under their feet seemed to echo along the mountainside. Surely, Piper thought, those men could hear them.

They moved on as the first light slowly grew from a pale gray to a pearllike luminescence, touching every clearing, the tops of the tall pines, the east faces of boulders. The shadows in the forest seemed to move then, crawling across the broken ground, slithering up tree trunks. There was a kind of dark magic to the forest, a magic that came only at dawn and dusk, the same magic that reached out and beckoned the unwary, leading them astray, turning them around in the forest, confusing them.

"You sure this is the way?" Dan asked her, stopping in the quickening light.

Piper gazed around, trying to see the distant peaks through the trees. "I . . . I think so."

Sound now began to awaken in the forest. A squirrel chattered. Birds chirped. Deer and elk moved from the cover of night along the trees at the edge of the meadows, their ears twitching, their eyes huge and dark. But the feel of the air was wrong, Piper thought. There was no morning haze lying in patches in the forest or slinking in the tall grass of the meadows. The air was too warm, too dry for morning. But then, it had been a drought summer.

They stopped in a meadow by a brook that was still running and cupped their hands, drinking the mountain water, splashing it on their faces. Piper soaked her wrists for a minute, grateful for the cold relief.

And then she noticed a doe and her fawn coming out of the forest only a few yards from them, cautiously making their way through the tall brown grass to the same brook. Piper nudged Dan and nodded and they both remained motionless, watching, unwilling to disturb the animals. It was only a minute later, however, that the doe abruptly raised her head and, frozen like a dun-colored statue, stared in the opposite direction.

Dan swore softly. "We better move on. She smells something," he whispered, and they made their way back into the trees.

It was midmorning when Piper finally stopped, slumping against a spruce, ready to cry.

"Exhausted?" Dan asked, coming up to her side.

"Yes," she managed to say. "I'm tired and I'm hungry and...and..."

"And what?"

"I think I got us lost."

"Lost."

She nodded, unable to meet his eyes.

"How? I mean..."

"Look," Piper said, sagging onto the pine-needle floor of the forest, "I don't know these mountains all that well. If we were on a trail, but as it is..."

"So, where do you *think* we are?"

She sighed. "I think we're on Twin Mountain. I thought we were on the back side of Hahn's Peak. I was looking for this old logging road, but I think we should have reached it by now."

Dan crouched beside her. "What if we climb up higher, get a vantage point, would that help?"

She laughed faintly. "A *map* would help."

"So what do we do?"

"Rest," Piper said tiredly. "We have to rest for a while or we'll never make it out. And then we better look for some berries or something. If we head lower into the valley we'll find some chokecherries, something to eat."

"I don't know," Dan began.

"Well, I do," Piper retorted. "We're tired and we're hungry and we're most likely lost. If we are, so are your pals. They'll have to stop, too. They could even be on another mountain entirely, or maybe they gave up. Maybe they tried to get back to the cabin."

"I doubt it," Dan muttered.

"I don't care," she said. "I only know we have to rest."

He regarded her solemnly, then finally nodded. "For an hour, okay?"

"Anything," Piper said and closed her eyes, stretching her legs in front of her, using a tree as a backrest.

She awoke an indeterminate time later, the hot midday sun striking her through the pine boughs. She jerked, remembering where they were, why they were there, and then realized that her leg was numb and that Dan's head was resting on her thigh, his body stretched out along her length. He was sound asleep.

She closed her eyes again, turning her face up into the strong sun, feeling its heat radiate through her, giving her body life. And then she looked back down at Dan, shifting her leg carefully to stimulate the flow of blood, and she reached out with her cuffed hands and touched his raven-dark hair with her fingers, feeling its silkiness, plucking a pine needle from it.

Against her leg she could feel his heartbeat, strong, slow, steady, and she could hear his soft snore. A hot breeze stirred the boughs above, and the sunlight cut across his shoulder and head, warming his sleeping body.

For a time Piper watched the dappled light on Dan and smelled the earth beneath her, slightly moldy, pine scented—a heavy smell. She listened, too, her ears sensitive to any out-of-place noise. Far off there was a squirrel chattering, and deeper in the forest a pine limb cracked high in a tree, giving her a moment of alarm. And yet for now, she knew, hidden on that side of the mountain, they were most likely safe. It was when they moved again, breaking cover to cross a meadow, that they would be exposed.

She kept watching the sunlight on Dan, feeling the warm dampness of his head on her thigh. This man had risked his life a few hours ago to save hers. He'd known the danger; he had to have believed his chances of survival were remote. And yet he'd come for her.

She loved him. Her heart swelled and her fingers caressed his hair and her handcuffed hands ventured along the muscled column of his neck, lightly, stroking him into a sounder sleep so that she could savor these few moments before... But she wouldn't think of that now. Somehow they'd make it to safety.

He must love her, too, Piper decided. It couldn't have been honor and duty alone that had spurred him to climb the mountain to her rescue. He *had* to love her, at least a little. She knew then that every experience in her life had been leading up to this moment, the moment she knew she was hopelessly, irrevocably, in love. If she died in the next few hours, if she lost her life in these mountains, Piper knew her last thoughts would be peaceful—finally, finally she knew what love really was.

And Dan. Maybe he didn't love her, maybe he did in his own way, but at least she'd given him everything she had to give. If only, she thought, if only *she'd* been the one to walk into that boot shop... If only she could make Dan understand what she now knew—that Diana would be happy for them. If only Dan could see his way clear to love her just a little.

He woke a few minutes later, coming to a sitting position with a start, his body instantly rigid, ready, before he realized where he was.

"It's okay," Piper whispered, smiling at him, loving him for the cop that he was at heart.

"God," Dan murmured, "I forgot where we were. I thought..."

"We're all right," she told him, "but we've rested enough."

"Yeah," he said, rising to his feet, taking her hands and helping her up.

Something passed between them then, a familiar current, and Piper felt her heart thump too heavily against her ribs. They were chest to chest, Dan looking down into her eyes, her hands still in between his. Slowly, his gaze locked on hers, his head descended and his mouth brushed hers, then moved along her cheek and down to her neck. His breath was hot on her skin; the sun beat down on her back. She sighed, pressing herself to him, and then her bound wrists were around his neck and his hands were stroking her back, her waist, her buttocks, bringing her hips to his.

Dan kissed her thoroughly, his lips twisting against hers, his tongue exploring the back of her mouth. Her senses reeled, and a deep, pulsing ache seized her belly. She pressed herself hard to him, her mouth hungrily moving against his, her fingers entwined in his hair, keeping his head to hers.

It was Dan who broke it off, coming to his senses, collecting himself, reaching behind his neck and removing her arms. "Not now," he said soberly. "We have to keep moving. Okay?" he asked, getting his breath.

"Okay," Piper said, her cheeks and neck on fire. "Okay." She, too, caught her breath. Then she asked, "Dan if not now, then . . . well, *when?* I mean . . . will we ever . . ."

For a moment he gripped her shoulders. "Don't ask," he said. "For God's sake, don't ask me that."

She had to accept that. He was right, of course; their future was unknown. And yet, he hadn't given her any hope. She knew he wanted her, but did he *love* her? *Forget it,* she told herself, turning from him, calming her heart. For now they simply had to survive. Later, if they made it, later she'd ask for answers.

They traversed the ridge they'd slept on, then made their way down to the groves of aspens and underbrush below, finding some wild berries to eat. It wasn't much, and Piper's stomach seemed to lurch and grip the food, making her nauseous for a minute, but still she ate, trying to fill the void in her belly.

Dan did the same, muttering that he'd kill for a big greasy cheeseburger and fries, and then they moved on, crossing the valley, climbing again, climbing up into the tall stands of pines, up, up to where Piper hoped she could get a fix on just where they were.

"I don't know," she said, edging out onto an outcropping. "I think that's Little Mountain over there—" she pointed with her cuffed hands "—and that could be Anderson over that way."

"Hey," Dan said, still behind her, "be careful. You're not a mountain goat, Piper."

"I'm okay," she started to tell him when suddenly there was a whirring sound near her ear, a *chunk* in a tree behind Dan and finally the echo of a rifle shot reverberating in the valley.

Piper fell backward, stumbling, scrambling to get under cover, half knocking Dan over as he tried to grab at her T-shirt and drag her down.

"Holy..." he swore, pulling Piper beneath him, edging them both back toward the trees.

Piper was gasping. Her shoulder scraped across a rock painfully. "It's them," she breathed. "My God, it was them!"

"Yeah, I know," Dan panted. "They've got the rifle with them. Scope and all."

"How...how did they find us?"

"You were sticking out like a sore thumb."

"It's not my fault!" Piper choked out as they scurried into the forest, Dan still pulling her, crouching, ducking behind a tree.

"I never said it was."

"Well, what do we do now? I mean, they're practically on top of us. Oh, God."

"They're across the valley," Dan told her. "I'm sure of it."

"How..."

"Never heard the shot until it had already slammed into the tree, that's how."

"They're pretty far, then," she said, catching her wind.

"Not far enough. Damn," he said, "I thought we'd lost them last night."

"Me, too," she whispered. "Me, too."

They moved fast after that, Piper hoping, praying she had them on the right track toward that logging road. If they could make the old, rutted road by nightfall, they could walk out to the highway by midnight. Sure. Hitch a ride. Call Dutch. No. Not Dutch. Call someone, though. They'd be okay. *If,* she thought as she and Dan ran along the ridge, *if* they made it to the road.

It was the same ridge that lay between Piper and Dan and the two men who were stalking them that almost proved the end of Dan's journey. He didn't know about scree, that loose, shalelike rock that looked innocent enough but could slide out from underfoot in an instant.

Piper was telling him to be careful when it happened—Dan lost his footing ahead of her, tried to right himself, slipped again, and a small slide started beneath him.

It could have been disastrous except that they were crossing the bottom of the rock face rather than the top. Dan slid only a few yards, then jammed his feet into the ground, halting his fall, coming to rest against a boulder. Piper scrambled down to him, her heart beating madly. He was cussing up a storm, holding his shoulder. The wound on his temple had reopened and was beginning to ooze.

"Are you all right?" she panted. "Dan..."

"I'm okay. I'll be fine," he muttered. Suddenly he sat up straight, forgetting his pain. "My gun," he said angrily. "The gun's gone." He checked and re-checked himself, then began to search the area.

Piper looked, too. They both walked up and down the rock face for nearly fifteen minutes, but there was nothing. Holding his arm, Dan finally called to her, "We gotta go. We're too exposed here. Come on, forget it."

She was standing some distance above him, crouched over, straining to see gray metal against gray rock. "We can find it," she said. "A few more minutes and we can—"

"*I said forget it!* Head on over to those trees and I'll meet you. Now, Piper."

She held back tears of frustration. "What're we going to do? We have to find that gun! Dan!"

"We can throw rocks at them, how the hell do I know!" he yelled back.

The going seemed to get rougher after that, steeper and more broken, and hotter. It *was* a hot afternoon, hot and bone-dry, without a cloud in the sky. Not even the dense stands of trees seemed to afford any relief from the heat. Piper kept wondering about that. Always, *always* in the mountains it was cool. And it was breathlessly still. The animals that had given life to the forest that morning all seemed to have burrowed into the shadows or gone so deep into the woods that no man could follow. Sweat trickled down Piper's neck and between her breasts; Dan's shirt was soaked through. They drank from a skinny mountain stream and walked on, never resting for more than a minute, rarely speaking. It was too hot to talk.

Evening came grudgingly. Piper shielded her eyes and looked at the sun moving tenaciously to the western horizon, a giant orange flame in the paling sky. She licked her dry lips and felt a quiver in her calves and thighs and began to wonder if, indeed, they'd ever make that road.

"Are you sure the road's across that valley?" Dan asked more than once.

"I think so" was all Piper could tell him. "I sure hope so."

They edged slowly along the side of what Piper was relatively sure was Twin Mountain. Through thick aspen stands and then higher, up to the pine forests they went, zigzagging across the terrain, trying to lay down a false path if, God help them, Sweet Pea and Frank got an occasional glimpse of them. Every time they had to cross a clearing they crouched on aching muscles and made a dash for it, rushing into the forest on the far side, panting, thirsty, exhausted.

"They can't be keeping up this pace," Piper said. "They just can't!"

"They can and they will," Dan told her grimly. "Don't underestimate them. There's too much at stake."

The sun dipped, moving quickly now, and the air held on to its stillness. In the valleys the shadows had gathered; only on the higher reaches did the sun's light still glow. The peaks on the western horizon became a sawtooth line, dark against an absolutely clear sky. Piper stopped, leaned against a tree and mopped at her face with her wrists, looking west. The sun sat on the slant of a mountain, bearing down on it, and the sky was a deep, glowing coral, shading away to pink and lavender. Gorgeous. Strange. In the mountains the sky was never red like this unless there were clouds for the light to reflect upon, yet there wasn't a single wisp overhead. It should have been cooling off, too, and it wasn't. Crazy weather—global warming, or something.

The sun settled lower, and the sky glowed red, orange, pink, as if a painter had washed it with a broad brush of his clearest colors.

"We have to get moving," Dan said beside her. *"Piper."*

"I know," she replied, "I know."

But it was hard. Oh, it was so hard for her brain to send the commands to her legs. And Dan. He had to be as tired as she was, but he staunchly refused to show it, walking ahead for the most part, leading the way, his back straight. How chivalrous, she thought, how male. And yet she loved him all the more for his courage. If Dan gave out, she didn't know what she'd do. An odd notion for a hard-core, independent female, Piper knew, but still, it felt good—Dan by her side, strong, capable. If she had to face death, Piper thought, who better than with the man she'd fallen in love with.

As the sun set, dusk gripped the Rocky Mountain wilderness, dulling the landscape, softening the boughs of the fir trees. Shadows grew deep, sinister in the forest, yet still the air remained too warm, too dry. There was even an odd scent to the woods, familiar yet unfamiliar to Piper. A strange, strange summer.

The bad news, Piper thought as she forced one foot in front of the other, was that it was growing dark, and the going would get rougher, as it had been last night. The good news was that now she had her bearings straight.

"Well," she announced tiredly, "we aren't lost anymore."

Dan turned. "You know where we are?"

She nodded and pointed with both hands across the valley. "See that cut just below that rock outcrop? Well, unless I'm crazy, that's an old mining road. Farrow's Road, I think."

"But you're not sure."

"I'm *pretty* sure. And if we head across that valley—" again she pointed "—we should make the logging road in a few hours."

"That's good news," Dan said.

She smiled wanly. "I was just thinking the same thing."

"You know," he said, "I'd be halfway to the Canadian border by now if it wasn't for you."

"If it wasn't for *me*," Piper quipped, "you wouldn't be on this mountainside in the first place." And then, holding his gaze in the last light, she said, "Thank you. If it wasn't for what you did last night..."

But Dan brushed her words aside. "It's my fault we're in this fix. Don't blame yourself for a minute."

She shook her head, denying his guilt. Then she reached out and put her hands on his arm and gave it a squeeze. "We'll make it," she said fervently. "We'll be okay and those creeps will get what's coming to them."

Dan covered her hands with his. "I plan on just that," he said in a low voice. "I plan on seeing them behind bars for good."

"All but Harry," Piper whispered.

"Yes, Harry," he said quietly.

The moon rose, a huge shining orb in the sky. Oddly, there was a kind of haze around it, a reddish ring of color that Piper had never seen before, but then, she decided, maybe she'd just never noticed it.

They moved on, carefully stepping over fallen logs, around rocks and protruding roots. And still Piper kept looking up at the sky, her nose twitching, as if she were unconsciously trying to recall something. Dan was looking, too, but always behind them, on the watch for Sweet Pea and Frank.

Exhaustion seeped through her muscles and bones and right into her very soul, a tiredness so deep she began to wonder if she *could* keep putting one foot in front of the other. She longed to rest, to stop for only a few minutes, but Dan seemed bent on continuing, uncomplaining, his stride only slightly less certain than it had been a dozen hours ago.

They did stop by a mountain stream, both dropping to their knees, drinking thirstily. Piper thought she must have gulped a gallon of fresh water before she finally came up for air. It tasted so sweet, so life-giving, so...

That smell, she thought, and cocked her head, her nose stinging. She gazed at the pink haze around the moon again and then sat up on her knees, her back ramrod straight. Something was not right.

"What is it?" Dan asked when his head came up from the water. "Is it..."

"No," she whispered, "it's not them." She turned and stared into the northern sky, a terrible, sick realization just dawning on her. The red sky, inflamed and feverish, the haze, the sharp odor of... "My God," she breathed. "Oh, my God." Dan followed the direction of her eyes. They both saw it then, in the darkening northern sky—the air was thick and choked with smoke. The mountains were on fire.

CHAPTER SIXTEEN

FOR HOURS PIPER HAD fought to keep panic from swamping her. She'd led them south, as close as she could figure, anyway, because civilization lay to the south. In every other direction the national forest stretched unbroken, on and on, endlessly. The air smelled of smoke, stronger and stronger now, and the heat seemed to pulsate in the air. But the fire was behind them, to the north, or what Piper *thought* was north. Unfortunately, the road she'd wanted to reach was also to the north.

She followed Dan as he moved, his shoulders slumped now, across a valley that was almost as bright as day under the full moon.

"How's your arm?" she asked.

"It's okay. A little stiff. I'll live."

She didn't make the obvious retort because she was too tired, too scared. And her feet hurt and her shoulders ached and her wrists were rubbed raw. She fought the awful writhing feeling of fear; it wouldn't do either of them any good.

On the horizon, on her right hand side, the red glow persisted, distant still, but the smell of smoke was pervasive, and when the wind changed they could hear the echo of snapping wood and the roar of the fire.

"Well," Dan said, pushing aside some branches, "if there's a fire there'll be people coming, fire fighters. That's good. Maybe helicopters and planes."

"Tomorrow, maybe, when it's light. Tonight—I don't know, I just don't know."

Dan must have heard the hopelessness in her voice, because he stopped and turned and took her by the arms when she tiredly halted. "Now, look, Piper," he said sternly, "we'll get out of this. It's only a few more miles. Hang in there, kid, we're going to make it."

She searched his face in the dim, silvery light. "Oh, Dan, that's what you said to Harry. Don't lie to me."

He pulled her close, fiercely, and held her for a moment then released her. "I'm not lying. We're going to make it. This fire will help us."

"Dan," she said, gulping, her mouth dry, her head light, "I'm sorry I got you into this. It's all my fault. You told me to leave and I came back and now you're in this awful fix and..."

"Shh," he said, "this isn't the time to compare who's at fault. You wouldn't be here if it wasn't for me in the first place. Now we walk, we go on. Later we trade blame." He tilted her dirt-smudged face up. "Okay?"

She tried to smile. He was right. Now they had to concentrate on getting to safety. "Okay," she said. "Sorry I'm being such a wimp."

"Lady," he said, his face close to hers, so close she thought he might kiss her, "you could work the South Philly district."

"And what does that mean?"

"That you're doing all right."

She wanted to smile. She wanted him to pull her against his chest and hold her forever. Maybe they should just stop. Stop right here and hold each other. Let those men behind them come. Let the fire come. Or maybe they'd fall asleep in each other's arms and in the morning it would be all right.

Somehow, though, they stumbled on, up hills, up and up, over boulders, around trees, her legs aching with tiredness, then down, down into another valley, and her thigh muscles screamed with overuse.

She tried to keep the faint breeze on her left side— that would mean it was blowing from the east, into the fire, holding the flames at bay. But there was hardly any wind at all, and it shifted a lot, confusing her. Besides, the prevailing wind pattern in the Rockies was always westerly, and if that pattern held true then the fire would travel and leap toward them.

She had to keep thinking, *One foot at a time, don't panic, keep going.* It was the hardest thing she'd ever done. But if she had to do it, she was glad Dan was with her. If he hadn't been there, Piper knew she'd have been a goner: panicked, alone, terrified.

"How come you're not ever afraid of anything?" she finally asked, panting, stepping over a fallen log.

"I'm scared," Dan said matter-of-factly.

"You are not. You sound perfectly calm," she retorted.

"Lots of practice," he replied.

A little while later she said, "Dan, I want you to know that I'm glad you're here with me."

"Thanks, kid. I'm glad I'm here with you, too."

"Liar."

He stopped and his eyes bored into hers, dark in the moonlight, and his face was smudged with dirt and dried sweat and a black growth of beard. He said nothing, and she wondered what he was really thinking or, if they got out of this mess somehow, if he'd ever want to see her again. But she wouldn't ask. The future seemed aeons away. Maybe there was no future.

On they trudged through the woods, the heat growing, the smoke wafting on the hot air, and once in a while they could see sparks or a particularly black billow of smoke off to the right, behind the shoulder of the mountain they were skirting.

Piper tripped and fell, unable to save her balance because her hands were cuffed together. She sat on the ground, feeling her palms scraped, her knees bruised. She hung her head and closed her eyes, pressing tears back.

Dan was beside her in a moment. "You all right?" he asked, kneeling.

"Damn these handcuffs!" she burst out. "I can't stand them another second!"

"I know," he said. "God, I wish I could do something. Piper, come on, get up. Hang in there. It won't be much longer. We'll get to a road soon."

And she had to believe him. She couldn't sit there and wait for Frank and Sweet Pea or the fire. She had to go on. She *would* go on. She was young and strong and so was Dan and she loved him and they were going to get through this together.

"Okay," she said, letting him help her up. "Damn it, let's get going. What're you waiting for?"

It seemed as if the night had no end. Time unrolled slowly, agonizingly. In a clearing, with the moonlight on them, Dan read his watch. "Eleven thirty-five," he said.

"Is that all? Are you sure?" she said. "I thought it must be three in the morning."

"Yeah, I know."

"Frank and Sweet Pea must have given up," she said. "They must have. In this heat, with the fire? They'd be crazy to follow us."

"Maybe," he allowed.

"You think they're still behind us? They're probably lost if they're still trying to follow us, don't you think?"

"Maybe."

"You're overestimating them," she said, shaking her head.

"Maybe," he said for the third time.

They climbed down a rocky face into a valley, where they found a stream. They both knelt and drank, cupping their hands, sucking in the cool, mud-flavored water. Nothing had ever tasted so wonderful. Piper drank and drank, filling her belly, feeling the cool liquid soothe her tongue and throat. She sank back on her heels with a sigh and let her hands rest on her lap.

"Oh, Lord, but that's good," she breathed.

"Fill 'er up," Dan said, wetting his face. Then he took his shirt off and splashed water on his torso, and rivulets of it cascaded, molten silver, down his chest.

Piper would have taken her T-shirt off and done the same, but she couldn't get it over the handcuffs, so she just splashed her face and neck and then drank some more until she felt ready to burst.

Then they both rose and went on, following the streambed for a time, veering off finally when it changed direction.

The moon was high overhead now, the air so thick that it appeared fuzzy and reddish. Smoke.

They climbed again, going more slowly, plodding, breathing hard, and the acrid air stung their throats.

At the top, where they should have been able to see into the distance, to the pine-covered, undulating mountains, Piper drew in a sharp breath.

"Look," she whispered, frozen in place.

"Son of a . . ." Dan swore.

Before them, across the valley, the forest burned. The smoke came toward them, carried on a molten-hot breeze, making them cough, tearing their eyes. The black trees were in tatters, torn by red-orange tongues of flame. The noise came to their ears, a far-off roar, so powerful it was unbelievable, a wild beast's roar of conquest and destruction. Sparks exploded in streamers, and the sky was a dull, angry red.

Piper stood there, her heart a lump of stone, her breath catching in her throat, unable to think or move. The fire's grandeur, its dangerous, unholy beauty, smote her first, then her mind snapped back to the present. "My God," she said, "it's so close! How did it get so close?" But the hot air fanning her face and rustling the leaves around her answered her question.

"Okay, we're going to have to move fast," Dan was saying, taking her arm. Then he coughed, choked by smoke, doubled over, and when he straightened up he swore. "Hit the road, kid."

Piper turned to him and started to say something—she'd never be able to recall what it was—when a sound distracted her, a sharp whistling, a thud. Then Dan was yelling something and throwing her to the ground, himself on top of her, and Piper's breath was slammed out of her and the rocks pressed into her chest and stomach and legs. It took her a second to figure out what had happened.

"They're still there," Dan said bitterly. "They're still behind us!"

"They shot at us again?" she asked stupidly.

"You okay?" He rolled aside and felt for her shoulders, her face.

"Yes," Piper said, "I guess so."

Dan put his arms around her for a moment then and held her, and Piper could smell the sweat on him, mingled with smoke and dirt, and she breathed it in, letting herself relax for one sweet, quick moment, letting herself feel the strength and hardness of this man.

"We've got to go. Keep low, no more standing on high spots," Dan said quietly. "We stand out too much against the fire."

Oh, God, she had to get up, strain her weary, aching body, lurch to her feet and start moving again. But Dan wouldn't let her walk. No, this time there was more urgency. The fire was like a locomotive roaring toward them, and they had to run to keep ahead of it.

"We have to get to the road," Piper said, gasping, panting, choking. "It'll act as a firebreak, or maybe there'll be some fire fighters there. Oh, God, there will be, there has to be! Dan, what do we do if there isn't anybody?"

"Never mind that. Just keep going," he said, his voice rough with tension. "I wish to hell we knew where it was."

Piper thought, tried to picture a map in her head, tried to figure how far they'd walked since sunset. "I...I think it has to be close now," she said. She stubbed her toe on a rock and almost fell, but Dan was there, grabbing her arm. Above them black smoke drifted across the bloody face of the moon. Piper blinked, her eyes burning. *Got to keep going,* she commanded herself. If Dan could make it, so could she.

They tried to run, but branches grabbed at them, and exposed roots yanked them off their feet. Each time it got harder to get up, until finally Piper fell and lay on the ground, coughing, utterly spent.

"Come on," Dan said.

"I can't. Go on . . . I just can't," she whispered.

"I won't go without you, Piper," he said roughly.

"Go!" she cried, pounding the ground with her fist, dragging the other hand with it. "Get out of here! Leave me alone, save yourself!"

He squatted down beside her, took a handful of her matted hair and pulled her head back painfully. "Look, Piper, maybe you want to give up, but I won't leave you, so you're responsible for me, too. Now decide what you want to do," he said coldly.

"No, no," she sobbed. "Get away from here!"

"Not without you," he repeated, letting go of her hair so that her head fell forward.

He was forcing her to go on. *It isn't fair,* she thought. *It's too hard. He shouldn't make me.*

But she got to her hands and knees, and Dan helped her, and then she was standing, rocking on her feet, tears streaming from her burning eyes, her nose running, her chest rising and falling in great, sobbing breaths.

"Don't pull that again," he said, and he shook her shoulders hard, so hard she felt a spurt of anger kindle in her.

They moved on, half running, mostly tripping, righting themselves, surging relentlessly forward.

The fire beast was louder, the air hotter and thicker by the minute. Sparks and ashes flew all over, drifting, settling, burning holes in their clothes, singeing their skin, graying their hair. They kept running, stumbling, Dan keeping a tight grip on her arm, her hands held awkwardly in front of her.

She became aware of movement and noise in the forest around them. For a split second she thought it was Frank and Sweet Pea, but then she realized it was all around them, a rustling in the undergrowth, sometimes a panicked crashing, the direction of which she couldn't judge.

"Animals," she breathed. "The animals are running from the fire."

A leaping shadow flashed by in front of them, a deer, and squirrels chattered, scampering. It was a frightening phenomenon, unnatural, because the animals weren't the least bit afraid of them. Fire now ruled their world and man meant nothing, just another puny beast fleeing destruction.

On their right was the huge black bulge of a mountain, its forests aflame. Anderson Mountain, Piper thought, hoped, prayed. They had altered their direction a bit, moving more to the east to get away from the fire, and she knew the road ran north and south here, so they had to hit it. *They had to!*

Which was she more afraid of? Frank and Sweet Pea or the fire? She didn't know. Both were merciless, but maybe they'd have a better chance with the fire. There were stories of forest fires leaping areas, leaving them untouched, so that there would be an oasis alive with small animals who'd sought sanctuary there. But how could you tell where those places would be? You couldn't.

A cave? A cave... Could you live in a cave until the fire passed by? Or would the oxygen be sucked out of the cave, suffocating you? That is, if there was a cave or rockfall or waterfall to hide in around here. But there wasn't.

On they went, slower now, weaker, falling more often, their hearts and lungs near to bursting. Piper kept her mind focused on making her body move, but she wanted to scream and sob and throw herself down and let death come and take her, just to have it over with. The noise grew, the thunder crashing on their eardrums, the heat and choking smoke blinding them. It was coming—closer and closer, pursuing them, a personal hunt, an insane vendetta.

"We're going to have to find someplace," Dan gasped. "Someplace to hide."

"Where?" she choked out. "There's no place, nothing!"

"How far to the road?" Dan asked, shouting close to her ear over the roar.

She shook her head. "Soon. I think soon. I'm not sure."

"Are there any culverts under the road, a drainage ditch, something like that?"

She shook her head again. They stumbled past a stand of trees and around brambles and chokeberry bushes. The sky was lit up. It was almost like day, an unnatural, angry day, and the moon was crimson.

There was a hillside and a rock slide ahead of them, a big pile of boulders and a dark bare streak above it. How odd, a bare spot…a familiar sort of bare spot…

"Mine tailings," Piper mouthed and stopped short.

"What?"

"Mines," she said. "*Mines*. There are mines around here! Gold mines, shafts, holes in the ground!"

"Mines," he repeated.

"Yes! If we could fine one." Her heart leaped in hope. "Do you think...?"

"Where? Where are they?"

"God, I don't know. But they're all along the road, so we must be close. That's one right there." She pointed. "But it's collapsed in, filled in."

"There've got to be others," Dan said.

"Yes, there have to be!"

They staggered on, searching the hillside, the lower reaches of Anderson Mountain. If it had been day... Piper was sure this area was familiar to her, but now, with the smoke and the noise and the red inferno, she couldn't recall. There were more dark streaks on the hillside, even some tumbled shoring timber, but no black openings.

Oh, she'd been up here with Diana, riding, jeeping. They'd come as kids to neck and drink beer. Some girls had even bragged about making love in the old abandoned mines. Where? *Where were they?*

A spark landed on a nearby bush and the whole thing burst into flame, a leaping candelabra. Piper gave a startled cry, shrinking away. Dear God, they had to find a place soon!

Piper wasn't sure when she finally saw it—was it a figment of her fevered imagination or was it real? "There!" she cried, pointing.

Dan looked. "Yes," he said, "let's go."

They scrambled up the hillside, sliding backward on the loose gravel, the greasy, gray mine tailings. But it was up there, a round dark hole.

Let it be deep enough, Piper prayed. They wouldn't have time to find another one; the fire was bearing down on them with its locomotive roar, and the air was full of ash. She didn't even feel the burnt spots on her skin, didn't feel the exhaustion and pain, her wrists bruised and rubbed raw from the handcuffs. She fought, gasping, her breath sobbing in her throat, clawing her way up the hill.

A whistling sound, a whine and *chunk*—particles of stone exploded into the air near Piper's hands. Her mind was slow to register it, but Dan was yelling something at her. She threw herself flat on the slope, falling awkwardly on her tethered hands, her breath knocked out of her lungs.

"Dan?" she cried, panicked, "Dan, are you all right?"

"Yes" came his hard voice.

"They're here!"

"Okay, we're almost there, take it easy. Can you crawl?"

"Yes, I'll try." Alarm filled her with hot spurts of adrenaline. She crawled, as she'd seen soldiers do in training, on her elbows, squirming along, hearing the thunder of the fire behind them, closer and closer, expecting a high-powered bullet to slam into her back at any second.

Then she was at the entrance, the black hole, and she rose, stumbling over debris and old timbers, and went into the mine shaft, into the shocking pitch blackness, the eerily cold dampness. Dan was behind her, his hand on her back, following as the shaft closed in around them, blotting out all sound and heat and light. Deeper, deeper they went.

Piper halted for a moment, her chest heaving. "Dan, I can't see," she whispered.

"I'll go first. At least I can hold a hand out" came his voice, echoing in the stone that buried them.

"How far, how far do we have to go?" she gasped.

"As far as we can," he said grimly.

"What if they follow us in here?" she asked. "What if they have a flashlight?"

"Hey, kid, you sure do worry. They could be half a mile away with that rifle. They couldn't have seen where we went," Dan said, but she knew he was lying, trying to relieve her anxiety. If they could see to shoot, then they could have seen the mine opening. They *must* have seen it!

Dan led her, blind, holding a hand out ahead of him, feeling with his feet. They went on for a hundred yards, almost two hundred, slowly. The air was cold and clammy in the mine, stale. Silence hung around them like a shroud except for water dripping somewhere, dripping monotonously. And occasionally there would be the rustle and squeak of a small animal scurrying away.

Piper kept listening behind them for sounds of pursuit, but there was nothing, only the same drip, drip, drip and the muted echo of their own footsteps.

Dan grunted and stopped. "There's some kind of wall here, a cave-in or something. This is it, I guess."

"Are we far enough?"

"Hope so. There should be enough air in here to last us till the fire goes past."

Piper sank onto the hard, damp floor of the mine. Dan sat beside her. They were enclosed together in utter darkness, held in the bowels of the earth. Dan put his arm around her shoulders and his mouth by her ear. "It'll be fine here," he said reassuringly.

She rested her back against the cold rock wall and sighed deeply. "I couldn't have gone another step."

"You did well," Dan said. "You'll be safe now."

"Oh, Dan, how did we ever end up in this awful, awful mess?"

"Funny how things happen" was all he said. "Now, look, why don't you try to get some sleep, Piper? Here, put this on."

She felt him hand her his jacket that he'd had tied around his waist. "Aren't you cold?" she asked.

"I'm fine."

She could only pull it around her shoulders because of the handcuffs, but it felt good. She leaned back and closed her eyes, then she opened them again to pitch blackness. "Dan? Dan, aren't you going to try to get some rest?"

She sensed him near her, then his hand felt for her face and he turned her head toward his. "Dan?" she asked again, uneasy.

"Look, Piper," he said, "I've got to go back."

"What?"

"I've got to go back to the entrance and try to find Frank and Sweet Pea before they find us."

She was stunned, sickened. "No," she said in a strangled voice. "Dan, no, don't be crazy."

"I have to," he said tiredly.

"They'll kill you."

Silence met her words, then she could hear Dan move. "Please, Dan, they'll kill you—or the fire will—and I'll be alone, and they'll kill me, too."

"No, kid, they won't. I'll see to that. I'll take care of it."

"No!" she cried. "They have guns!"

"You stay here. You'll be safer," he said.

"Dan, don't go," she cried brokenly.

But she could hear him move away from her, and she sat there, hugging her knees, disbelieving, tears running down her dirty, burned cheeks, stinging. *No,* her mind cried in a futile monotony, *no, no, you can't do this!*

But he was doing it. His footsteps, slow, labored, were retreating from her. To do what? And then in a flash of insight Piper knew what she had to do. She couldn't, wouldn't, stay there alone. If Dan faced death she would face it with him, because she didn't want to live without him.

"Wait," she said to the silence and blackness, then louder, "Dan, wait!" She pushed herself up and, holding her cuffed hands in front of her, she stumbled after him, her heart pounding like a drum, her limbs heavy, trembling with effort, her nose running from her tears.

Back along the mine shaft, step by halting step. Where was he? Was he gone already, shot or burned to death? "Dan," she whispered to herself, "please, Dan. I love you."

Then she saw it, blinked, squinted. Light. A reddish flickering ahead of her. The entrance was there, and the fire had reached their hillside. Oh, Dan! Oh, my God, was he out in that? She tried to run, a lurching stagger. "Dan!" she cried, but the noise of the fire was getting louder, the air hot and smoky again. "Dan!" she screamed, stumbling, coming up against something solid.

"Piper, for God's sake!" Dan said. "I told you—"

"I couldn't wait, I couldn't."

He cursed under his breath. "Stay here, damn it. I'm going to try to get out there."

"The fire's here. You can't!"

But he plunged forward, and now Piper could make out his form in the glare from the fire. She took a step

toward the entrance, another. A roaring filled her ears
and a hot, sucking wind tore at her. And Dan was
ahead of her, fighting it. Even if the flames didn't
touch him, there'd be no air to breathe!

Smoke billowed, obscuring Dan, but when it cleared
she could see him, doubling over, coughing. Flames
licked at the entrance, reaching a tongue out to the pile
of discarded shoring timbers, igniting them in an explosion.

"Dan!" she screamed as he flung a hand up to his
face and stumbled backward, the flames reaching out
for him. And Piper ran and grabbed his arm and
dragged him back, beating desperately with her bare
hands at the small flames in his hair and on his back.

She held him then, cupped his face in her manacled
hands and looked straight into his eyes. "Dan, you
can't," she said.

He slumped, his face haggard. "They're out there,"
he said, anguished, the fire flickering wildly on him.

"I know."

"They'll be killed...."

"But we'll be alive," she said. "There's nothing
more you can do."

He turned his head toward the entrance, and Piper
thought she saw the fire glint off moisture in his eyes.
Her heart went out to him, only guessing at the pain
he must be suffering.

"Dan," she said, "let's go."

He turned and took a step, then stopped and twisted
his head to look toward the entrance one last time.

"Dan," she pleaded, and he straightened his
shoulders and took her arm and led her back into the
mine shaft, to safety, and all the way he never spoke a
word.

They huddled together, their backs to the cave-in, Dan's jacket draped around both of them. Piper reached up her hands to stroke his bristly face, but he seemed to stiffen at her touch. She said nothing, for there was nothing to say, his pain so sharp that her words could never alleviate it. She only wanted him to know that she was there for him.

Finally they slept, completely worn out, uncomfortable, shivering in their sleep. Piper dreamed in odd snatches—strange, frightening dreams that she didn't remember when she woke.

And then, when she did stir and open her eyes, groaning at the thousand small agonies in her body, she panicked, because it was pitch-black and she couldn't see.

"Shh, it's okay," Dan said next to her, and she remembered, shuddering, astonished that she was still alive, feeling absolutely drained. Cold and shaky, weak, with a raging thirst.

"Is it over?" she asked, her voice cracking.

"I don't know."

"How long did we sleep?"

She felt him shrug beside her. "Can't tell. A few hours, maybe. How are you feeling?"

"Great," she muttered.

"I thought we should take a look."

"Yes. Dan?" She hesitated, considering her words. "You couldn't have done anything."

"Sure," he replied. "Maybe they got away."

"Yes, maybe they're fine," she agreed.

But Frank and Sweet Pea weren't fine. Piper and Dan came across their bodies at the base of the hillside, strangely enough not charred, but lying together unharmed, their guns and knapsacks intact, only a few scorch marks on them.

"Smoke inhalation," Dan said, staring expressionlessly down at them.

Piper averted her gaze. "I'm sorry, Dan," she said.

He didn't reply, only stood there, his head slightly bowed, a lonely figure in the charred wasteland, ash everywhere, the trees grim, black, denuded spears pointing up to the smoke-heavy morning sky.

The ground was still hot, the stench overpowering. And Dan stood there, saying goodbye to his brothers.

Piper looked around, and now she was sure where she was. Yes, there was the valley leading down toward the headwaters of the Elk River. She knew where to go now, and even if it took a long time at a slow pace, they'd make it to the road. Yet the knowledge that they were out of danger did not lighten her heart. She felt shell-shocked, divorced from reality, as if her mind had retreated, unable to handle all the input.

Then Dan did a strange thing. He knelt in the black ash next to the bodies and felt around in their pockets. Piper shuddered and looked away.

He held it up at last, a grim smile cracking his burnt, black, filthy face. The key to her handcuffs. He rose and came over to her. She held her hands out, and in a second it was done. She was free. She rubbed her wrists and swung her arms. God, that felt good! "Thanks," she said.

"Hey, kid, you're welcome," Dan replied, then he knelt again and rummaged around in a knapsack. He held up a canteen. "Water," he said.

They each drank half, carefully alternating swallows. It wasn't enough, but it helped.

"So, do we just...leave them here?" Piper asked.

"Not much else I can do. We'll report them.
And—" Dan twisted his mouth and looked away
"—their families will want to claim the bodies."

"Yes, sure."

"You know where you are now?"

She nodded and pointed.

"Okay, let's go," Dan said wearily.

They hadn't walked a mile down the dirt road before a fire-fighting crew from Hahn's Peak found
them. The crew was in a truck, dressed in bright yellow fireproof gear, armed with picks and shovels and
water tanks, and it headed toward them raising a
rooster tail of ash behind them. Dan and Piper halted
and waited. The truck driver saw them, slammed on
the brakes and leaned out the window. "Lord in
heaven!" he yelled. "What on God's earth are you
two doing out here?"

They were given water and food and driven back to
Hahn's Peak, where the fire-fighting effort was head-
quartered. It seemed the fire was under control now,
burning to the east, although if the weather didn't
change it could break out again.

Piper was in a kind of daze, clinging to Dan's hand.
They got out of the truck and she almost collapsed,
her legs going rubbery. Dan held her up, an arm
around her. "You okay?" he asked.

"I'll be fine," she breathed.

And then there was Dutch, his face oily and
smudged with black, in fire-fighting gear. He looked
at Piper, then at Dan, then back at Piper. "My God,"
he whispered, "I thought you were dead."

"Pretty close," Dan said.

"We found your Cherokee," Dutch said, "and the
Jeep. And a body near that cabin..."

"There're two more up there," Dan said calmly.

"By the mines on Anderson Mountain," Piper added.

"The fire?" Dutch asked.

"Yes."

"Good God!" He ran a dirty hand over his face, and Piper could see that it shook. "Those men, the ones you said were here to..."

"Yes," Piper replied coldly.

Dan looked at her questioningly.

"I went to Dutch," she explained, "but he wouldn't come."

"Christ, I'm sorry," Dutch said, his face drawn. "I knew when I saw the cars and the body..."

"Harry," Dan said slowly. "His name was Harry Tegmeier."

Dutch just stared at him.

"He was my friend," Dan said.

"Look, I..." Dutch began, but fell silent, and Piper studied his face. There was none of the usual bravado left in Dutch. "I'm sorry," he finally said, and his eyes went from Dan to Piper and back. "I'm so sorry."

"We almost died up there," Piper said.

"I—I know," Dutch admitted, staring at the ground. "Piper, I..."

"You what," she started to say, but Dan took her arm and gave it a squeeze. He was right. There was no more to be said.

It was Dutch who finally led them to the county vehicle and told the driver to take them to the hospital.

They were silent all the way, Dan's arm touching hers as they sat in the back of the car, watching the smoke that tinged the horizon a sickly gray. And in that silence they sat there together, and they mourned.

CHAPTER SEVENTEEN

PIPER RAISED HER HAND to knock on the door of Dan's hospital room. She hesitated, frowning, and wondered why it was so difficult to face him. Oh, she'd seen him on and off yesterday while the staff had put them both through a battery of tests—chest X rays, blood workups, lung diagnostics—but there had been so many people around, and it seemed as if she and Dan had been mere acquaintances. The events of the past few days had receded into a distant and unreal past. It was almost as if none of it had happened.

Except for the way Piper felt, the soreness and exhaustion, the singed eyebrows and hair, the scrapes and abrasions and bruised wrists and blistered burns all over her body.

She sighed and knocked finally, feeling foolish just standing there in the hall.

"Come in," she heard him say.

She pushed open the door and put a smile on her lips, an unsure smile that trembled at the corners. "Hi," she said, just standing there, twisting the tie on the generic hospital robe in her fingers. "How are you doing?"

He sat on the edge of the bed, his torso bare, wearing a pair of green hospital surgical pants. Burns dotted his arms and face, and his hair, too, was singed. He looked at her and grimaced, moving his heavy shoul-

ders in that offhand shrug of his that so often took the
place of words.

"Did they finish all those tests?" she asked.

"Yeah. Ridiculous."

"So you're okay?"

"Sure. Are you?"

"Uh-huh." She tried to smile. "Did you sleep last
night?"

"Enough."

"I didn't, not much. I hate hospitals, never could
sleep in one. I hope they let me go home soon," she
babbled. "Uh, did you call the ranch? Is everything
okay there?"

"I called Rick. He and Luis have everything under
control."

Piper wanted to ask if she was coming back to work
on the ranch. She wanted to ask if she was still fired,
if he still wanted to sell the place, if he hated her or
loved her or was glad to be rid of her now that they
were safe. But she couldn't. The words were stuck in
her throat, held there by fear. For once, Piper Hilyard was terrified to face reality.

Dan stood, his feet bare, his chest bare. He stretched
a little, as if his muscles were sore. Piper looked away,
feeling a tightness in her chest. "I, uh, actually...
Could I sit down?" she asked.

He looked at her for a moment too long, and she
could read nothing in his expression. He gestured to a
chair then, and she sat gratefully, jiggling a bare foot.
"I had the radio on in my room this morning," she
said, "but the news was real sketchy about everything. They talked about Joey Washington and Frank
and Sweet Pea, but half of it sounded all wrong."

"That's typical."

"Well, what really is going on now?"

"Internal Affairs in Philadelphia is handling the whole thing."

"You talked with them?"

He nodded. "For over an hour yesterday. Of course, there's no one left alive to indict."

"But they'll set the record straight?"

"Oh, yeah, that's for sure."

"And Diana? Did you tell them about that?"

"Yes," he said slowly, "I told them. They checked the airlines' reservations two years ago and called me back. It was Sweet Pea. He did it alone. Flew out here and came after me."

"And got Diana instead," Piper said very quietly.

"So," Dan said, "it's over."

Piper shook her head. "What about Harry?"

Dan crossed to the window and stood with his back to her. "I told them that Harry saved our lives, that he was killed doing it."

"It's true."

"Yeah, it's true, all right."

"Will his family get his pension?" she asked.

"I hope so. I'll do everything I can to see to it that they do. Harry was a good cop, a good friend. His family deserves what he worked for all those years."

"Do you think—I mean, did Harry know about..."

"Diana?" Dan turned and folded his arms across his naked chest. "I doubt it. Not until afterward, and then it was too late. Then he was in too deep."

"Poor Harry," Piper said. "And Captain Mac-Murray, did he know? What's going to happen to him?"

"There'll be an investigation, and my guess is that he'll be nailed. He covered up the Joey Washington thing deliberately. He'll lose his job, or if IA doesn't think they can make the charges stick, they'll shunt him off to some desk job where he'll shuffle papers till he retires. MacMurray is history."

"So," Piper said, "it really is over."

"Yeah." Dan moved restlessly, prowling the room on bare feet. He was a stranger to Piper, and she could hardly remember making love to him, holding him, running through the mountains with him. She couldn't conjure up those emotions, those sensations. It was as if everything had gone up in flames with the forest, and nothing was left but cold, dead ash.

"Dutch Radowsky came to see me last night," Dan said then.

"Me, too," Piper said. "I've never seen him so humble."

"He's resigning as sheriff."

She nodded. "He told me. Going to Denver, he said. He's going to go to the police academy and try to get a job on the force there. I guess he learned a hard lesson. Poor Dutch."

Dan sat on the edge of the bed again and ran a hand through the burnt stubble of his hair. "That all he tell you?" he asked.

"That's enough, isn't it? Dutch apologizing. That's plenty."

"He didn't say anything about who he was recommending to take over for him?"

She cocked her head. "No, he just said he was leaving."

"Um."

"Dan?"

He sat, head lowered between his shoulders, elbows on his knees, hands clasped. When his voice came it was so quiet Piper almost couldn't hear him. "What?" she had to ask.

Dan raised his head slightly and regarded her somberly. "Me," he repeated. "He recommended me for sheriff."

"You." Piper's mind whirled for a moment, but then her thoughts slowed, settled into place, and she had to smile a little. "Well, sure, why not?" she asked. "You're going to take it, aren't you?"

"I don't know."

"Ha! Sure you are. You wouldn't say no if you had to pay *them* to be sheriff," she said.

"Piper, I don't know."

"Okay, right, you don't know," she said. "Give yourself some time to decide. Five minutes or so."

"I think I'm going back to Philadelphia," he said then.

Shock held Piper silent. Dan was leaving, moving back East. It was his home, after all, and now that everything was cleared up, he could go back. Why not? Oh, God . . .

"The ranch?" she finally asked. "Diana's ranch?"

He moved restively and sat up straight. "I can't run it, you know that. It's still for sale."

"So you're moving back East and selling the ranch and that's that."

"I don't know," he said tiredly.

And me? she wanted to ask. *What about me?* But she didn't. She wouldn't beg or cling. Dan was through with Steamboat Springs, through with the ranch, through with her. He wanted out. Maybe she shouldn't blame him.

"Okay," Piper said, getting up, giving her ugly robe a yank to straighten it, but then she couldn't think of anything else to say. Her face was stiff and it was hard to talk. "Well, fine, so you'll be out of here pretty soon," she managed to say, and when he didn't answer she turned to go, feeling brittle, brimming with sick disappointment. "Well, I guess I feel a little tired, so I think I'll try to get a nap. See you, Dan."

"Yeah, sure" was all he said.

BETTY AND JOHN HILYARD came to pick Piper up early the following morning. They'd flown home from Santa Fe the day before and retrieved their red Cherokee from the county impound lot. They'd spoken to Piper by phone before they'd left Glen's house, but they were still somewhat stunned by the reporters and TV cameras and media vans outside the hospital.

"Holy cow," John said, "this is a three-ring circus!"

"You and Dan are heroes," Betty said. "Well, hero and heroine."

"Terrific," Piper muttered.

"Cheer up, honey. Your hair will be fine in a week or so. All you have to do is get those frizzled ends trimmed off," Betty said.

"Has the doctor checked you out?" John asked. "You've got a clean bill of health?"

"He's coming by in a few minutes, Dad. Then I can go."

"You're sure you're okay? You had a chest X ray and all? Smoke inhalation can have very bad side effects," her father persisted. "Pneumonia, all sorts of things."

Dr. Schiller listened to Piper's chest once more, gave her some prescriptions for her burns and signed her out. "Well, young lady, I wouldn't suggest doing this sort of thing too often," he said.

"I'll try to remember that," Piper said. "How's Dan Bourne this morning? Is he checking out, too? I thought maybe we could..."

"Oh, Mr. Bourne's already gone," Dr. Schiller said. "Signed himself out. He really should have waited to get some prescriptions."

Gone. He's already gone. Had he left for Philadelphia already?

"Honey?" her mother was saying. "Here, I brought you some nice comfortable, loose clothes, so they won't rub your burns. You want to go now, Piper? Piper?"

"Oh, sure, Mom," Piper said, but her mind was still numb and full of pain. Dan was gone. He hadn't even stopped by to tell her or to say goodbye. He'd just left, all alone, not caring about her, not thinking about her. He'd just walked out.

At home the phone rang incessantly—friends, relatives, reporters. But not Dan. Betty and John fielded the calls, telling everyone Piper was still too ill from her ordeal to talk. But the truth was that she was only too weary emotionally.

Two days after she'd returned home her dad came up to her room to tell her that he'd heard from Bob at the gas station that Dan Bourne was still at the ranch. "So I guess he didn't go back East yet," John said.

A quick, sweet gladness stabbed Piper for a moment, then the familiar heaviness settled back onto her. He hadn't left yet, but he hadn't phoned or asked about her or contacted her in any way. It was almost worse, because he was so close, and he'd had so many opportunities, days' worth of opportunities when he could have come by or called or... "That's nice, Dad," she said.

Her father looked at her strangely. "Well, honey, I thought you'd like to know."

"Uh-huh, thanks," she said.

It was her mother who offered the solution. She marched over to Piper's room the following afternoon and plumped herself into a chair. "Your Jeep's in the drive," she said, "in case you didn't notice. That man, Luis, I think it is, dropped it by."

"So?" Piper said, staring out the window.

"So, I want you to get in your car and drive out to the ranch."

"What for?"

"What for? To talk to Dan, that's what. You're too tough a kid to sit here moping. It's making you sick, not to mention your poor old parents."

"It isn't...Dan," she lied, ashamed.

"Oh, it isn't Dan. I see," her mother said. "Right. Now do as I say and pull yourself together. You need him. And I imagine he needs you."

"He doesn't—"

"Yes, he does. I may be old and incredibly stupid about these things, but trust me on this. The man needs you."

An hour later Piper was in her Jeep driving up the Elk River Road, her hands gripping the steering wheel, her heart knocking against her ribs, her courage ebbing and flowing with each turn of the vehicle's wheels. But she knew this was something that had to be done, this final confrontation, something she had to get off her chest. Her mom had been partly right, anyway.

After everything she and Dan had been through together... You couldn't survive that with a person and remain unchanged. All these months, Piper realized, she'd been fighting her attraction to Dan—because of guilt and Diana's memory all mixed up in her mind—but now it was out in the open. They'd made love, they'd been threatened, hounded, shot at and burned. They'd faced death together. Now she realized exactly how she felt. It was as if everything superficial had gone up in flames with the wildfire.

She needed to tell him that. No matter how *he* felt, Piper needed to tell him. She took a deep breath and turned into the driveway under the crossbar. And then, as she drove toward the house, she began for the first time in days to feel her temper starting to percolate. *The coward,* she thought abruptly, *turning tail and running like that! Not even facing up to me! How dare he?*

She pulled up in her usual place and didn't wait for the dust to settle, but got out of her car and marched toward the porch steps.

He must have seen her, because he came to the door just as she stamped up the steps and pushed it open. He just stood there, his expression dispassionate, a beer can in his hand.

"Dan," she declared, "you didn't even—"

"Hi, kid," he said, interrupting her, "I see your temper's back."

Her anger deflated a little, but she kept on. "Dan, you didn't...even..."

"I know."

She met his gaze, but there was nothing she could read in his blue eyes, no love, no hate, nothing. It was as if a dam burst inside her suddenly, and all her energy flowed out onto the ground. He just didn't care about her at all. How was she going to tell him how much she loved him, how much he'd hurt her? She looked at him and felt only pain, her anger draining away along with her strength.

"Oh, Dan," she finally said, "you could have called me. Why, *why* didn't you?"

"I..." he said, then fell silent, staring straight ahead, that muscle working in his square jaw. "Look, how about I get you a beer or soda or something?"

"Sure," she said, letting her breath whistle out between her teeth. "Sure, a Coke, whatever."

She sat on the porch steps, rested her chin on her fist and waited. Her soul was so sick and empty that she wanted to cry. How did people survive this pain?

He came back a minute later and popped open a can for her, then sat down himself, staring into the great beyond, drinking his beer. She sipped on the Coke and waited and waited for him to break the dreadful silence. The air seemed to grow heavier, and Piper felt it stick in her throat. She thought of leaving. But no, she wasn't going to walk away until she heard from Dan's own lips that he didn't give a hoot about her. She couldn't leave and be wondering for the rest of her life.

"Look," she said after a long time, "why did you just walk out on me in the hospital? And I thought you were going back East. Are you?"

His discomfort filled the air. She could feel it radiating from him.

"*Dan,*" she persisted.

"Look, I..." But his voice faltered.

"You what?"

"I hate this," he said.

"Hate what? Talking? I know that," she said, "but for God's sake, please try."

He compressed his lips, annoyed, embarrassed, completely out of his element. Her heart hammered sickly, but still she had to hear him say aloud that he didn't care.

"All right," he finally managed to say. "I thought about telling you I was checking myself out of the hospital. I really did. But I figured... well..."

"What?"

"I figured you needed some space," he replied very quietly.

"Space."

"Yeah." Suddenly he crushed the metal can and got to his feet. "You want another drink?"

"No."

"Well, I do." He disappeared inside again, then reappeared, a fresh beer in hand, the can sweating moisture. He sat back down on the steps, not looking at her, just staring out across the fields.

"Space, you said," she prompted.

"Yeah, well," he said, "what I meant was I took too much for granted that night."

"That night?"

"Ah—" he cleared his throat "—you know, the night we were, ah, here together."

"Oh," she said, then added, "What, exactly, did you take for granted?" Her heartbeat had begun a heavier pace.

"Uh... you... us."

"You mean a relationship between us," she said carefully.

"I guess."

"And you wish there wasn't one—a relationship, that is."

He looked away.

"Dan," Piper said very slowly, trying to say it the right way, scared, risking more than she'd ever risked before. "Dan, you must know that there's a relationship between us whether you want it or not."

"Yeah," he mumbled, looking down, "but I made a mistake before."

"Diana."

"Yes, Diana."

Piper blew her breath out between her teeth. "I need to know, Dan. You have to tell me. Do you . . . do you feel anything for me, anything at all?"

He said nothing.

"Darn it," Piper said abruptly, "tell me what you feel. Do you *hate* me?"

"Hate you?" He straightened, slammed down his beer can and got to his feet. He began pacing the driveway in front of her, back and forth, his hands jammed in his trouser pockets. Finally he turned toward her, and his blue eyes pinioned hers. "I've liked you a whole lot, too much, ever since you showed up at my door last spring."

"Oh," she breathed, stunned.

"Yeah, and I knew it wasn't real clever of me, so I . . ."

"You tried to chase me away," she said wonderingly.

He shrugged.

Piper got up from the steps and went to stand in front of him. She looked into his eyes, mustered up every ounce of courage in her and spoke her piece. "I love you, Dan. It's the kind of love that can't be bargained with. If you were to walk away from me now, I'd still love you. Forever."

He stared at her long and hard. "Look," he said, "I made a mistake before. Or, let's say Diana and I both did. We jumped into—"

"Dan," she interjected, "do you really believe what we've both gone through was a mistake? That we're jumping into anything?"

He shook his head slowly.

"Diana would approve, you know," Piper said. "She'd want you to be happy. She'd want me to be happy. You know that, don't you?"

But he didn't answer her question directly. Instead he said, "I took that job."

"As sheriff?" she asked, astonished.

"I didn't really want to leave," he admitted.

"You're going to be sheriff?" she asked again, incredulously.

"I guess so."

She put a hand on his arm. "And the ranch?"

"I can't run it, Piper."

"I can," she said quietly.

He turned his face away. "I, uh, I thought of that."

"Well," she said, "well, then..."

"I, uh, don't think it'll work," Dan said slowly, still not looking at her.

"Why not? Tell me, why don't you?"

He turned abruptly toward her, his face as angry as she'd ever seen it. Inadvertently Piper stepped back. "Because, damn it," he said, "because I can't have you around here all the time. I can't deal with it."

"You don't want me here," she said slowly. "Oh, I see."

"No, you don't see. I want you here *all* the time. I want you with me. Mine," he said harshly.

Piper stared at him in wonder. "You really love me? Is that what you mean?"

"Yes," he said, "that's what I mean."

"Well, then," Piper replied, "if we love each other, there's got to be a solution."

"I thought of one," Dan said slowly, "but..."

"Dan?"

"If we... well, if we got married, then..."

"Yes," Piper said ardently.

PIPER TOOK the handkerchief from her mother and sniffed. "Thanks, Mom."

"I don't know why you always do this," Betty whispered in her ear.

"I can't help it," Piper said, blowing her nose, un-ladylike.

"Oh, Lord," Betty said and walked away to talk to her new son-in-law.

It was a glorious autumn evening in Steamboat Springs, the aspen leaves quivering, pure gold, the sky a perfect bowl of darkening blue overhead. An early September snow had cloaked the mountain peaks in a mantle of dazzling white. An absolutely idyllic evening—mild, cloudless, perfect, Piper thought as she headed across the lit-up lawn toward her husband of an hour. It was silly of her to be crying.

Dan looked so handsome, she thought, tears filling her eyes once more. So strong and beautiful, talking to her mother, smiling, those two adorable lines on each side of his mouth deepening. She was so happy, so terribly, deliriously happy. As she walked she dabbed at her eyes, trying not to smudge her makeup.

"Lord, she's crying again," Betty said to Dan disdainfully.

He turned and looked at her and his smile broadened. Piper grinned back through her tears. "Never mind me," she said. "I told you I'd cry."

"You did," he said, nodding.

"Do I look awful?" she asked.

"You're beautiful, kid," Dan said.

Piper did look beautiful, everyone at the wedding agreed. She'd chosen an informal dress, knee length, in off-white silk charmeuse, a soft, flowing fabric that draped from a round-necked and long-sleeved bodice to her waist, where a wide belt of seed pearls and sequins set off the full skirt that swirled and clung around her long legs. In her hair she wore a circlet of baby's breath.

The informality of the wedding had been Piper's idea—a few close friends and family for the service in her parents' living room, a small catered reception on the lawn under the willow tree. A two-week vacation in Mexico, where Dan was going to let her visit some famous horse-breeding ranches, and then home, to their new home together—the Elk River Ranch.

"Go on, you two." Betty said, "Dance or something."

Dan took Piper's hand in his and led her to the makeshift floor in the center of the lawn. Everyone clapped and urged them on. Piper blushed and Dan shook his head at her and they danced, holding each other close, smiling shyly, lovingly, their cheeks pressed together. Piper allowed her fingers to brush the hair curling slightly above his shirt collar. She drank in his scent as other couples joined them dancing on the floor, including her parents. She saw her mother move by once, and Betty was crying. Piper smiled. She nudged Dan.

"Women," Dan muttered in her ear.

"Men," Piper countered. "If I hadn't made you ask me to marry you, we never would have..."

"You got that backward." His mouth brushed her neck and sent ripples up her spine.

"Uh-huh," she whispered lazily. "Maybe we should go somewhere private and argue it."

"Um," Dan was saying in her ear when suddenly the rude beep of a pager sounded from his pocket—it was the sheriff's department.

"You didn't switch it off?" Piper said, standing back.

"Well, I... Look," he said, "I'll just call in and tell the dispatcher not to beep me again. Okay?"

"Sure," Piper said doubtfully.

He called from the living room. Piper stood in the door and listened. Dutch would have dropped everything and gone straight over to the office—wedding or no wedding. Oh, she hoped Dan...

"A barroom brawl," Dan was saying into the receiver. "Why can't Larry go on over there? Well, I know Dutch wanted to handle everything himself, but I'm not Dutch, am I?" A pause. "No, Denise, I wouldn't fire you if you'd given this to one of my deputies. And, Denise, I'm switching off the pager. You guys handle it. Sure, I'll tell her. Good night." He hung up.

"Thank heavens," Piper said with relief.

Dan turned toward her, and a slow grin gathered on the corners of his mouth. "Thought I'd leap into the squad car and ride to the rescue, didn't you?" he asked.

"Why, Dan," Piper replied, "never in a million years."

"Uh-huh," he said and crooked a finger at her. "Come here, kid."

"Yes, sheriff," Piper said, and went toward his outstretched arms.

HARLEQUIN SUPERROMANCE®

HARLEQUIN SUPERROMANCE WANTS TO INTRODUCE YOU TO A DARING NEW CONCEPT IN ROMANCE...

WOMEN WHO DARE!

Bright, bold, beautiful...
Brave and caring, strong and passionate...
They're women who know their own minds
and will dare anything...for love!

One title per month in 1993, written by popular Superromance authors, will highlight our special heroines as they face unusual, challenging and sometimes dangerous situations.

It takes real courage to mend a broken heart in #566 COURAGE, MY LOVE by Lynn Leslie

Available in October wherever Harlequin Superromance novels are sold.

HARLEQUIN CELEBRATES
THE SEASON OF SHARING
AND FAMILY WITH

Friends, Families, Lovers

Harlequin introduces the latest member in its family of
seasonal collections. Following in the footsteps of the popular
My Valentine, *Just Married* and *Harlequin Historical Christmas
Stories*, we are proud to present FRIENDS, FAMILIES,
LOVERS. A collection of three new contemporary romance
stories about America at its best, about welcoming others into
the circle of love.... Stories to warm your heart ...

By three leading romance authors:

KATHLEEN EAGLE
SANDRA KITT
RUTH JEAN DALE

Available in October, wherever
Harlequin books are sold.

THANKS

HARLEQUIN SUPERROMANCE®

THE MONTH OF
LIVING DANGEROUSLY

LIVE ON THE EDGE WITH SUPERROMANCE
AS OUR HEROINES BATTLE
THE ELEMENTS AND THE ENEMY

Windstorm by Connie Bennett pits woman against nature as Teddi O'Brian sets her sights on a tornado chaser.

In Sara Orwig's *The Mad, the Bad & the Dangerous*, Jennifer Ruark outruns a flood in the San Saba Valley.

Wildfire by Lynn Erickson is a real trial by fire as Piper Hillyard learns to tell the good guys from the bad.

In Marisa Carroll's *Hawk's Lair*, Sara Riley tracks subterranean treasure—and a pirate—in the Costa Rican rain forest.

Learn why Superromance heroines are more-than just the women next door, and join us for some adventurous reading this September!

HSMLD

Calloway Corners

In September, Harlequin is proud to bring readers four involving, romantic stories about the Calloway sisters, set in Calloway Corners, Louisiana. Written by four of Harlequin's most popular and award-winning authors, you'll be enchanted by these sisters and the men they love!

MARIAH by Sandra Canfield
JO by Tracy Hughes
TESS by Katherine Burton
EDEN by Penny Richards

As an added bonus, you can enter a sweepstakes contest to win a trip to Calloway Corners, and meet all four authors. Watch for details in all Calloway Corners books in September.

MEN MADE IN AMERICA

Fifty red-blooded, white-hot, true-blue hunks from every
State in the Union!

Beginning in May, look for MEN MADE IN AMERICA!
Written by some of our most popular authors, these
stories feature fifty of the strongest, sexiest men, each
from a different state in the union!

Two titles available every other month at your favorite
retail outlet.

In September, look for:

DECEPTIONS by Annette Broadrick (California)
STORMWALKER by Dallas Schulze (Colorado)

In November, look for:

STRAIGHT FROM THE HEART by Barbara Delinsky
(Connecticut)
AUTHOR'S CHOICE by Elizabeth August (Delaware)

You won't be able to resist MEN MADE IN AMERICA!
